T0277975

NOT ABOUT A BOY

MYAH HOLLIS

An Imprint of HarperCollinsPublishers

HarperTeen is an imprint of HarperCollins Publishers.

Not About a Boy
Copyright © 2024 by Myah Hollis
All rights reserved. Printed in the United States of America. No part of this book may be used or reproduced in any manner whatsoever without written permission except in the case of brief quotations embodied in critical articles and reviews. For information, address HarperCollins Children's Books, a division of HarperCollins Publishers, 195 Broadway, New York, NY 10007.
www.epicreads.com

Library of Congress Control Number: 2023943954
ISBN 978-0-06-334198-2

Typography by Julia Tyler
24 25 26 27 28 LBC 5 4 3 2 1

First Edition

For my Alex,
the one I lost

PART
ONE

1

A STATE OF DELUSION

He does not stay over. He shows up at 12:30 a.m. and leaves by two, long after the apartment has gone still. When I can watch his silhouette move like a phantom through my room, pulling on clothes, knowing he'll have no problem getting from here to the front door. I yawn, mumble something synonymous with goodbye, and roll over. It's a simple system.

Tonight he'd fallen asleep so I figured I could give him, like, thirty minutes to rest before kicking him out. And this is why you should give boys nothing.

"Hayden!"

I crawl over the body in my bed to turn on the lamp. Soft, golden light pours onto a face completely swaddled in the sheets. Head nestled into the pillow. Comforter pulled up to his chin. He looks so peaceful.

I slap him.

"Damn," he groans. His fingers lock around my wrist to keep me from hitting him again. "Was that necessary?"

I grab his phone with my free hand and hold it up for him to see. He blinks at the clock on the glowing screen. 5:27. Finally, his eyes flicker to mine with the appropriate amount of alarm.

"Are they awake?"

"I don't know." I'm usually the first up because I don't sleep much. I lock the dead bolt to cover Hayden's tracks, make coffee, and retreat to my room. Dave's alarm goes off at 5:30 and by 5:35, Sue's in the kitchen grabbing an assortment of skincare products from the fridge. So we could have time. A minute or two. Maybe.

I run through every alternative escape plan in my head, and short of pushing him out of the twenty-nine-story window, there's no option that gets him out of here undetected. Not now, at least.

In the hallway, bare feet shuffle on the hardwood floor, but they're not moving in the direction of the kitchen. They're getting louder. Closer. Hayden stills. I barely allow myself to breathe. The knob jiggles, and for a split second, I'm not sure if I remembered to lock it.

"Mel, are you up?" Sue asks from behind a door that is very much still closed. Thank god.

I exhale. "Yeah."

"You want an omelet?"

Hayden nods. I cover his face with a pillow. He isn't flailing his arms like in the movies so I'm probably not pressing hard enough.

"No, thanks."

I wait until Sue's podcast is playing through the Sonos before removing the pillow from Hayden's head. He purses his lips. "You couldn't have let her make the omelet? I'm starving."

"To death, I hope." He stifles a laugh. I yank my wrist free and climb out of bed. "Do not move. Do not make a sound."

Blithely ignoring my warning, his long limbs stretch out to fill the space that I left.

I slip into the hallway and shut the door, taking a moment to compose myself before I have to face my guardians. Everything is actually completely fine, and I am not having a heart attack. I may reside in this apartment for the time being, but I prefer to live in a state of delusion.

I spent the four years since my last foster placement splitting time between the Laurelle Academy dorms and my friend Rena's house—both of which offered an alarming lack of supervision—so adapting to life with a couple in their late thirties over the past three months has not been without its challenges.

Sue's in the kitchen wrapped in a black silk robe, brown hair slicked back into a tight bun, with a silicone mask on her forehead and thick globs of cream under each eye. This white woman is going to age like a Cullen if she and Tata Harper have anything to say about it.

She dumps diced tomatoes into a sizzling pan of garlic and onions. The oil pops and she flinches, turning down the flame. "Did you see the email from Debra about rescheduling your check-in call?"

I cross the kitchen and grab a mug from the cabinet by the sink. "Call? I usually just say her name three times in the mirror."

3

"It's Thursday at four," she says because she knows I haven't read it. She leans her hip against the counter, watching me go through the convoluted process of making a flat white with their fancy espresso machine. "You can't just have coffee every morning. You have to eat something. A piece of toast, at least."

"I eat at school."

She raises her eyebrows.

"I do!" If I make it in time for breakfast, which I won't today. I'm running later than usual and there's still the issue of the boy trapped in my room. It's starting to feel a little "Tell-Tale Heart." I need to get back in there before she hears the pulse thumping under the floorboards.

"They're going to think we're not feeding you."

"Who? Debra? Debra doesn't care."

"Debra doesn't care about what?" Dave asks, emerging from their room fully dressed for work, even though he's been awake for . . . what? Three seconds? Men.

"Whether or not she's malnourished," Sue says.

Dave runs a hand through his wet hair and sits at the kitchen island. Sue pours him a cup of orange juice, which he downs with a handful of vitamins.

"You're giving her too much credit," I say. "She's not that good at her job."

Dave smirks, prepared to make a sarcastic comment until Sue shoots him a chastising look. I escape to my room with my coffee, making sure they're both out of sight before I open the door. To my complete and utter bafflement, there is, once again, a boy dead asleep in my bed.

I don't have time for this.

I shower and dress quickly, pairing a vintage band tee and a tangle of gold jewelry with my favorite pair of Levi's. I twist my curly hair into a bun and pat a berry-colored balm onto my lips and cheeks. A little concealer to hide the dark circles under my eyes and a few swipes of mascara. If you look like you've slept, then your body can't be tired. That's science.

Hayden's awake, still under the covers, scrolling on his phone when I leave the bathroom. Not a care in the world. Imagine having the audacity.

"I think I heard them leave," he says.

I do a quick sweep of the apartment just to be sure. The glass tray on the table by the door where they keep their keys and Dave's wallet is empty. I check the peephole too because I am nothing if not paranoid. Once I have quelled my anxiety to manageable levels, I blow through my room like a tornado, hastily grabbing everything that I need for school and shoving it into my bag.

Hayden moves at a much more lethargic pace, collecting the things he has somehow managed to scatter everywhere and following me out to the kitchen.

"You know," he says, "you're very cute when you're mad."

I glance over my shoulder at him. "I'm not mad." He gives me a *yeah right* look because of course I'm mad. "You don't take anything seriously." My hands shake as I pour the rest of the lukewarm coffee from my mug into a travel cup. A little of it dribbles onto the marble countertop. "Do you know how bad that could've been? They cannot catch some random boy in their apartment. They're not my parents, Hayden. This shit is complicated."

"I'm sorry," he says. When I don't respond, he comes over and spins me around to face him. I guess he does look a little contrite, but he also looks calculating. "Maybe . . ."

"What?"

"I don't know. Maybe I should meet them."

I take a step back and bump into the cabinet. My elbow hits the cup and almost spills its contents all over the floor. He grins, and seeing Hayden smile is kind of like staring directly into the sun. You forget it's a bad idea until you do it and then it's like, well, I guess I'm blind now.

"Then I wouldn't be some random boy in their apartment."

"You want me to introduce you as what? The guy I'm hooking up with? Do you think that's better?"

He shrugs. "You could just say we're dating."

"We're not dating."

"It doesn't matter."

I stare into warm brown eyes, trying to assess what is going on right now. "It does matter because I'm starting to think that you think we're dating."

He doesn't deny it. He couldn't if he tried. His face is giving him away. I turn back to my coffee and snap the lid on.

"Why are we still sneaking around?" he asks, leaning his

6

elbows on the counter. "It's been over two months. Aren't we past that now?"

"There's no getting past it."

"Why?"

"Because it is what it is, and honestly you're kind of ruining it."

I check the time on my phone. It's finals week, and if I don't leave right now, I'm going to be late for my first exam. He waits by the door while I turn off all the lights in the apartment. In the hall, one of the neighbors, Mrs. Miller, eyes us conspiratorially, towing a small dog behind her.

Hayden hits the button for the elevator. I adjust the strap of my bag, aware of his eyes on me.

"Just end it, Mel. Clearly we don't want the same thing."

I don't know what else there is to want. This was supposed to be simple. Transactional. I can't fall for someone when the last boy I loved is still curled around my neck like a hand. I told Hayden this could only work if we keep it casual, and he agreed to my terms. Nothing has changed.

When I meet his gaze, he tilts his head provokingly, calling my bluff.

"You end it."

His face breaks into the defiant smirk I've come to know so well. "Nah, I'm good."

The elevator door opens and the older couple inside steps back to let us in. The woman stares like she's never seen Black people before and cannot fathom our existence, let alone why we would be occupying the same elevator as her. I stare back until she looks away.

"Why are you so against it?" Hayden asks once we're in the lobby. "I want to hang out with you during the day. Clothed. And have conversations that consist of more than twelve words. Why does that seem more unreasonable to you than hooking up and then pretending we don't know each other?"

"Because we don't know each other." He rolls his eyes. "We don't!"

"Isn't that the point of dating?"

He jogs ahead of me to grab the door. Outside, the spring breeze tugs a few strands of hair loose from my bun. I start in the direction of school, but Hayden pulls me back.

"I am sorry about this morning," he says. "Seriously. I'm not trying to mess things up for you."

I know I can't blame him for falling asleep in the middle of the night. It's on me. I should've been more careful. Not just today, but from the beginning. I thought I'd accounted for everything. I tried to be cautious. To set clear boundaries, but I knew this could happen. Someone always catches feelings. I just thought it would be me. I've been proud of my ability to keep this casual.

Whatever. "It's fine."

He doesn't try to hug me because we don't hug, but he does reach out to smooth down a rogue curl blowing across my face.

The problem is, I know what it is to want someone when you shouldn't. To get so caught up in their fire, you turn to ashes on the floor. My last relationship burned so bright it destroyed us both. Like a cosmic explosion. I can still see the light flickering through the dark, even so many miles away.

I'm trying to protect myself. I want to protect him too.

I duck away from his hand. He smiles, his gaze fixing on something behind me. "What's up, Fred?"

I spin around to find my doorman strolling toward us with his hat tucked under his arm, sipping from a Starbucks cup. "Good morning, Mr. Thompson. Miss Cœur."

Oh, absolutely not.

"Hi. Bye," I say to Fred and Hayden, respectively, and sprint away, digging through my bag for my phone. I FaceTime Rena, and she picks up on the second ring. The screen is black. I can barely see her.

"He's friends with my doorman now."

Rena turns on the light and removes her eye mask. There are crease marks on her face and a heart-shaped pimple patch on her chin. Her purple hair has mostly fallen out of the bun that is now dangling limply from the top of her head.

"I left them talking in front of my building. What could they possibly have to talk about?"

She takes out her retainer and chucks it toward her nightstand. She goes through retainers like hair ties. "The tall boy is sleeping over now?"

"First of all, don't say that like there are several boys. Secondly, no. He's not supposed to be. It's getting messy."

She rolls onto her stomach and closes her eyes. "It's been messy."

"It wasn't supposed to be. It was supposed to be easy. That was the whole appeal of Hayden."

"*That* was the appeal?"

"I mean, yes. He's obviously gorgeous, but plenty of boys are cute. I vetted him like a fucking politician. I made sure there was no weird ex drama. No major red flags. His circle is small. He doesn't run his mouth—"

"I remember." Of course she does. She made a spreadsheet of all of the contenders, titled *The Thirst Games*. Hayden scored tens across the board. "Which is why it might not be the worst thing in the world to just see where this goes."

"That wasn't the plan. What good is recon if we're not going to follow the damn plan."

"Plans can change."

I gape at her. This is the same girl who asked me why I would stick to one boy when I could build a roster. "Are you serious?"

She sits up and takes a long, *long* drink from her water bottle. Buying herself time to figure out how to voice whatever thought is making her peer at me like that. "I'm just saying. You're allowed to move on."

What does that mean? To move on? What does it look like?

When Darren and I broke up, I thought that was moving on. Removing his number from my phone. Deleting text threads. I thought losing him was moving on. Letting his mom cry in my arms. Waiting for my own tears to come.

And when the sobs wrung my body out like a rag, wasn't that moving on? When I buried myself in the memory of him and felt him coat my skin like dust, layer by layer until I was lost too.

Clawing my way out. Blinking into blinding light. The air in my lungs. That felt like moving on to me.

I stop at a crosswalk, watching the cars speed through puddles from last night's rain. Dark, swollen clouds threaten to bring more. New storms on the horizon.

"It's okay to let people in," Rena adds, her voice soft. "If someone cares about you enough to want to know you, maybe you should let them."

Maybe she's right. Or maybe this is the worst advice she could've given me.

2

CHAMBERSON

The bell for the end of fourth period rings and I blink the classroom back into focus. Around me, some students scramble to finish the exam. Others stand and stretch, dropping their packets in the pile on Mrs. Nelson's desk on their way out. I finished the final with ten minutes to spare, even with the throbbing headache building inside my skull. Sue was right. I probably should've eaten something.

As soon as I clear the doorway, someone falls into step next to me. "Your mind is terrifying," he says, handing over the biology notebook I lent him last week. "Don't share your notes with anyone else. No one should have to see that. Have you ever known peace?"

I don't have the same exact curriculum as I did at Laurelle, but it's close enough. I consolidated all my notes from both schools to prep for finals, because as hard as I've been trying to keep up, I wasn't sure what to expect this week. I've spent the past few months studying my ass off in an attempt to salvage my GPA—which plummeted fall semester due to the events of last summer. Of all the elements of my life that I'm trying to change, decent grades is the least daunting goal to strive for.

I round the corner toward the courtyard and he does the same. "You're welcome, Trey."

"Melie, I'm in your debt." Hayden's best friend throws an arm over my shoulders, his tone grave. "I just worry that you have the makings of a serial killer. Who catalogs information like that? There were chapters. Footnotes. A glossary. You're not well."

"I have a Virgo moon," I say, shaking off his arm. "How'd you do?"

"Mrs. Nelson loves me. It'll work itself out."

Trey has half the faculty wrapped around his finger. He weaponizes his charm and good looks in a way I personally find concerning. He'd be an incredible cult leader. "What will you do when you can't use pretty privilege to your advantage?"

"Aw, you think I'm pretty?"

"Maybe then you'll actually have to put in effort."

"I'm also rich, so probably not."

I press my lips together to keep from laughing because it's not funny. "That was the most disgusting thing you've ever said."

He flashes me a dimpled smile. "Ever? Nah."

We push through the heavy doors and descend the steps to the courtyard, where half the student body is lounging in the grass or gathered around the tables scattered throughout the grounds.

As private schools go, Chamberson's a different breed. I

thought Laurelle was lax, but we still had uniforms. We were expected to eat meals in the dining hall and pretend we had some reverence for the structure of a school day. Physically being on campus at Chamberson seems to be optional. It's not uncommon for people to return after free period with giant shopping bags or waddling around in flimsy pedicure flip-flops. We're even allowed to attend classes online if we're out of town for an extended period of time. A policy begging to be abused.

Trey stands in line with me while I wait to buy a sandwich. My head feels like it's going to explode. I unwind my hair tie and let my curls loose, massaging a tense spot at the nape of my neck.

"Heard about your close call this morning," he says, lips curling into a smirk. "Oversleeping, Melie? Come on."

He's minding my business right now but that doesn't mean he's wrong. "The thing is I never oversleep." I wouldn't admit it to him or anyone, but I think I slept better with Hayden next to me. I put a mental bookmark there. I'll revisit that issue later. "I didn't even bother to set an alarm."

"An amateur mistake." He examines the display of fruit on the concession stand and chooses an apple. "I'd say I'm disappointed in you both, but I didn't think you'd make it this long without getting caught."

I can't help but grin. "You underestimate me."

"And I'll never do it again."

I order a chicken and pesto on ciabatta and sparkling water, swiping my student ID to pay. Trey's eyes spark in a way that lets me know who's standing behind me before she even opens her mouth.

"Are you done for the day?" Shaine asks me, without so much as a glance in Trey's direction. There's a thin line between love and hate and it's called lust. These two walk it like a tightrope. "Want to get massages?"

I met Shaine through Sue, who styled her for a *Teen Vogue* shoot a few years ago. She and Shaine's mom became the type of friends who go to spin classes, send each other floral arrangements on birthdays, and conspire to get two reluctant teenage girls to hang out.

It was my first week at Chamberson, and I refused to be set up on what was essentially a playdate. Shaine refused to do anything her mother specifically asked her to do. It wasn't until we were partnered together in English two weeks later that I spoke more than a couple of words to her. We were both devastated to discover that Sue and Mrs. Aoki were right.

"I have a review session for calc."

She weaves her arm through mine, leading me to our usual table on the far left of the courtyard. "No one goes to the review sessions."

"I'm being tested on a year's worth of material, and I just got here in March. I can't not go to the review sessions."

She pouts, slumping next to Justine and Olivia, the other half of our foursome. A few tables away, Trey joins Hayden and their fellow basketball players. Hayden doesn't have an exam until later in the day. I'm sure he went home, took a leisurely shower, changed into a fresh pair of sweatpants, and arrived in time for lunch.

I nudge Shaine's arm. "You and Trey have a lot of tension for two people who dated in ninth grade."

"And three weeks in tenth," Olivia says, sipping from a can of Diet Coke. Shaine kicks her under the table. Olivia smiles sweetly, brushing her thick blond hair behind her shoulders.

"It's their thing," Justine says. "They get off on it." She eyes Shaine, daring her to kick her the way she kicked Olivia.

Shaine scoffs. "Excuse me. I'm in a relationship. Besides, who hasn't dated Trey?" The three of us raise our hands. She glares at us one by one, starting with Olivia. "Bitch, you're gay." Then Justine. "You don't date." She turns to me. "Give it time."

Justine rests her cheek on her folded arms, staring at us over her sunglasses with sincere curiosity. "Allo girls always seem so tortured. Are y'all miserable?"

"Yes," Shaine and Olivia say in union.

I nod, unwrapping my sandwich. "Mostly. Yeah."

"Anyway," Shaine says, angling her body away from two out of three of our collective problems. Olivia scans the courtyard for the third but Rowen's nowhere to be found. "Since Mel's staying with me this weekend, we can all get ready at my place on Saturday and go together."

Every year on the Saturday after finals, someone throws a massive party to celebrate the end of the semester and the beginning of summer break. The three of them have been talking about it for weeks, but this is the first I'm hearing of my plans to crash at Shaine's. I haven't decided if I'm going to the party yet.

Shaine narrows her eyes at me. "You're going. And don't tell me you have nothing to wear. You live with Susan Romano. I don't want to hear it."

Sue is the type of famous stylist that JLo would play in one of those early 2000s rom-coms, with the power outfits, the chic Manhattan office, and the brilliant lawyer husband. She took my measurements one morning with her eyes. Like a fucking robot. Now new clothes just materialize in my closet.

"Pick your battles, girl," Justine says. "If you don't go, she'll quite literally never get over it."

Shaine slams her hands on the table, startling a group of girls studying nearby. "Is it a crime to want to shake ass with my friends? Am I a criminal?"

"I'll go," I say, if only so she'll stop screaming.

I've been to parties with them before, and each time has required a level of restraint I've never had to exercise before. I can't afford to fall back into old patterns. I made promises when I moved here. Promises I'm trying very hard to keep.

"And you'll sleep over," Shaine says. A demand, not a question.

"Yes, I'll sleep over."

She smiles serenely, a sated lion after a kill. "Wonderful."

3

YOU'RE KILLING ME

Hayden's been over for the past two nights because I never fully learn a lesson. I need to be traumatized in the exact same way no less than three times for me to modify my behavior.

It's Thursday and with all my exams done and papers submitted, I've spent most of the afternoon in bed rereading *The Bell Jar* for my summer assignment: a five-page essay on the fig tree allegory and its impact on Esther's life. I'm almost to the end of the book but I can't focus because Debra's still talking.

". . . will be very important, Amélie. But so far everything looks great on our end. There's still the home visit in August, but if all goes well, Susan and Dave should be able to move forward with the adoption process in the fall, given that's what the three of you want."

When she doesn't continue, I remember that I'm supposed to express excitement and genuine hope for the future. So I say "love that" and practically hear her purse her lips through the phone.

It's not that I don't want to be adopted. It's just that I don't find myself particularly adoptable. I don't think Debra does either.

Since I was a kid, I've been made to believe that this is what I'm supposed to want more than anything. That made sense to me until around eleven when the blind optimism of childhood gave way to the cool disillusionment of adolescence. I wasn't small and cute anymore. I was anxious and resentful. For years I acted in complete opposition to whatever was expected of me out of sheer spite. Last winter, when I was at my lowest point, willing to accept any hand extended in my direction, I promised her I would try one last time.

My placement with Sue and Dave is a Hail Mary. A last-ditch effort before I age out of the system in nine months.

I imagine that, for Debra, being my case manager must feel like being a car salesman trying to get that shitty old Ford Focus off her lot. It's particularly frustrating because Laurelle Child Services is the Bentley dealership of private adoption agencies, so why is the Ford even there? Do they expect her to sell it? In *this* economy?

I sympathize. LCS's record is phenomenal. Among their clients are some of the country's wealthiest and most influential families. This is very largely due to the fact that Laurelle Academy, the institution that birthed the agency, has become one of the most coveted boarding schools in the world.

Mildred Laurelle was an orphan who, despite the odds, went on to become a rich, childless woman with lovers she refused to marry and too much disposable income to spend in a lifetime. Laurelle is her legacy, and although her vision of an elite school for orphaned girls was pure, less so were the intentions of the board in charge of her nine-figure estate.

The whole point was to give the less fortunate a chance at a brighter future or whatever, but it wasn't long before the school opened its doors to the children of parents willing to pull college-admissions-scandal-level fraud to get their kids accepted. With the influx of tuition dollars and property-allocated funds, the New Canaan campus became just shy of a palace.

"How are you doing?" Debra asks. "Emotionally, I mean."

"Is this the part where we talk about our feelings?"

There are few things that Debra hates more than the emotions of a child. One of those things just so happens to be a checklist left unfinished, so she perseveres. "I see here in your chart that you've stopped your antidepressants."

"They make me nauseous. Besides, I'm not depressed. My life was depressing."

"Amélie—"

"Richards said it's fine, but if you want to take a deep dive into my trauma, I've got time."

The Laurelle kids who are under the guardianship of LCS are all assigned a Debra. If they're very lucky, like me, they also get an overbearing psychiatrist named Richards.

"I will discuss it with him. I can't imagine that's the best course of action, considering what you've been through. . . ."

I turn back to my book because this is a convo Debra can have with herself, but my phone vibrates with a text from Shaine.

Shaine: wyd?

Me: nothing. what's up?

Shaine: got in a fight with Lucas

Shaine and Lucas's breakups are as consistent as the phases of the moon. I could track my period by them.

Me: what did he do now?

Shaine: he still has his dating app

Shaine: the one he said he deleted two months ago

I tune back in to Debra, who is in the middle of the longest monologue she's ever performed. Good for her.

Me: never check a boy's phone. it'll only bring you pain

Shaine: I didn't check his phone

Shaine: I have a burner account

Me: ???

Shaine: a burner account

I stifle a laugh because *whew, girl.*

Me: I can read

Me: I just don't understand

Me: you made a fake dating profile

Shaine: yes

Me: so you could swipe endlessly on the off chance that you see your trash boyfriend

Shaine: mhmm

Me: to confirm that he's doing what you already knew he was doing

Shaine: correct

My beautiful, smart, funny friend. Going full Interpol over a boy who won't even cross the Brooklyn Bridge for her. A tragedy.

Me: that is psychotic

Shaine: the point is I need to shop

Shaine: come with meeee

Shaine: I'm sad

I start to explain why Lucas is not worth a single human emotion, but Debra is calling my name.

"Amélie. Are you listening to me?"

"I heard every word you said."

Sad isn't the word I'd use to describe Shaine right now as she rips through the racks at Bloomingdale's. Long, black hair whipping around like Medusa with the snakes. Amex burning a hole in her Prada purse, while sales associates swarm, calculating the potential commission.

I'd call her enraged, maybe? Deranged?

"What is it about me that makes boys think they can lie to my face? Do I look like an idiot?" She spins around, holding an arm full of dresses, skirts, a few swimsuits. Her eyes are daggers, red lips in a pout. "Seriously. Do I look stupid?"

The question is clearly rhetorical, but she waits for me to answer. "Well, what are the consequences of a boy lying to you? Because they'll do it if they can get away with it."

She stands frozen for a second. Blinks. "Maybe I am an idiot."

"You're not an idiot."

"Bozo the fucking Clown."

"We're all clowns when we care about someone."

"I gotta care less." She holds up one of the items from her pile. An olive silk cami. "Do you like this?"

"Don't you have that?"

"Not in this color."

A sales associate with a wide smile and a predatory vibe comes slithering out from whatever hole he was hiding in. This is why I shop online. "Can I start a fitting room for you?"

"No, thanks," Shaine says. "Can you take these to the register, please?"

His eyes light up as he takes the pile of designer clothes from her. Shaine walks aimlessly through the accessories department, picking things up and putting them down again.

"It's exhausting," she says, trying on a tiny pair of six-hundred-dollar Dior sunglasses, flicking the price tag out of her face like she's swatting a fly. "We have the same fights over and over. He does something to piss me off. I call him out on it. He makes me feel like I'm delusional—and I am, obviously, but it's not my fault. I'm just trying to operate in this world as a heterosexual woman and it's hard!"

"It's a cursed endeavor, for sure."

I don't know a thing about Lucas. Never met the boy. Couldn't pick him out in a lineup. I've always considered it a stubborn tenacity that keeps him in Shaine's life, but you forget about the soft things. The fragile hope that grows in the spaces between what others consider to be significant. Shaine only shares the worst of it. The good she keeps for herself. I don't know what he means to her, but I get it. Wanting someone so badly that you break into pieces. Promising yourself that the end result will be a mosaic.

Shaine studies her reflection in the display mirror. Although

I can't see her eyes through the dark lenses, I know she's looking at me when she tilts her head in a silent question. I shake my head and back the glasses go. "I think I'm done. For real this time." She moves on to the Gucci display, gazing at the options without really considering them. "I don't want to feel this way anymore, you know? Isn't dating supposed to be fun?"

"Allegedly."

We meet the sales associate at the register. He already has the sensors off and the clothes wrapped in tissue paper. Shaine swipes her card without checking the total.

"Can we get dinner after this?" she asks. "There's that new Argentinean place down the street."

My phone buzzes.

Hayden: I thought about what you said

Hayden: about us not knowing each other

Hayden: you're right

My eyes narrow at the texts. I don't know where he's going with this, but I'm sure I won't like it.

"Mel." Shaine glances at me as she scribbles her signature on the receipt. The sales associate comes out from behind the counter to hand her the bags, already scanning the floor for his next sale. "Dinner?"

"Oh, yeah. Sure."

Me: of course I am

An ellipsis pops up on the screen. Disappears.

Shaine and I squeeze through the doors of the Lexington Avenue exit with her many bags, turning right and heading uptown toward the restaurant. She walks with purpose, the way most native New Yorkers do. I have to jog to keep up with her.

Hayden: what are you doing this weekend?

Me: why?

Hayden: come to the hamptons with me

The Hamptons? Why would we go to the Hamptons? What about *we are not dating* was unclear to him? I'm confused.

Me: you're killing me

Me: is this a thing you do?

Hayden: what?

Me: take girls to the hamptons

Hayden: haha

Hayden: I'll pick you up on saturday

Hayden: 8am

The boy has lost his mind.

Me: bye

Hayden: it's a 2.5hr drive. you can sleep in the car

Me: I didn't say yes

As we enter the restaurant, Hayden's response flashes across my screen and I'm back in the hall of my apartment building with him again, waiting for the elevator. That infuriating smirk. The challenge in his eyes.

Hayden: then say no

4

TOO FAR FROM GOD'S LIGHT

The way I see it, I have two options. Go to the party with Shaine, Olivia, and Justine, or go to the Hamptons with Hayden. I've been to enough parties for a lifetime. The few that I've attended with the three of them have never gotten too out of control, but I've been told to expect a certain level of debauchery tomorrow night.

It would be a mistake to go. I know that. It hasn't been long enough since I was sixteen. That me still lives too close to the surface of my body, inextricably nestled between skin and muscle. The girl who was in so much pain that she sought distraction or relief at any cost.

This new me is fragile. I built her from nothing. From scraps. I moved to New York to create the life I could never have in Connecticut, but you can't outrun yourself. It takes more effort than I have some days to keep the darker parts of me from waking.

The Hamptons is probably the lesser of two evils. Better the devil you know, right?

And then there's the fact that the thought of spending a whole day with Hayden, being with him in a place that's not my apartment, seeing him in his element, has me curious. Unfortunately, curiosity often gets the best of me. When I texted him earlier today to confirm, he simply said: **8am. I'll bring coffee.**

I stuff a bikini and another pair of shorts in a bag that is already way too full, considering we're only staying overnight, and zip it shut. Now there's nothing left to do but establish my alibi.

The kitchen smells like garlic and rosemary. The windows are cranked open, a warm breeze billowing through the curtains. Sirens blare from the street below.

I drop the bag near my shoes by the door. Dave looks over from where he's sprawled out on the couch, still in his work clothes, watching TV. "Where are you going?"

"Shaine's for the weekend."

I join Sue by the stove, loading a plate up with chicken, mashed potatoes, and broccoli. Dave moves his feet to let me sit in the corner of the couch that I've claimed as my own. Sue sets both of their plates on the coffee table, returning to the kitchen for a corkscrew and the saltshaker. She snuggles into the left side of the couch and throws one of her many chunky knit blankets over her folded legs.

I've never seen either of them use the kitchen table. I'm pretty sure she only got it for the aesthetic.

"Oh, what did you buy yesterday?" she asks, pouring a glass of white wine.

"Nothing."

With Sue disappointed beyond words, it would appear, Dave takes the opportunity to assure me, for the hundredth time, that I can use the credit card they gave me when I moved in.

Growing up in LCS means living in close proximity to wealth, both at Laurelle and with the families I'm placed with. I know how rare it is to be a foster kid that has never wanted for anything in my life. All my needs are met. The luxuries I'm expected to have—a phone, computer, credit card—are provided, but none of it belongs to me. It has never come naturally to me to spend someone else's money like it's my own. It's hard enough to live with the guilt of constantly taking and taking and never having anything of value to offer in return.

"I was there for moral support," I say. "Shaine's dating an asshole."

"Dave was an asshole at your age," Sue says. Dave chokes on a piece of broccoli. "We dated our senior year of high school and broke up right after graduation."

We both stare at Dave. He clears his throat. "Everyone breaks up after graduation."

"We got back together nine years later. Once his brain fully developed."

He laughs. "I was processing a lot of trauma."

Dave's a foster kid too. He was adopted when he was sixteen. I think that's the reason I'm here, but I've never come right out and asked him. During my first month here, he tried to talk to me about my experience in the system, but I couldn't bring myself to share war stories with him when his experience must have been so much worse. Dave's a man of few words, and I'm a girl of fewer. He hasn't pushed the topic, and I appreciate that.

"This is good," I say, biting into a piece of garlic herb chicken.

Sue grins. "Thanks. I ordered it and put it in that cute dish."

"It's what she does for Thanksgiving too," Dave says.

"I can cook, I just don't want to."

"That's not very Italian of you, Sue," I tease.

"Who are you, my mother-in-law?"

Dave snorts. "My mom has never said that to you."

"I took his last name. I did not take on the responsibility of cooking lasagna from scratch every night."

I nod. "That would be so much lasagna."

Dave stifles another laugh.

There's an awful and highly derivative alien invasion movie playing on the TV. We all know it sucks, yet we sit here and let it happen to us. I find it fascinating that, with all the problems in the world, there are people who read a script like this and think, *Yes, that is how I should spend a few million dollars.* This is truly the darkest timeline.

Unable to stomach a second more of what may be the worst film I've seen in my life, I take my dishes to the kitchen and load them into the dishwasher.

"What are you and Shaine doing this weekend?" Dave asks.

"There's a party tomorrow night that I'm socially obligated to attend."

Sue turns to me, holding a glass that contains no less than

half a bottle of wine. "As your guardians, we have to remind you not to do drugs, get drunk, or be stupid."

Dave takes a swig of his beer. "Don't do anything we would have done."

"Be better than us."

"That's all any parent can hope for."

I roll my eyes. Not an adult among us, I fear.

While I wait for someone in Shaine's apartment to answer the door, I text the Romano group chat to let Sue and Dave know I made it downtown safely. Dave responds with a thumbs-up.

The door swings open and Shaine's arm shoots out to pull me in—which, now that I think about it, may be the only way I've ever entered Shaine's apartment.

"What took you so long?" she asks, half dragging me across her living room. I kick my shoes off as we go, tossing them back in the general direction of the other shoes lined up in the entry-way. "They're driving me crazy."

"I was eating dinner."

I wave at her mom as she heads up the stairs of their gorgeous Tribeca loft. Mrs. Aoki is Shaine plus thirty years and two divorces. They're identical in looks only. In every other way, they're oil and water. Shaine is loud and dramatic. Mrs. Aoki is quiet and refined. Two queens ruling one three-bedroom kingdom, finding peace mainly in their mutual resentment of her father—a taboo topic in this home.

"Hi, Mel. How are you?"

"She's fine," Shaine says on my behalf. Mrs. Aoki gives me a look that I interpret as *good luck with that*. Shaine's fingers tighten around my arm. "Come on."

There's a rolling rack in the middle of her bedroom. I didn't know she owned a rolling rack. Justine's lying next to Olivia in the middle of the king-sized bed wearing an expression of pure exasperation.

Olivia offers me some of the gummy bears she's eating. Her hair is braided into a golden crown with a few loose tendrils framing her face. Clearly Justine's work. Liv is more of the messy-bun type.

"Okay," Shaine says once she has our undivided attention. She angles the rack so I can see all the options hanging up. "I need you to choose. They are incapable of making decisions."

"Apparently so are you," Olivia says.

Shaine ignores her. She holds up an impossibly tiny pink dress. It would be a long shirt on my five-six frame. Shaine is five nine. No way it covers her boobs and butt at the same time. "So this one is a little short," she says. The bed shakes with Olivia's silent laughter. "But I have tights—"

"I can see your cervix in that dress," Justine says.

"If I don't bend down, sit, squat, or walk up steps, I should be fine." When none of us respond, Shaine huffs, throwing the dress in a growing pile of clothes in the corner. She grabs the next option, a pair of black leather pants. "Okay. Love these, but—"

"It's June."

Justine smirks at me. "That's what I said."

"You can wear leather in any season," Shaine says.

"Right, but do you want to?" I ask. Shaine tosses the pants to the side too. "What about that two-piece set you got yesterday?" She stares at me blankly as if she doesn't remember what she purchased less than twenty-four hours ago. "You're kidding."

"I honestly have no idea what I bought yesterday. I was in a fugue state." She hauls the bags out of her closet and rips through the layers of tissue paper until she finds the periwinkle crop top and matching skirt. "Wow, I have great taste."

"Perfect," Justine says, closing her eyes. "Let's be done now."

Shaine tears open a bag of cheddar potato chips, douses it in the hot sauce she keeps in the bottom drawer of her nightstand known as *the bodega*, and shakes it up. The girl will put hot sauce on anything. "Mel, what are you wearing?"

I haven't told her about the Hamptons yet. I probably wouldn't tell her at all if I didn't need her to cover for me. My friends know about me and Hayden but only conceptually. Like how I know about space. I understand it's out there and I can name the planets or whatever, but I'm not NASA.

"I'm not going to the party."

She cocks her head to the side, chewing slowly. "Why do you *think* you're not going?"

"I'm going to the Hamptons."

They all look at each other. Justine sits up, her long faux locs swinging. "Hayden's taking you to the Hamptons house?"

Before I can respond, Shaine lets out a feral laugh. "Oh my god. The boy will stop at nothing."

Olivia scoots over to me, propping her head up on one arm. "Wait, does this mean . . ."

"No, we are not dating."

"But he wants to be. It's very obvious," Shaine says. She kicks all the clothes and bags back into the closet, pushes the rolling rack in, and shuts the door. "It's almost painful to watch."

"Don't freak her out," Justine says. "We need her to get back the Hamptons house access we lost when you broke up with Trey."

Shaine glares at her. "He cheated on me."

"That house has a saltwater pool. We have all suffered greatly for his transgressions."

"Look, Mel," Shaine says, sitting at her vanity and opening one of her many skincare PR boxes. She's been modeling professionally since she was a kid. Receiving an excessive amount of free products is her favorite perk. "When I dated Trey, I strayed too far from God's light." Justine starts humming a church hymn. "But in that forsaken place, I learned a few things. The first is that no boy is nearly as funny as he thinks he is. The second is that Hayden's actually a good guy. He's a cishet male, so take that with a grain of salt, but my point is . . ." She trails off, staring at Olivia, who's grinning like an idiot at her phone. "What are you smiling at?"

"Huh?"

Shaine jumps up and takes the phone. Olivia snatches it

back, but not before Shaine reads the name on the screen. "You are not texting Rowen."

Olivia's cheeks turn bright red, blue eyes wide. "I was just asking if she's going to the party."

I had a few classes with Rowen. I don't know much about her except that she's the school drug dealer and seems to operate with strange impunity at Chamberson. The only way you can get away with that is if you're the kid of someone who gets away with worse.

Another thing I know about Rowen is she's almost as notorious with the girls at school as Trey.

"Rowen is not the girl you date." Shaine enunciates each word carefully. "Rowen is a community resource. Like the library. How many times must we explain this to you?"

"I don't know," Olivia snaps. "How's Lucas?"

Shaine tackles her.

"Hey!" Justine jumps up, pulling them apart. "You." She points at Shaine. "Don't date Lucas. He has the IQ of a gingerbread man. We are tired."

"I'm not with him anymore."

"Lie to someone else."

Shaine swivels her chair so that she's facing the mirror again, opening a jar of moisturizer and smearing it all over her face. Justine shoves Olivia.

"Ow!"

"Shut up, that didn't hurt. Do not date Rowen. Have you lost your mind?"

Olivia frowns. "You guys don't know her like I do."

"By that do you mean we don't know what her bedroom ceiling looks like?"

Shaine snickers. Olivia glares at her, tossing a pillow, which Shaine bats away easily.

Justine turns to me next. "You. Date Hayden. Mostly for the pool, but also because deep down in your little ice-cold heart, you know you want to."

"Right," Shaine says. "What's the problem?"

It's moments like these that make me wish I'd kept whatever this is between me and Hayden to myself. I intended to at first because my friends in New York are not my friends back home. There's so much they don't know. So many things I haven't told them about me. But they found out about Hayden, and when they brought it up, I didn't see the point in denying it.

I chew on my lip, unsure of how much to tell them. "My last relationship . . ." Defined me. Consumed me. Erased me. "Didn't end well."

Olivia scoffs. "What relationships end well?"

"Boring ones," Shaine murmurs.

Justine laughs. "Girl, get help."

"The best way to get over someone is to get under someone else." Olivia delivers this cliché with the enthusiasm of someone who came up with it herself.

"She's doing that already."

"Is it bad?"

Top of the list of things I'm not discussing? This. "Mind your own chaotic sex life."

"You never feed us," Olivia whines, plopping onto her back. "We need sustenance."

Shaine, busy braiding her hair into such a horrible fishtail that Justine is forced to intervene, says, "If you think he's not talking about it . . ."

Honestly, I'd be insulted if he weren't.

"Will you cover for me or not?" I ask Shaine.

She grimaces as Justine brushes out a knot in her hair. "I will make this one exception but never cancel on me for a boy again."

Next time I need an alibi, I'll call Rena.

5

GOT TO BE A SCORPIO

I know what summer's supposed to feel like. I remember being a kid, feeling it waft in like gas. How it would cause eyes to glaze over. Make people high. I remember choking on it. Having my routine ripped from me by adults who thought they were doing me a favor. Laughing lightly, calling me studious. Telling me to go live. That I'd worked hard. I'd earned it.

But every summer I lose time. I tumble from one moment to the next, and it's terrifying to look up and not know how I got there or what to expect in an hour, two weeks, a month. It's the first official day of break and already I feel restless.

Hayden picks me up in a chauffeured black SUV I've never seen before. He's leaning against the side, one spotless white sneaker crossed over the other, with a small coffee in his hand. I'm tired and emotional, so when he reaches for me with arms I've spent too many nights in, I don't think twice about what any of this might mean or who we might be after this weekend. I just go to him and feel my body click into place.

I didn't sleep much last night. Shaine had been thrashing

around, ripping the sheets from the bed. I'd been thinking of this time last year. The first time summer felt like it could mean something new to me. I had just broken up with Darren and I knew it was the last time I ever would. I was proud of myself for going through with it. So in awe of what I'd done. It was over. Finally. And I was sad, but more than that, I was hopeful for a season of blue sky.

Two months of blue-gray. That's all I got before the flood came.

Hayden opens the car door and throws my bag in the trunk with his. I close my eyes as we pull into the morning traffic and sleep the entire way.

Gravel crunches under tires. My head bounces on Hayden's leg. I don't remember lying down or having the middle seat belt strapped around my torso. Hayden has one hand on my hip, the other tapping out a series of texts. I tug on the seat belt to free myself enough to peer out the window as the car comes to a stop.

The Hamptons house sits on more than an acre of land. Massive and hedged off from the rest of the street by a steel gate and lush, towering trees. I don't go in with him right away. I walk around the back, along a flower-lined walkway made of giant slabs of stone. I want to see the pool. It's been forever since I've floated in anything larger than a bathtub.

The backyard is broken into two levels. The pool and sundeck are on the lower level. I stand at the top of the sloping lawn, but I don't go down. Once I do, I'll want to swim, and I'm starving. I retrace my steps to the front yard. The SUV is gone and the front door is wide open. I close it behind me, glancing around the sun-drenched foyer.

"Hungry?" Hayden asks, appearing on the second-story landing.

I nod.

"Still tired?"

I nod again.

He smiles, jogging down the stairs. "Let's pack food and take it to the beach. We can bike there."

There are fresh-cut flowers in a crystal vase on the entryway table. The same ones that grow in the garden outside. The silky pink petals are still damp with early morning dew. "I've never ridden a bike before."

Hayden stops midstride, waiting to see if I'm joking. I'm not. "How do you not know how to ride a bike?"

"I've been on a bike, but no one ever taught me how to ride one."

He studies my face, and once again, his looks calculating. "Hmm" is all he says as he heads for the kitchen.

He packs fruit and cheese and bread and meat. He packs two types of water and some fancy Italian soda in a glass bottle. Salads, chips, and cookies. I don't know who's eating all this. He adds ice packs to the cooler bag and zips it up.

We both came in our swimsuits, so we don't need to change. He finds a blanket and towels in one of the hall closets and stuffs those in a second bag.

"You're gonna have to learn how to ride a bike," he says, holding the door to the garage open for me. "That's ridiculous."

"Why do I have to learn how to ride a bike? What circumstances in life will require me to know how to ride a bike when I can just walk?"

He continues like I hadn't spoken. "You can use my mom's. I need to put air in the tires."

Hayden searches the shelves along one of the walls for an air pump. While he scavenges, I spot an old Polaroid camera sitting in a box of DVDs and random cords. I don't expect there to be any film in it, but when I aim it at Hayden and press the little button on top, it flashes and spits out a small, rectangular picture.

"There's more film for that thing somewhere," he says. "I went through a phase where I documented everything. Half of those DVDs are probably home videos of my dad eating cereal or my mom brushing her hair."

I shuffle through the box, and sure enough, there's a pack of film under a collection of photos of his family doing various mundane things.

"Hayden the photog."

"It was very short-lived." He grins as I snap another picture.

"This will be perfect to capture my last moments on earth."

He grabs me by the waist to adjust the height of the seat. I snap another picture in his face. "It's a bike. Children ride them all the time. You'll be fine."

"Rena knows all my social media passwords. Tell her to delete everything."

"Are you done?" I am, actually. He presses a button on the wall and the garage door opens. "There are no hills. The ground is completely flat. If you lose your balance, just put your feet down."

"Oh, that's it?" He steadies the bike while I climb on. "This is not natural for me. I don't ride things."

"We both know that's not true."

"Wow."

He laughs and tows the bike forward. "Feet on the pedals. Keep the handlebars straight. You won't fall unless you freak out."

"I'm going to fall."

"Fall toward the grass."

"That's comforting. You're a great teacher. I love this so much."

"Ready?"

"No." But he picks up the speed while my feet do their best to keep up with the pedals. "Do not let go."

"I have to let go or you're not actually riding the bike."

"I'm fine with that."

He shifts his grip from the handlebars to the back of my seat. "Keep pedaling. We're going three miles an hour. You're good."

I notice the moment when he takes his hands off and yes, I do freak out. But for those two incredible seconds, before I crash into the bush, I feel fucking free.

He runs over, laughing until tears form at the corners of his eyes. I'd make a smart remark about how that is not the appropriate reaction in this situation, but I'm laughing too.

Hayden helps me to my feet, picking a few leaves out of my hair. His smile burns a hole in my brain. I pry the bike from the bush and grin at him.

"Again."

There's a bruise the size of a golf ball sprouting on my thigh from my time in the bushes. I don't mind it much, but I grab an ice pack from the cooler anyway and press it to my leg. My hair has blown dry from lying on this blanket for hours. My skin is a warm, golden brown and speckled with sand. My fingers are stained red.

I made it two blocks on the bike, falling half a dozen times, before Hayden agreed that it was best we walk before I broke something. By the time we returned the bikes to the garage and set off on foot, I felt more at ease. I knew he could sense the energy shift. I suspect that may have been his plan from the start.

I grab another handful of berries and pop one in my mouth, tracking Hayden from across the beach. He's on the phone, pacing up and down the shore, his face contorted in irritation. I watch him curiously. I've never seen him upset before. He catches me staring and gives me a half smile, muttering a few words that I can't hear and hanging up.

"My dad," he says, lying next to me. He keeps his voice light, but I can feel the stress coming off him in waves.

"Is everything okay?"

He bites into a wedge of watermelon. "He's mad because he wanted me to go to some gala tonight."

"What time?"

"Seven."

I check my phone. It's a little past three. "Should we go back to the city?"

"Why would we do that?"

"Is he going to be pissed?"

"He'll get over it."

Apparently, Hayden had more than one ulterior motive for planning this trip.

"Interesting." I fold my arms over his chest, resting my chin on top of my hands. The remnants of his irritation melt away, replaced by roguishness and something softer. He dips his head to look at me. "Is that why you wanted to come today? So you didn't have to go to the gala?"

"Partially," he admits, sweeping my hair out of my face. His expression is so serene. So completely content. It's mesmerizing.

I don't know what to do when he looks at me like this. It isn't hard to lose yourself in someone else. It happens before you know it, and then it's too late.

I lie back on my side of the blanket so he can't feel my stupid heart racing. "Part of the reason I came was to avoid a party too."

"What was the other reason?"

"I heard about the pool."

He smiles. "It's a good pool."

We spend the whole day at the beach. By evening, I'm draped over the edge of the patio, taking in this small stretch of East

Hampton. The glare of the sun as it dips low on the horizon. The air, thick with water and salt. The quiet. It's been too long since things were quiet.

Rena FaceTimed me twice while we were out. I call her back.

"I have two drafts of a post that needs to go up tomorrow," she says in lieu of hello. "I need you to help me choose which one is the least shitty. I swear I did them in five minutes, but I've worked with this brand before, so I know what they . . ." She trails off, craning her neck like we're speaking through a window and not a phone. "Where are you?"

"The Hamptons."

I slide the patio doors open, bringing the sunset inside. The wall of glass folds like an accordion into the house's wooden frame.

Hayden's in the kitchen making dinner. When he said he was cooking, I thought he meant he was putting a frozen pizza in the oven. Whatever is happening over there is far beyond my comprehension.

"For how long?" Rena asks.

"Just tonight. I told you this."

"No, you didn't."

Maybe I didn't.

"I told you in my head. It doesn't matter. Send me the drafts. I'm positive neither is shitty, but I'll tell you which one is better."

"One sec." The video freezes as she clicks out of the convo.

I wander through the room, fingertips trailing over the gold frames on the mantel and the books on the built-in shelves.

Hayden said this place belonged to his great-grandmother. Before she died, she made her kids promise that they would never sell it. I guess some people inherit engagement rings and some inherit multimillion-dollar property. The only thing my mother left me, the only proof I have that she ever walked this earth, is my life. I wonder what she'd think of how I've squandered it.

"Okay," Rena says, reappearing on-screen. "I sent them and a picture of you that I need you to approve so I can post it. We haven't posted in weeks."

Once Rena hit influencer status, she took it upon herself to be my unofficial social media manager—because I couldn't care less and she cares too much. I barely even open the app anymore.

"Got them. I'll review after dinner."

"Thank you. Love you. Have fun with the tall boy. So glad we picked him."

I roll my eyes. "I'll call you tomorrow."

"Don't get pregnant," she says, and the call ends.

"What did she mean by that?" Hayden asks, one foot in the kitchen and the other in my conversation.

I walk over to where his phone is charging and unplug it to charge mine. "She means she doesn't want me to have a baby right now. Isn't that ridiculous? I'd be a wonderful mother." He shakes his head, grating fresh parmesan into a pot of . . . what is that? I bump him out of the way so I can see. "Are you cooking risotto? Why do you know how to cook risotto?"

Opening drawers until I find the silverware, I hop up on the counter next to him and eat straight from the pot. He watches, amused, as I chew the first bite slowly. I glare at him. "It's good." But it isn't just good. That tire company should give him at least one star for this. "I can't believe you."

He laughs. "What?"

"You can cook."

"And you're mad about that?"

"Uh, yeah. I am extremely upset to not have learned this about you sooner. Think of the midnight snacks I've missed out on." He can probably make pizza dough from scratch. A waste. "I starve at night for what?"

"Do you have a kitchen in your bedroom?"

"I'd have built one. Or at least ordered one of those burners people put in their college dorms. And a minifridge. And . . . what else do you need? A toaster oven?"

He turns the stove off, scoops a few spoonfuls into a bowl, and hands it to me. "What did Rena mean about picking me?"

"Mm," I hold up a finger because I have stuffed my mouth full of this damn risotto. So good. "You were drafted," I say between bites. "Thank you for your service."

"Drafted? I asked you out."

I lean back against the cabinet, biting my lip to keep from giggling. "Oh, my sweet, sweet summer child."

"I did."

"I know. You were supposed to."

"But you turned me down."

He's not wrong. I did turn him down, but only because dating him was never the plan. The truth is, upon moving to the city, I found myself incredibly bored. Boredom is a dangerous thing for someone like me. School was a good distraction, but I didn't know what to do with the hours in between. I didn't want to revert back to old habits. The excessive partying and the numbing drugs. Things had gotten so bad after Darren's death that Richards sat me down in his office, and with a look I had never seen before, asked if I was trying to die too.

I eat half my food while Hayden moves around the kitchen—putting away ingredients, wiping down the stove and counter, loading the dishwasher. His wheels are spinning as he replays those first few weeks in his head. "You wanted me to ask you out?"

"Yes."

"So you could say no?"

I smile. I had planned it perfectly. Spent my first week at Chamberson observing. Figuring out who's friends with who. What the social dynamics were. I dropped subtle hints in conversations. I let people say more than they should, and I took mental notes. I made a short list of five boys who could work. Boys I didn't intend to love and didn't think I'd grow to hate.

I texted the list to Rena, who looked into each boy carefully and sent a spreadsheet less than forty-eight hours later. The rest was like hunting. I've never been hunting, but I think I'd be good at it.

"I presented a counteroffer," I say. "That's just good business."

Hayden scoops another spoonful of risotto into my bowl and pours the rest of the pot into his. "I'm feeling extremely objectified."

"Are you?"

"Yes." I pout sympathetically. I, a woman, can't imagine such hardship. He smirks. "I should send Rena a gift though."

"A fruit basket at least."

We sit across from each other at the table, and it's the strangest part of the entire day so far. Have we ever eaten a meal at a table together? I don't think we have.

"Seems like a lot of work just to hook up with someone," he says after a moment. His gaze is expectant, waiting for a response to a question he hasn't asked.

I take a long sip of water until the bubbles burn my throat. What does he want me to say? "I'm an Aries. Rena's a Sag."

"I don't know what that means."

"It's our dynamic. If I were to commit a felony, I'd do it with Rena. Actually, maybe we have. I don't know what counts as a felony, but if she were ever to go to jail, I'd have to go too. We'd have to be in the same prison, but we couldn't be cellmates because we'd kill each other. We'd be in side-by-side cells."

"I have no idea where you're going with this."

I'm not sure either, but I'm on a roll.

"My point is, it's not a lot of work. I mean it is, but it's what we do."

"Why?"

"Because we're thorough."

"But why would it matter if you're not trying to date the person?"

Here we go. Did I find the one boy on earth who cannot be content with a friends-with-benefits relationship? We are alone in an empty house on a beach and this is the mood we're establishing?

He's got to be a Scorpio.

"What's your birthday?" I ask. "I don't have my spreadsheet."

"November seventeenth."

Like I said.

"Such a red flag. I'm surprised you made it through our vetting process."

"I'm honored," he says dryly.

"You should be."

Hayden twists the cap off a fresh bottle of the fancy Italian soda, which, as it turns out, is the best thing I've ever tasted. He leans over to fill my empty glass first. "Is there really a spreadsheet?"

"I'd never lie about spreadsheets."

"Who else is on it?"

My eyes narrow. "How many girls have you brought to this beach house?"

"Only a few dozen."

"That's really special."

I know he's joking but part of me wishes he were serious. That I was one of the countless girls he'd done this with.

I glance out the window toward the wall of trees, the

neighboring houses, and the ocean on the other side. Before I moved to New York, I rarely spent longer than a week away from the water. I wonder what part of my body betrayed me and told him how much I needed this.

When I turn back to him, he's watching me, smiling. "I figured you'd like it here."

"It kind of reminds me of home."

If I had been given the option to go anywhere in the world, this city wouldn't have been my choice. There are worse places to live than Manhattan, but there's so much I miss about Connecticut. I miss riding in cars down long, winding roads. I miss fall leaves on front yards and the sound of sprinklers in the morning. I miss those days when you can be outside for what feels like hours before you see another person. Impromptu picnics in empty fields. The smell of cut grass and wildflowers. You don't get any of that here.

"Why did you move?" he asks. "Did you have to or did you want to?"

"I didn't want to. I also didn't really have to." I'm old enough to have some say in the families LCS places me with. It has to be a good fit or it won't work. "I was kind of going through it." I don't know how to tell him that I left to save my life. I don't think he could understand the way I would need him to, so I just say, "Moving away seemed like the best thing to do at the time."

He leaves it at that, sensing that this isn't a topic to push, and we eat in silence. It's awkward. Almost unbearably so.

I open my mouth to try to break the silence, but he beats me to it.

"Five questions."

"What?"

He wipes his mouth with a napkin and tosses it in the empty bowl in front of him. "I get five and you get five and we answer honestly."

This is the emotional equivalent of standing in front of a firing squad. Hayden doesn't miss much, even when I wish he did. He's honest. He has the rare ability to articulate his feelings exactly. He doesn't hide anything. He isn't mysterious. He's open. Even though there are things I can't tell him, I know if I did, they'd be safe. He wouldn't hide them away in the pockets of his mind and use them against me later. He's like glass. Clear all the way through. Light reflecting. This is only problematic when I catch my reflection in his glow.

"Fine," I say. "But you have to ask all of yours right now and I get to save mine for later."

"That's not how the game works."

"The game is made up. The rules are arbitrary. What's your first question?"

I try not to anticipate what he could want to ask me. I work very hard to keep my face impassive and my heart at a steady rate.

His brown eyes lock onto mine. "What are you afraid of?"

"Like, in general?"

"No."

He wants to understand why fear seems to be the singular motivating force behind every action he has known me to take. Why I always seem to hold myself together like I'm awaiting the inevitable moment when my pieces become disjointed and I scatter across the floor. How I know it's really only a matter of time before the sky falls. Why I don't seem to fear the fall itself, just the idea that I may survive it again.

"I'm afraid of losing myself."

He tilts his head. "What does that mean?"

"Is that your second question?"

"No, it's a clarifying question."

I didn't agree to clarifying questions, but I also didn't forbid them.

"I can't explain it."

"Try," he says.

I push the pad of my thumb into my palm, feeling the delicate bones on the back of my hand. The bluish-green veins there. They say we're made almost entirely of water. Most days I feel more liquid than solid.

"Have you ever dropped something without realizing it until way later? Something important like your keys or your wallet. You spend all day retracing your steps trying to figure out where you lost it. What were you doing? How were you so distracted that you didn't notice sooner? It's like that, but scarier because it's you. Different parts of who you are." I doubt any of this makes any sense, but he nods like he gets it. "When it happens, there isn't much you can do about it."

Hayden stands, gathering our dishes and carrying them to the sink. "What keeps you from sleeping?"

It's easier to answer him with his back to me. "I'm not any good at it."

"You're not good at sleeping?"

"I can't be good at everything."

"Has it always been that way?"

I purse my lips. "That's definitely your third question."

"Fine."

I can't remember a time when sleep came easy to me. "It's gotten worse as I've gotten older, but I'm used to it now."

"You talk in your sleep sometimes."

I can't bring myself to be embarrassed by that because there's something hidden in his tone that I can't quite decipher. When Hayden sits down again, I know the next question will be too much. I can see it in the way his brows knit over his eyes. Like he doesn't want to hurt me. Like he doesn't know what could hurt me.

"Is Darren the reason you left Connecticut?"

His words are a whisper. Barely audible, but they cause a ringing in my ears that drowns out everything else. Every thought in my head. Every idea I had about how any of this would go. Any faith in myself that I could be strong enough to get through two more fucking questions.

"Whatever happened between you and him—"

I push my chair away from the table. I've never told Hayden about Darren. I don't have the words to describe the feeling of my two worlds crashing into each other and exploding. I want to run, but there's nowhere to go. I want to ask him to leave but this is his house. I'd leave but I can't.

"I'm going to take a shower," I say.

"Mel—"

I hold up my hands to stop him from talking but drop them when he notices how badly they're shaking. I grip the back of the chair for support. "I know what you're trying to do but you cannot push me. If you do and I give in, we will both regret it. We will. So, please just . . ." I will myself to hold the tears in for five more minutes. I'll cry in the shower if I have to. I don't want to cry in front of him.

We stare at each other, and I can see that he had expectations for today. This is not how he hoped things would go. I hoped we could have a moment to exist outside his expectations. Neither of us has gotten what we wanted.

It's a big deal to let someone know you. It's a lot to give people custody of the pieces of your heart. To tell them how it broke. And that you're not looking for glue, just learning to breathe. Why each inhale feels sharp. Show them where the shards punctured your lung. To tell them this and then bring them in. To make the space. To let them share what little air you have.

I'm not ready for that. I told him. He didn't listen to me.

6

SORRY IF THIS IS WEIRD

We sleep on opposite sides of the bed, our backs to each other. So much space between us.

I shouldn't have reacted the way I did, shutting him down without any discussion or explanation. It's just that hearing Darren's name come out of Hayden's mouth was too much. This is all happening too soon. I shouldn't have come here with him. I should've known better. I knew better.

I lie in bed until a little after six a.m. Tiptoeing to the bathroom, I change into my bathing suit and pad down the steps and out the back door to the pool.

I watch the dawn set the sky on fire. Floating on my back in the cold water, I watch rays of pink and orange rip through the clouds. I watch the moon concede to the day. I feel the world warm.

I stayed with Rena the night I found out I was leaving Connecticut. We lay around her pool, and looking up at the starless sky, I tried to see beyond where I was then. To imagine what could be if things were different. For so long, all I'd dreamed of was a life with Darren. I didn't know how to want anything else anymore.

Feet dipped in the still water, I longed so badly for the quiet fury of the ocean. I was newly sober and didn't know any other way to cope with the waves of despair lapping over me than to feel actual waves break against my skin. It helped me remember that the emotions were in my head. They weren't real. The heaviness couldn't really crush me. It was only in my head.

We scattered Darren's ashes in Eden, the place where he and I used to swim. All I could think as I watched him blow away was it must be lonely in a black sea. Who would he talk to when darkness fell? What would he see? There'd be no difference between the water around him and the sky above. Just floating in a cold, endless abyss. It would be lonely but peaceful. The world is lonely too, but it's chaotic.

I wanted peace for him, even if it caused me pain.

I kick off of the wall of the Thompsons' pool and bob slowly to the middle. I have a strange feeling that I'm being watched. I open my eyes to find Hayden standing on the edge of the balcony. Looking up at him, I'm suddenly overwhelmed by a deep sadness that I can't explain. We stay this way for a long time, silently communicating all the things that we need to say out loud. My feet hit the tile again and I push off, diving under the water. When I come up for air, he's gone.

He emerges ten minutes later from the kitchen with a cup of coffee, taking long strides across the lawn. "The car will be here in an hour."

He sets the cup on a nearby table and turns back toward the house.

"I broke up with him a year ago," I tell him.

Hayden and I have spoken maybe ten sentences to each other all morning. I've been going over all the other questions he could've asked me last night. Whether I should've told him about Darren. What I would've said.

"We were together for three years. It was a hard relationship. It's not something I like to relive."

He looks at me for the first time since we got in the car. He'd been sitting so still, I wasn't sure if he was sleeping. "I shouldn't have brought it up."

I lean my head against the window and close my eyes. My phone vibrates.

Rena: are you home?

Me: not yet

Me: in the car

Rena: call me the second you get home

Me: is everything okay?

Rena: call me when you're alone

When the car pulls up to my apartment, Hayden grabs my bag from the trunk. I tell him thank you for the trip. I tell him bye. He waits until I'm inside before the driver pulls off.

I FaceTime Rena once I'm in my room. She's in her dad's office wearing the blue-light glasses she got after her social media addiction gave her computer vision syndrome. Her phone is propped up against something, but her focus is on her laptop. Next to that is her iPad. And next to that, the desktop monitor glows brightly in what is a strangely dark room considering it's the middle of the afternoon. She takes one look at me through the screen and says, "Check your DMs."

I open my Instagram app, finger hovering over the inbox symbol. There's something in Rena's expression that's setting off alarms in my chest. Rena is dramatic, but she wouldn't do anything she thought would worry me unless she had to.

I click the only message in the request folder and read.

It's from someone named Brie Mitchell.

Hey, sorry if this is weird. I didn't know how else to contact you. Are you in the city?

I go to Brie's profile, and I don't understand what I'm looking at.

It's me, smiling at the camera, with my hair cropped short, just below my shoulders. My face, a little more angular, chin pointier, cheekbones more defined. More freckles on my nose. My hazel eyes, but brighter.

Me with people I've never met. Me in a leotard and pointe shoes, arching over a ballet barre. Me in countries I've never visited, eating food I've never tasted. Immersed in a life I've never lived.

There have been times in my life when I was way too high— like, forget-your-own-name high—but there's no way I got so high I went to Italy and forgot about it. I've never heard of a pill that turns you into an elite ballet dancer and then wipes your memory. If there's a drug that makes you as happy as this girl seems to be, I've never found it. That's clearly not my life, but it's more than that. I can't find myself in her eyes. They look the same, but I could never mistake them for mine.

She looks so happy.

I go back and read the message four more times.

Hey, sorry if this is weird. I didn't know how else to contact you. Are you in the city?

It was sent over a month ago.

"She lives here?" I ask Rena because I'm sure she's discovered everything there is to know about this girl short of her Social Security number by now.

"Yeah. In Brooklyn."

"Is she . . ." I can't bring myself to finish the sentence because it's both ridiculous and so blatantly obvious.

"Your twin? Please be serious. Look at her."

She's right. Brie doesn't just look like me. It isn't a resemblance. We're identical.

I wait for the panic to start. For the questions to flood my mind. I wait for my body to react, muscles tensing, limbs shaking. I wait for this information to register in some real way, for the full magnitude of the situation to hit me, but I feel nothing. Just a spongy kind of numbness. White noise in my brain.

"You guys must have grown up together, right? If you went to Laurelle when you were four, she must have been there with you."

"I don't know, Rena. I guess so."

"Richards and Debra never mentioned her?"

I shake my head. There's so much about my early childhood that I don't remember. There are bits and pieces of memories, but no whole moments. Flashes of people and places. I remember how things felt, but I can't form a clear picture of anything in my head until maybe six or seven. That can't be normal.

"What did you find out about her?" I ask.

Rena emails the dossier she's been compiling in the ninety minutes since she texted me. Every piece of info she found on Aubrie Mitchell. Her birthday, which is the same as mine. Her parents' names. What they do for a living. The neighborhood she lives in. The boy she dated last year but "didn't seem that into." The more I scroll, the more Brie solidifies in my mind. She's a whole person, existing merely miles away from me, living an entire life.

What am I supposed to do with all this? What do I do now?

"I found a video of her dancing on the account of a ballet school in Dumbo," Rena says. "Down for a stakeout?"

The video was posted on a Monday. Rena checked their class schedule and saw that there's an advanced class at four p.m. on Mondays. That's how I ended up here, crouching behind a bench waiting to catch a glimpse of Aubrie Mitchell.

I've been here for almost two hours. I brought snacks, as one should for any good stakeout. Exactly twelve people have come in and out of those doors during that time. I tear open another bag of mini chocolate chip cookies and lie back on the blanket. I can see through the gaps between the planks of the bench. I sit up on my elbows when the door opens again, but the only people who leave the building are a small child and her mother.

I may be turning into the villain in a psychological thriller, but I've made my peace with this. If there is a reasonable, sane reaction to finding out, after seventeen years, that there may be someone walking around this earth with your face, I'd love to know what it is.

It's so humid, my hair's getting bigger by the minute. The blanket is damp with sweat, and I'm ready to go. I won't go until I see her, so my exhaustion has turned into restlessness.

"Do you see her yet?" Rena whispers through my earbud.

"Why are you whispering?"

"Oh. I don't know. Do you see her?"

"No."

"What are your coordinates? Check your twelve o'clock."

"Twelve o'clock is in front of me, Rena. It's just looking straight ahead."

The only way I could persuade Rena not to drive all the way to the city for what may be a fruitless mission is if I kept her in my ear the entire time.

"Wait. Something's happening."

Students pour out into the street, clad in leotards and sweatpants with their hair twisted into tight buns and large bags slung across their backs. I scoot as close to the bench as I can without passing through like an apparition. I get a few suspicious looks from people walking by, but I choose not to acknowledge them because minding your business is free.

"What's going on?" Rena screams. I turn down the volume on my phone.

"They're leaving the school."

The crowd begins to thin. There's a very real possibility that she's not here. I stand up, ducking behind a car and peering through the windows. This looks even shadier than the bench thing, but it works because I see her. She's one of the last to leave the building. She's not in a leotard. She changed into shorts and a T-shirt, her curly hair loose and blowing around her face. She reaches into her bag and takes out her phone.

"Oh my god." I can't help but move closer. I want to follow her to wherever she's going, but I left all my stuff over by the bench.

"Oh my *god*," Rena echoes, operating off of nothing but the sound of my breathing and vibes. "Go talk to her!"

"I can't confront her on the street."

She's me if life had happened differently. She's me with a last name belonging to people who knew where she came from and wanted to share their name with her anyway. She's me if I'd grown up in a city rather than in the suburbs. If I'd found a passion and applied myself to it. If I had a future I was fighting for.

But then she zeroes in on me. She has stopped completely in the middle of the sidewalk, earning her own dirty looks from strangers. I don't take my eyes off her, but when I zoom out enough to orient myself, I realize I'm standing in the middle of the opposite sidewalk. I've wandered out from the safety of the car's shadow. Lured toward her like a spell. Something over which my body had no control.

This was a mistake.

Brie starts to cross the street, waiting for a gap in the passing cars. She moves hesitantly, but she's moving. Closing the space between us. Each step that she takes causes my world to sway.

"What's happening?" Rena asks.

This was so stupid. Why did I come here? What did I think would happen? Why did I think I could do this?

My legs are shaking now. Not a tremor, but a full shudder rippling through my body. I can't focus on anything. The connection between my brain and limbs seems to have been severed. My heart is racing at twice its usual speed.

I spin around and slam into a woman carrying an armful of groceries. The handle of the paper bag rips and her produce falls all over the sidewalk, oranges rolling into the gutter and cucumbers accidentally trampled by people who look but have no intention of helping. She glowers at me with that special brand of New York ire that's always bubbling just below the surface. I think I'm hyperventilating.

"I'm sorry," I say. I want to help her pick up everything, but my urge to run is greater.

"Nah, you busy? You got someplace to be?"

"I'm sorry. I didn't mean—"

"Mel!"

Brie's voice shuts my body down. I stare at the woman dumbly as she curses me out, but I can't hear what she's saying over the buzzing in my ears. I have to get out of here, but my legs won't move.

A full scene in the middle of the sidewalk. The lady's yelling at me. Rena's screaming in my ear. Brie's calling my name. I'm going to be sick.

Body convulsing, I bend down to scoop up the last of the fruit. The woman snatches it and storms away. Before I can leave too, Brie catches up to me and grabs my wrist.

The sensation brings me back to myself. It settles my stomach. Builds a fire in my chest. This isn't my fault. I didn't ask for this. I didn't torpedo her life. Casually. Like it's no big deal. I yank my arm away.

She takes a step back, glancing at the crowd that has begun to scatter now that it's clear this family dispute will not be worth their time.

I didn't expect to meet her today. I hadn't prepared myself for the shock and confusion on her face. Our face.

"What are you doing here?"

Her words are like an axe to my chest. I didn't anticipate that she could be angry, but there's more than just anger there. Some other emotion I can't identify.

What am I doing here? Suddenly all the events that led to this moment seem like a series of bad decisions.

"You DMed me," I say indignantly.

"Yeah and you never replied. Now you're running from me?

Really?" I can't slow my racing thoughts long enough to form a coherent response to her. She starts to say something else but snaps her mouth shut, looking away when tears begin to pool in her eyes. "You know what? I'm not doing this right now." She brushes past me, heading back in the direction from which she came.

What the fuck just happened?

Numbly, I watch her jog across the street and mix into the flow of foot traffic until I lose her.

It's that easy to lose someone. They're here one minute and the next you're alone again.

7

UP TO ONE HUNDRED

Me: come over

The first time I got high I was fourteen. I was sitting in the grass in Darren's backyard, knees pulled up to my chest, watching him roll a joint between his fingers. It was the middle of the afternoon, but it was summer so he had just woken up. He slept a lot that summer. Smoked a lot too. Didn't talk. I got used to sitting with him. I learned not to ask if he was okay or if I'd done something. I didn't want to upset him but I missed him. He was right there, and I still missed him. I didn't know what had changed.

In that silence, I spent more time in my head than I ever had before. I thought too much about everything. Talked myself out of the things I wanted to say to him. Tried to calm myself down when sadness would inch up my spine and cause my limbs to go heavy because I didn't know if I'd have him to lean on if I started to fall. There were so many times in that first year that Darren had come through for me when everything felt like it was caving in. I didn't know what was going on with him, but I wanted to be there for him too in whatever way I could.

I didn't realize he could see the way the weight of this was crushing me. It was embarrassing. As many times as he held the two of us up, I couldn't do it when the situation was reversed. It was the first time I really felt like a burden to him. So when he held the joint out for me—his one way to offer me support, the one thing that seemed to be helping him through whatever it was that I couldn't—I took it.

The pills started a few months later. I took those too. I'd have stopped if it didn't help so much. Because it helped, it made everything so much worse. For him and for us.

When I got sober last winter, I flushed almost all of my stash down the toilet in Richards's office. I didn't think I had a problem, although Richards disagreed, but that felt like the only way I could break my bond with Darren. I didn't want to feel him in the way the pills caused my mind to slow. It had become the only way I could sleep, and although I was exhausted, I was so tired, I promised myself I would find another way to live. And I did. I have.

But a half hour ago I opened the little wooden box tucked away inside my drawer. The one I told myself I would never open. I only kept one pill as a precaution—an ejection seat to save me if I ever found myself free-falling again. I just want to sleep, but whenever I close my eyes, I see Brie's face. I hear the hurt in her voice. I feel the storm of emotions in my body, none of which I can name or understand. So I swallowed it and came up to the roof to hear the city buzzing below. I didn't want to be alone.

I rake my fingers over the angry red skin of my arm and

wait for Hayden's reply to my text. I don't usually text him this late. I'd gotten nervous the pill wouldn't work and needed a backup plan. I didn't think about the fact that it's almost one in the morning. Sue and Dave have been asleep for hours. He's probably sleeping too.

Hayden: can't tonight

He's never told me no before.

We haven't spoken since he dropped me off yesterday. Maybe I should've expected the conversation over dinner to change things between us. I laid down a boundary, and it's only fair that he be able to do the same. Any other night I may have accepted it. If my pride were intact, I may have left the text unanswered. I think that's what he expects because when I write back **please**, a full three minutes pass before he responds.

Hayden: you okay?

My fingernail rips through flesh and I wince, wiping the blood off my arm with the palm of my hand.

Me: can you stay?

Hayden: the night?

Me: yeah

The ellipsis pops up and disappears. Once. Twice. I'm about to tell him never mind when my phone buzzes with his reply.

Hayden: be there in 20

I wait for him to text again telling me he's here before I get up. My legs are rubber. I take the elevator to my floor and when I turn the corner, he's there with a backpack hanging from his shoulder. He looks like he's about to pass out, and I feel a twinge of guilt that I dragged him out of bed this late. But I'm so happy to see him that I hug him. He stumbles back. Surprised, he hesitates for a moment and then squeezes me back, resting his chin on top of my head.

"One sec," I say, slipping into the apartment alone. I open the fridge loudly, pour a glass of water and wait, listening for Sue and Dave. Dave's white-noise machine is whirling. I keep my eyes on the space under their door. Sue would turn the lamp on if she got out of bed. Dave's footsteps would be heavy on the floor.

After another minute of silence, I let Hayden in. He follows me down the hall to my room, locking the door behind us and kicking off his shoes. I set the glass down on the nightstand and climb into bed. My body feels dense and formless like a block of clay. I can't keep my eyes open but I can't sleep. I can't stop seeing her face. I feel unmoored.

Hayden doesn't speak, just unzips his bag and pulls something out. Then he's next to me and the lights are off. He taps my arm. When I roll over, he offers me one of his earbuds. I take it and glance numbly at his phone screen. The opening credits to some stand-up comedy special I've never seen start, and I shift closer to him. He presses me to his side, fingers trailing through my hair. I turn my face into his neck to block out the light.

When Brie walked away, it took me five minutes to get enough control over my legs to make it back to the blanket. Twenty minutes before my body stopped shaking. Even now, I can't regulate my nervous system. I've never felt anything like that before. The panic, yes, but never that tenacious pull toward another person. The snap of that tether when they turn their back on you. I didn't know I could hurt in this specific way, and I don't know what to do to stop it.

Is this what she felt waiting for a DM that never came? Did I hurt her this way too?

Laughter fills my ear. I squint at the phone drooping in Hayden's hands. His eyes are closed and his breathing is deep and even. I take out our earbuds and put them next to his phone on the nightstand. When I lie down, his arms wind around me like vine and I start to cry. They're enervated, aimless tears. I hold my body still so that I don't wake him. I feel stupid. I don't even know why I'm crying.

Laying my head over his heart, I count the beats up to one hundred and back down to one. I breathe slowly with him, in and out. It doesn't lift the weight from my chest, but it helps.

When morning comes, we're still tangled around each other. I slept, but I can't be sure how long. When I peek at Hayden, he's awake, looking out the window. The apartment is quiet. Sue and Dave must have left for work already. I want coffee but that would involve getting up. I'm stiff and my eyes feel dry and swollen. The covers are too heavy to move. The pillow is too soft. Hayden's too warm.

He meets my gaze, and we stare at each other. It reminds me of the way he looked at me when I hugged him last night. Confused, his eyes full of unasked questions. I start to roll over but he lifts me onto his chest. He slips his hands under my shirt, rubbing my back.

"Are you okay?" he asks. "I was worried about you."

"Sorry."

"What's wrong?"

"I had a bad day." He doesn't say anything, just holds me tighter. "I shouldn't have texted you so late."

"I'm glad you did. I had a bad day too."

"You did?"

"Mm-hmm." He presses his lips to my hair. "I got into it with my dad."

"Told you he'd be pissed."

"Trust me, it doesn't take much to piss him off. I should thank you for getting me out of the house."

"In that case, you owe me one."

His laugh shakes some of the tension out of my body. We stay like this for so long that I'm starting to fall back asleep when my phone vibrates. I groan. Hayden takes one hand out of my shirt to unplug the phone from the charger. It's a text from Rena with her ETA.

"I have to get dressed." I push off his chest so that I'm sitting on his lap. "Rena's on her way."

This isn't a regular visit. Rena insisted on driving down with Cal even though I told her not to. I hate that she feels like she needs to drop everything to check on me. The empty box on my dresser taunts me from across the room. Shame greets me like an old friend.

Hayden's thumb brushes over the scratch on my arm. Then over the ghosts of others peppering my skin. Tiny, faded marks you can't see unless you're close enough and really looking. He lines his nail up with one. And then another. And another. I pull my arm away.

His eyes are dark and intense, scanning over my face. "You never answered my question."

I keep my expression neutral. "What question?"

"Are you okay?" The concern in his voice reminds me of how I used to speak to Darren. Constantly checking for any cracks in his facade, wondering if I could believe a word he said. "You can talk to me about stuff. I'm not trying to pressure you. I just want you to know that."

"I know. I'm okay."

"You're sure?"

"I'm sure," I say. "I promise."

But neither of us believes me.

A few hours later, Rena's analyzing me, her blue eyes slits—which could be from suspicion or the edible she ate earlier. We're at some random park in Harlem scarfing rice and beans, the braided metal of the chain-link fence digging into my back. My butt is going numb. I readjust, scooting over so I can lay my head on her leg, my half-eaten food abandoned on the grass.

"You like him." She says it like an accusation.

I don't want to talk about Brie so we're talking about Hayden instead. I filled them in on the trip and everything that happened this morning, downplaying my reason for texting him. Omitting the whole pill situation. I kept it as light as I could, and Rena took the bait. She loves boy talk.

"What?" I ask, although her words were perfectly clear.

Cal, having finished his own food, reaches for Rena's abandoned rice, which she lets him have. "She said you like him." He goes for her plantains too, but she swats his hand away.

"She heard me," Rena says, running a hand through her wavy lilac bob. "I'm all for a rebound, but you cannot date the rebound."

"I agree. Weren't you the one who told me to give him a chance?"

She tilts her head. "Did I say that? Doesn't sound like me."

Cal yawns. He pretends he's not into these types of conversations, but he's as much of a gossip as Rena. Truly one of the girls. At the ripe age of eighteen, they are already an old married couple starved for entertainment. Rena's all about the drama. He's here to make sure we don't lose the plot. "Well, M, you're gonna have to end it because he's not going to."

"I didn't say end it," Rena says. "Have you seen him?"

"Let's break up and then you can date him," he mutters.

She rolls her eyes.

"No, I have to end it." I mean it as a statement, but it comes out more like a question. They stare at me, waiting for an answer I don't have. "Right?"

Rena shrugs.

Cal stuffs our trash in the bag before the wind can blow it

into the other trash littering the street. "He clearly likes you. A guy's not gonna try that hard if he doesn't. Especially if you're already hooking up." Rena hits him. "What? Am I lying?"

I'm not confused about whether Hayden likes me. The question is, what do I do about it?

Cal sets off in search of a trash can. Rena waits until he's out of earshot before she says, "He's right."

"I have to end it."

"But you don't want to."

That's the thing with Rena. She always gets right to the heart of the things I don't want to say. Why do I need a therapist if I have her?

"I do." Do I? "I think I do." No, yes. Yes. "I do."

"So what's stopping you? Could it be that he's stupid hot?"

"You're not helping."

"Don't listen to me. I'd go to hell for a hot boy. You know this." She tugs lightly on a chunk of my hair. "I meant what I said about moving on. Even if it's not with Hayden."

A group of kids tear down the street on bikes, the youngest barely keeping up, pedaling frantically with little legs. As the distance between her and the others grows wider, I want to yell for them to wait for her. Can't they see how hard she's trying? Can't they tell she's struggling?

"I'm so angry, Rena."

I know you can't be angry at someone for dying, but when I think of the fact that Darren's not here, it makes me furious. I don't know what it was about the alchemy of our relationship.

I don't know what made us so toxic, but it changed us both in an irrevocable way. How is it I was left to deal with the aftermath of us alone? It isn't fair.

"I get that," she says with a sad smile. "I'm still a little angry at Darren too."

I think of all the things I did to be with him. All the battles I won. The casualties of those battles. All the times I conceded. The things I lost.

"I'd have been something different if I never met him."

"Is that what you want?" she asks. "To be different?"

"I don't think life is supposed to feel like this. It can't be this way for everyone. How do people . . ." I don't know what I'm asking. How do people survive? How do they deal with the immense burden of existing? "I don't know how long I can do this."

"Do what?" When I don't answer, her voice becomes shrill. "You don't know how long you can do what?"

"I didn't mean it like that."

I'm not trying to freak her out.

"No, you can't say shit like that to me." It isn't often that I have to be careful with my words. Only around the people who really know me. Rena and I have been through so much together. "Amélie."

I stiffen at the sound of my full name coming out of her mouth. I can count on one hand the number of times she's used it, each time out of desperation. "I'm sorry."

"Don't be sorry, just . . ." She takes a deep breath, fiddling nervously with the ring on her finger. It isn't only about me. Darren was one of her best friends. She lost him too. I squeeze her hand.

"I'm okay. I really am."

After a minute she squeezes back. "No more existential breakdowns, please. My god, I can't take it. Let me see the boy again."

I let her use my phone to stalk Hayden. He barely posts so she's deep in his tagged pictures before she finds a clear shot of him. She holds the phone up and yes, he's gorgeous, we get it.

"You are screwed," she says.

"Thank you so much."

By the time Cal returns, juggling three half-melted ice cream cones, Rena's in the middle of a photo shoot. The only reason any photos exist of me at all is because Rena and Shaine won't allow me a single moment of peace. I keep pace with Cal as we walk to the subway. Rena, completely enthralled by the tedious job of editing the pictures she took, falls behind.

Cal drapes his heavy-ass arm around me. It's too hot for that, but I've missed him so much, I decide it's fine. His blond hair is sticking to his forehead. I can't tell if the sweat on my neck is mine or his. Nothing but love could resign me to this.

"When do you leave for London?" I ask. His mom has family in the UK. They usually visit for a few weeks every summer.

"I'm not."

"Have you seen her since you got back from school?"

"I call every few weeks."

My pending adoption into Cal's family was shot to hell after the home visit four years ago when it became increasingly obvious his parents were headed for a brutal divorce. They each left with half their collective assets and one whole traumatized kid. Sad thing is, that was the most functional house I'd ever been in.

Since Cal left for college last year, he only visits Rena.

"What about your dad?"

He doesn't answer.

"I'll take that as a no."

He groans. "They're both fine. When I call, we don't even talk about anything. How is it my responsibility to make shit feel normal? I did it for years and then I moved out. Now I'm done. They're the adults."

"You're an adult now too," I say. "But you're right. It's just sad, you know? They're your family."

"You're my family. You and the girl back there who cannot for the life of her walk at a normal pace."

It's not that Rena is walking slowly. It's that she's not walking at all. She's almost half a block behind. I can't take her anywhere, I swear. "Rena!"

She jogs to catch up to us. "Sorry, I'm done. Look how cute."

She chose a shot of me lying on my back with my head on her lap. I'm midlaugh, my eyes squeezed shut and my hair blowing across my face. It's only a moment, impermanent and fleeting, but it's happiness.

God, I needed them. I'm so glad they're here.

"I miss you guys." The words burn my throat. Maybe it wasn't the right choice to leave them. Maybe I should've stayed.

"We miss you too." Rena links our arms together. "Are you ready to deal with the Brie thing or are we still pretending she doesn't exist?"

"Chill," Cal says. "She's working through it."

I'm not working through anything. I'm avoiding it. I open Brie's message again.

Hey, sorry if this is weird. I didn't know how else to contact you. Are you in the city?

I stop at the top of the subway steps and take a deep breath. Rena and Cal exchange one of their telepathic looks. Cal moves me out of the way of the people trying to pass. Rena rests her chin on my shoulder, reading the words as I type and delete and rephrase. Before I can think too hard about it, I hit send.

can we meet?

8

GOOD LIGHTING. WATER. NO BREAD.

Rena slams her iPad on the coffee table. "This is the floor plan of the restaurant."

Cal, who's sitting on the floor with his back against the couch, looks up. He had been tuning her out up until now, preoccupied with something on his phone. "You're not serious."

"She has an anxiety disorder! I can't send her in there blind. We have to account for every variable. Look at her!"

They both look at me, curled up in a ball on the couch.

Rena's not wrong. I know I'm the one who suggested Brie and I meet, but part of me thought she would say no and then I could say I tried. She was so angry the last time I saw her. I didn't fully consider the fact that if she said yes, I would have to go. I've had less than a week to mentally prepare for this.

We decided to meet halfway at a restaurant in Little Italy. I suggested this particular restaurant because it has good reviews, and it's so popular that they kick you out after ninety minutes. Rena said ninety minutes is the perfect amount of time to decide if you hate someone and it ensures we have a built-in excuse to leave if things aren't going well.

"Where did you get a floor plan?" Cal asks as Rena props the iPad up so we can see the screen.

"I emailed them saying I was interested in throwing an event. The pricing quotes are very reasonable." She zooms in, tapping one of the rectangles on the floor plan. "The host desk is here. The reservation is under your last name. Show up ten minutes early. Request to be seated at one of the booths by the windows. You sit in the booth so she has to sit in the chair. You'll be facing the windows. Great lighting."

Cal sighs. "Babe."

"It's important. It's also a power move. After the Dumbo showdown, we need a rebrand."

I'm sweating through my shirt. I don't have the mental or emotional constitution to deal with this. "Too much information." I fan my face with one of Sue's magazines. "I'm not going to remember all of this."

"I wrote it in a text. Check your phone." Cal reaches back for my hand. I wipe my palm on my shorts and let him take it. Rena plows on. "When you sit, order water. Room temp. No ice. No lemon. Drink half of it. It'll give the impression that you've been there forever and she's late. This will be even more effective if she actually is late. Don't let them bring bread because you will get nervous, eat it all, get a stomachache, and be a bitch."

"That's true," Cal says. "You're rude when you're sick."

I drop his hand and he grins. Rena marks the floor plan with red arrows as if I'm supposed to know what they mean. She sends the document to my phone.

"Is there anything else?" I ask.

"Let's discuss the menu."

The front door opens as the menu is loading. We all turn at the same time. When Cal and Rena are here, it's normal for Sue and Dave to find us spread out in the living room with the quilt and pillows from my bed, empty take-out containers, and several laptops playing different shows. What stops them in their tracks is the unhinged look in my eye, the weary expression on Cal's face, and Rena physically hunching over the iPad at an angle that is unnatural for the human body. They glance around like they have no idea what they just walked in on. Sue puts her keys in the glass tray.

Cal and Rena look at me like, *Are you gonna tell them?*

I should talk to Richards first. Or Debra. Find out what they know. I should wait until after my lunch with Brie to decide if there's anything worth telling. I should find a better way to tell them. A better time.

The thought of doing any of that exhausts me.

Dave turns one of the kitchen stools around to face us. "What's going on?"

I don't know how to say it out loud, so I pull up Brie's Instagram profile and hand him the iPad. He stares at it uncomprehendingly. Sue, who's still taking off her shoes by the front door, walks over so she can see. Her eyes shoot up to meet mine.

She takes the iPad from Dave, scrolling through Brie's pictures. "She lives here," I explain. "I . . . met her. Kind of. It was . . ."

"A disaster," Rena says.

I shoot her a look. She mouths, *Sorry.*

Sue shakes her head like she's trying to get her thoughts together. "Met? You didn't know about her?"

"No. Did you?"

"No, they never told us." She gives me the iPad. I hand it back to Rena, who immediately loads a pdf of the restaurant's menu and begins slashing red X's through various items. "Mel, this is . . . How are you handling this?"

"I'm not. Rena's handling it."

Rena's head jerks up at the mention of her name. "Do you wanna see the dossier I've compiled?"

Sue gapes at her. If you know Rena for an extended period of time, you find that you meet her twice. First, you meet the bubbly, adorable girl she appears to be on the surface, and then you meet this creature who wears that poor girl's skin like a cloak. This is that moment for Sue.

"Have you spoken to Richards?" Dave asks. "Or Debra? We should call them. I don't understand how they didn't tell us about this?"

"Please don't call them," I say.

"They need to—"

"I know but . . . let me do it."

I've barely had time to process anything. I feel like I'm losing my mind, and if anyone from LCS starts coming at me with questions I can't answer, I cannot be held accountable for what I may do. I need to meet Brie. Then I need a minute to sort through all this. I will talk to Richards when I have a clearer idea of what I want to say to him.

"When's your next appointment?" Dave asks.

"Thursday."

I can't believe a few days ago I was lying on a beach and my most pressing issue was that a boy likes me too much.

"Sorry," Rena says. "I don't mean to interrupt the moment but, M, you need to get ready to go."

Sue's face scrunches. "Go where?"

"I'm having lunch with her. Brie."

"Do you think you should wait until you've spoken to Richards? Maybe there's a reason they haven't told you about her."

"Like what?"

Sue looks down, searching the floor for a reason that most likely doesn't exist.

"Besides," I say. "It's too late to cancel now. She probably wouldn't see the message in time, and I'm not going to stand her up."

Rena sends me a few more things from her iPad before finally powering it off. She crawls over to Cal and he opens his arms to her. "I left three outfit options on your bed. Pick option two."

After a quick internal pep talk and another glance at my concerned foster parents, I unfold myself from the couch and head for my room. Cal's voice trails behind me. "Why are there three if you know which one you want her to pick?"

"Free will is an illusion," Rena says. "But it's important for morale."

The second I walk into the restaurant, I forget every single thing Rena said. I step back outside to scan her text. Check in. Booth by the windows. Good lighting. Water. No bread.

Okay. I can do that. That's . . . Mm-hmm.

All right.

The host gives me the type of smile that says she's been working here too long and has mentally divested. I wait for her to greet me. She doesn't.

"Reservation under Cœur," I say.

She stares at me for a beat too long and then checks her computer.

"Right this way. Your guest is already seated."

I'm eight minutes early. How is she here already? This was not the plan. Rena didn't account for the possibility of her beating me here. How long has she been here? Did she order bread? Is she also a bitch when she eats too much gluten? Am I going to get a bitchy Brie because I'm two minutes late to being ten minutes early?

We wind our way through the dining room. It's midafternoon on a Saturday so the place is packed. I'm surprised Rena managed to get a reservation, but then again, Rena gets what Rena wants.

Brie is sitting on the booth side of the table facing the windows. Rena was right. The lighting is great. I take the chair. This is not how this was supposed to go.

"Hey," I say, working hard to keep my tone casual, like meeting your long-lost sister is a completely normal thing to be doing. As if I didn't have a meltdown the last time I saw her. Whatever she's thinking, her expression gives nothing away.

"Hi."

I fill my glass with the carafe on the table and chug. Rena didn't say anything about how much water I should drink in front of Brie. Is it okay to have ice if she's already here? Brie watches me shift in my seat. For her to be my literal identical twin and still be impossible to read is the most bizarre thing I have ever experienced. Have I ever truly seen my face until today? I put the glass down.

Brie opens her menu and casually, without a hint of emotion, asks, "Do you know what you're going to order?"

I don't know what I'm going to order because the host never gave me a menu. I'd use the one Rena sent but I don't want to have my phone out if Brie doesn't have her phone out.

"Uh, no." I fold my hands on the table where my menu should be and look around to see if I can get someone's attention, but all the servers are preoccupied. "Can I . . ."

She slides the menu to the middle of the table so we can both read, but it may as well be in Italian. I can't get my eyes to focus on the page.

"Good afternoon," our server says, appearing out of nowhere. "I'm Marco. I'll be taking care of you today." Marco stands over us with his pen and pad in hand. "Can I get you started with something to drink or would you like to order?"

I choose the first thing I see. "I'll have the cacio e pepe. I'm good with water. Thanks."

"I'll have the chopped salad with dressing on the side. Water is fine for me too." Brie closes the menu and hands it to Marco. "Thank you."

Once Marco's gone, a chill settles over the table. Brie studies me with guarded eyes. A chain-link fence around whatever it's costing her to be here with me. The emotions she's trying to contain. But I know all about fences. Enough to know how feeble they are. How easy they are to climb. It's how I first learned to build walls. Laying the bricks down one by one. Sealing it with concrete. Becoming a fortress.

Lately, I've been trying to learn how to exist outside those walls, but right now I'm grateful for them. For the trained blankness of my face while my eyes graze over Brie. Her hair, the same chestnut brown as mine. Her curls springier without the additional six or so inches weighing them down. The precise cut of her black winged eyeliner. The way it makes doe eyes look deadly. Her perfect posture. The tension she holds in her body.

Her eyes harden, clashing against barriers that have taken me years to build. The other side is pure pandemonium, but she doesn't need to know that.

"How did you find me the other day?" she asks.

I lean back in my seat, determined not to let the panic I felt the last time I saw her take over again. "I have an obsessive friend with too much free time."

"How long were you waiting?"

"A while."

"Would you have said anything if I hadn't seen you?"

I press my clammy hands into my thighs. I can feel my heartbeat racing through my palms as I tell her the truth. "Probably not."

She closes her eyes. When she opens them, the chain-link fence is gone. There's nothing standing between me and the full spectrum of her emotions. Anger. Hurt. Disappointment. My nails claw against skin.

"What do you want, Mel? You clearly don't want to talk."

She's right. I don't want to. And still. "I'm talking."

"You're not saying anything."

"What am I supposed to say?" She opens her mouth only to clamp it shut. "No, really. Tell me. What did you expect when you DMed me out of the blue like that? I wasn't ignoring you, by the way. I didn't see it until the other day. I've left my psychiatrist on read longer than that. Also, in my defense, what the fuck was that message? *Hey, sorry if this is weird.* Like, don't worry about it, just losing my mind because who even are you? Rena had to basically pull your dental records for me to know for sure that you exist and I'm not suffering from a dissociative disorder. To be real, I'm still not one hundred percent sure."

Brie looks dazed. She starts to say something but Marco reappears, dropping a basket of bread at our table. I mirror his easy smile the best I can.

I didn't come here to fight with Brie, but for her to be so angry with me when I haven't done anything to deserve it makes me want to give her a reason to be angry. The last time I saw her, she walked away from me. She was the one who didn't want to talk.

"When I saw you on the street, something felt off. I don't know how to explain it. I couldn't process it at the time, but . . ."

Brie's voice is so low, I have to focus to make out her words. She takes a shaky breath. "It was the way you were looking at me. How you're looking at me now. You used to get really bad nightmares when we were little. I'd wake you up and you'd be so disoriented that you wouldn't remember where you were or who I was. Only for a few seconds. Then you would blink and rub your eyes and you'd know me again."

Her eyes are far away, recalling memories that I've lost to time. Her chin trembles. "How do you not remember me?"

That question is like a battering ram to the wall holding me together. A wall that has withstood so much throughout the years, but isn't without its cracks and fissures. I cannot fall apart here. I need to get through this lunch.

Brie stands abruptly and heads in what I assume is the direction of the bathroom. I ignore Rena's advice, dousing a piece of bread in vinegar and olive oil and shoving it in my mouth. I don't have an appetite but I feel like, by eating, I'm feeding the thing inside me that's keeping me calm. Well, maybe not calm, but calm-ish. As adjacent to calm as I'm capable of right now. I take a sip of water to force it down and check my texts.

Rena: soooo

Rena: do we hate her?

I send her a pic of my bread and my non-window-facing view.

Rena: oh god

I put my phone away when Brie approaches. She slides into her seat. Her mascara is smeared and the tip of her nose is red. She won't look me in the eye.

"I didn't mean for this to be so awkward," I say.

Something between a laugh and a choking sound bubbles up in her chest. "Okay."

She combs her fingers through her hair. It's the same nervous gesture I do. Unfortunately, I am in no position to comfort her considering I'm barely keeping it together. You have to put the oxygen mask on yourself first and my mask hasn't dropped yet. We sit in silence, breathing as best we can.

By the time Marco brings our food with a graceless clatter that makes us both jump, I've been sitting so still, breathing so deeply, that I've damn near entered a state of hypnosis. He offers us an apologetic smile, replaces our half-empty carafe of water, and strides away.

The smell of the pasta turns my stomach, but I pick up the fork just to have something to do. Brie doesn't touch her salad. Although she's looking at me, it's like she's not really seeing me.

"Our apartment. Our mom. Moving to Laurelle." It's like she's playing the supercut of our childhood in her mind. "Nothing?"

I clutch my glass of water, sending little ripples across the surface.

"We roomed together for a year. We pushed our beds into one giant bed against the window and filled our drawers with snacks we stole from the dining hall. Every morning, we would—"

"You were only at Laurelle for a year?"

Kids like us are typically adopted young or not at all, but

still. A year? Was she placed with the first family she met? If we were together at the time, if her parents could fall in love with her so easily, what was wrong with me? Why didn't they want me too?

She looks down, finger tracing the rim of her glass. "I left right before our sixth birthday, but there was a period of time between the last time I saw you and when I left. You were moved out of our room one morning and no one told me why. No one told me where they were taking you or when I'd see you again. I didn't understand, but that's the way I remember it happening with our mom, so I thought that's just the way people leave you."

I don't remember anything about our mom. I don't remember sharing a room with Brie or being moved out of the room. I do remember where they moved me because it became my room for the next year until I was placed with the Baxters. That only lasted three months. When I got back, I started seeing Richards every Wednesday afternoon at three.

"You really weren't avoiding me this whole time?" she asks in a small voice.

"Why would I do that?"

She rips a corner off a piece of bread and puts the rest back in the basket. "Do you remember other stuff from back then? Friends? Your favorite movies? Classes you hated?"

I understand what she's doing. Trying to find in me the sister she lost, but I'm afraid to conjure ghosts. Just the thought of it sends a chill over my skin. Goose bumps up my arms. "Can we talk about something else?"

"Sure. Sorry." Her smile is sympathetic. It's the first time I've seen her smile, aside from her photos. She picks up her fork and starts eating. "Tell me stuff about you."

"What kind of stuff?"

"I've been keeping tabs on you over the years, but there's obviously a lot we don't know about each other. Stuff we can't learn from stalking each other's profiles."

Rena would take this as a personal challenge.

"You've been keeping tabs on me?"

"Since I was old enough to have a phone." She dips a forkful of lettuce in the small cup of dressing and scrapes half of it off. Who eats like that? "You don't post a lot. I had very little to work with."

I don't bother telling her my entire social media presence is a carefully curated lie. I wonder what she thinks she knows about me.

"If you've been following me this long, why didn't you say anything before?"

She runs a hand through her hair again. I have to stop doing that. It's such an obvious tell.

"Because you never did. I thought you might not want to see me."

Why would she think that? If we were as close as she says we were, why wouldn't I want to see her?

"I left you there," she whispers. "I thought you might hate me for that." She crosses her arms over her chest like she's bracing for a blow. "Do you think that's why you don't remember me?"

I laugh and it sounds insane even to my own ears. I have no idea what I feel about Brie getting adopted before me. Or that she's been out there all these years and has never reached out. I don't know how she can have such clear memories of me when I don't have a single one of her. Basically, I don't know shit.

I do know one thing though.

"Brie, if hate could make me forget someone, I wouldn't remember half the people I've met in my life."

This does very little to ease her guilt. Probably because it's not really an answer to her question. She pushes her plate away even though she's barely eaten anything. "The family that you're with now . . ."

"They're cool," I say. Brie relaxes a bit at that. "We're basically the same age. It's like living with camp counselors."

Not that I would know. I've never been to camp.

"Should I pretend I don't know your foster mom is Susan Romano?"

I roll my eyes. "Yes."

She grins. "Have you met any celebrities?"

"Like who?"

"She works with everyone."

"She doesn't bring them to the apartment."

Brie refills her glass and drops a wedge of lemon in. "My parents are both doctors. The only person I've met through them is a really great nutritionist."

"Do they know about me?"

Her smile fades. "LCS didn't tell them. I told them later. If they had known, I'm sure they would've taken us both."

Before I can respond, Trey walks in with two adults who I'm assuming are his parents. "Shit." He must feel someone staring at him because he turns and looks right at me. Then he sees Brie and his eyes widen.

"What?" Brie tries to follow my line of sight, but Trey's face is just another random face in the crowd to her.

"I'll be right back."

Trey sees me coming and breaks off from his parents. "Hey, Melie. What's up."

"You can't say anything."

"Say anything about what?" His eyes drift back over to our table. "Oh, Second Melie?"

"I'm serious."

He loses the smirk and eyes me skeptically. "The fact that you have a secret sister is one thing. The fact that you don't want me to tell anyone . . ."

"Please, Trey."

I don't know why I'm asking him to keep this from everyone, from Hayden, but when he nods in agreement, I believe he will.

"Boyfriend?" Brie asks when I get back to our table.

"God no."

I steal another look at Trey, but he's seated with his back to me.

"So," Brie says, once we've finished eating and there's nothing else for us to focus on. "What now?"

I pass her my phone. "I guess we can start with phone numbers."

"What? You don't want to take four weeks to respond to each other's DMs?"

"I'll text back really slowly, I promise."

She laughs, typing in her number.

We pay and make our way to the door. Outside, she puts on a pair of black sunglasses and gathers her hair in a low bun. Neither one of us knows how to say bye, so we don't. She takes a picture of us standing in the shade of the awning, leaning in close, and sends it to me. I hug her and it's like stepping through a portal into another world. This time when she walks away, it doesn't hurt.

I have no idea what happens now. Just because we're biologically related doesn't automatically earn us a place in each other's lives. What if I get to know her better and I don't like her? Or what if she doesn't like me? Will we wish we'd left things as they are now? Will we wish we never met at all?

9

SOMETHING ABOUT PEPTIDES

"**M**y apologies, Amélie. Thank you for waiting." Richards steps back into view of my laptop camera, taking his seat and pushing his glasses up the bridge of his sweaty nose. "We have some contractors fixing the AC unit. I appreciate your patience."

I've had a few days between my lunch with Brie and this session to consider all the times Richards could have told me about her and chose not to. The times I cried to him about how alone I felt in the world. The questions I had about where I came from. Who created me. What they'd thought of me. The way I never found much comfort in his clipped responses.

So I'm not patient right now. I am seething.

"No problem. Do you have anything very pressing that you'd like to discuss over the next"—I check the time—"forty-three minutes?"

The last time I spoke to Richards in this tone, he insinuated that I was manic. I wasn't. I was high, but happy high not sad high. Where I am now is kind of like the teapot before it starts screaming.

"Well, I—"

"Great. Let's talk about Brie."

"Aubrie?"

I know Brie's full name from the file Rena compiled. But that's not what I said. I smile. "I said Brie."

"I'm sorry, I don't und—"

"One sec. Before you gaslight me, I want to show you this cute picture I took on Saturday." I hold up the selfie of me and Brie outside the restaurant, adjusting the angle of my phone until my computer focuses. "My skin looks great, right? Shaine gave me this night cream, something about peptides. I don't know. Anyway, I wake up glowing now." He stares dumbly at the picture. "Oh, sorry. I'm the one on the right. Her hair is shorter, but it's pulled back so it's hard to tell."

I don't know what I expected his reaction to be. Guilt, probably. A little shame. I'd have been good with remorse. But the way his eyes flatten, the shutters that close over his face—I didn't expect that.

"Were you ever going to tell me about her? Was anybody?"

"You've always known."

Technically he's right. On some subconscious level I must have known about her. If those memories are repressed or missing, why have we never dealt with that? Why was he so content to let me live this way for so long?

My fingernails dig into the palms of my hands. "How is it possible that I don't remember her?"

Richards is quiet for a beat, turning my question around in

his head. Crafting his response with practiced precision. "The mind is mysterious and complex, designed to protect by any means necessary. The dissociative amnesia you're experiencing is likely the result of stress you experienced as a child."

"Then shouldn't this be happening to Brie too? Why is it just me?"

"You and Aubrie had the same upbringing, that is true, but that doesn't mean you share all of the same experiences or process things the same way."

I run my hands through my hair, massaging my scalp to ward off the migraine building in my skull. All the confusion, the uncertainty, the emotions I don't have names for—everything rises in my throat.

"You knew about her. You knew I didn't remember her and you never said anything."

He readjusts his glasses. "It's not always helpful to force the mind to face things before it's ready. Amélie, my number one priority over the years has been keeping you on a healthy path, and that effort has required my full attention as well as yours. Everything we do is with your best interest in mind. I'm glad you and Aubrie have found each other. I think that's wonderful. My job is to make sure you remain in a good place and nothing jeopardizes the progress you've made or the goals we're working toward."

The loneliness I felt before Brie has somehow been both mollified and intensified by having her in my life. For every way knowing her helps, it hurts. For every answer it provides, it offers endless questions about who I am and who I've been. Or who I could've been. It chips away at everything I thought I knew about myself. It builds on every insecurity I've ever had.

I wipe away my tears with the sleeve of my hoodie. Anger is exhausting. I hate that I can't sustain it for long.

"Have you been spending a lot of time with her?" Richards flips to a fresh page in his notebook. I shake my head. "Do you want to know her better?"

"It's too late."

"Too late for what?"

Too late for me to do any of this right, the way I would've wanted. Too late for me to be a good sister to Brie. A good pseudo-daughter to Sue and Dave. A good partner to Hayden. I don't know how to be who any of them think I am. I don't even know who they think I am.

Richards's brow creases. "You're still sober, right? You haven't relapsed?"

"Richards, I'm not an addict."

"That doesn't answer my question."

"I'm not doing drugs."

"I want to be frank with you," he says, leaning toward the camera. "I'm a little concerned. There are so many positive things happening for you, but it's a lot of change in a short period of time. That can be difficult for anyone to navigate, let alone someone with your history. I respected your decision to take a break from your medication, but that is contingent on you being honest with me. That's the only way this works. If you're struggling with all of this, you have to tell me. You cannot compartmentalize."

"You're being ridiculous. I've never been happier."

He stares at me and I stare back. I know what I must look like to him. Makeup smeared. Hollowed face. Listless eyes. As bad as I look, I don't look as bad as I *could* look, and that's the only thing keeping him from sounding the alarm.

"I'll have Debra talk to Sue and Dave about Aubrie."

"I already told them."

He nods. "Then I'm sure they have questions."

"They get an explanation but I don't?"

"I can't discuss another child's history with the agency. It's confidential. We show you the same respect. Debra will only be providing a little more context for Sue and Dave. We'll reach out to Aubrie's parents as well to make an introduction."

I'm not asking about Brie's history. I'm asking about mine. The things written about us in my file—which Sue and Dave would've seen too if they ever read it. Which means . . . "Sue and Dave have never seen my full file."

"Certain information has been redacted, but nothing that would impact a potential adoption or the development of your relationship with them."

It's like talking to a doll with preset phrases and marble eyes. I've never felt like this with him. I don't know what to believe anymore. "How do you expect me to trust people when you're the one who raised me?"

Finally, emotion blooms across his face. Richards is the

closest thing I've had to a parent. The most constant person I've had in my life. He's the one who taught me how the world works. He set up the goalposts and showed me which way to run. He built the parameters for me to operate within. Pulled me back when I crossed the line. I may not always like him, but I never thought there'd come a time when I didn't trust him anymore.

I needed to get out of the house for a while after my session with Richards. I went to a few coffee shops, a book store, a vintage shop, and eventually ended up here in the park. I'm on Face-Time with Rena and Cal breaking down everything Richards said, or more specifically didn't say, about Brie. I would have thought once he knew that I knew about her, he wouldn't keep so many secrets from me.

"Have you talked to Brie?" Rena asks.

"We've been texting here and there but it's still kind of . . ." I'm struggling to find the right word. It doesn't feel as awkward between us anymore, but it's definitely not natural. "Forced, I guess. We don't know how to be normal with each other. Or even what normal is."

"It'll take time," Cal says. His head is resting on Rena's arm so that they're both in frame. "You may be twins but you're also two individual people. You can't expect to know somebody right away."

He's right but that doesn't make it any less maddening.

"I knew I should've stayed with you," Rena grumbles. I

smile. Whenever Rena comes to visit, it takes the jaws of life for Cal to pry us apart.

"We were there for a week," Cal says.

"She needs me. Besides, Susan said I'm welcome back anytime."

"You have to leave to be welcomed back, babe. That's how that works."

Rena pushes Cal off of her, tilting the camera so he's out of view. "I will get in the car right now."

The couch groans as Cal gets up, probably to go rummage through the fridge. "You two are so codependent."

"She's the love of my life," she yells after him.

It's always been this way with us. When Cal first introduced me to Rena, his then best friend—although who were they kidding—it amazed me how instantly we clicked. I'd never had close friendships before. Never trusted anyone to be a vault for me and never felt trustworthy enough to be one for them in return. I didn't understand what it means to have someone's back and to know with complete certainty that they have yours too. I was always supposed to know her. Our relationship was the first thing in my life to really make sense.

So when she says she'd get in the car for me right now, she means it, even though it isn't necessary.

I lie back on the blanket and roll to my side. She brings the phone really close to her face so that if I block out everything around me, it's almost like we're kids again, sharing a bed and whispering secrets into the dark.

"He's mad because I like you better than him."

I laugh. She doesn't like anyone as much as she likes Cal, although I'm a close second. "Bye."

"Call me tomorrow."

The second we hang up, my smile fades. I don't like to worry Rena and Cal. They worry if I don't tell them what's going on, and they worry if I tell them the truth. I've found that if I tell them what happened in extreme detail, they don't always notice that I haven't told them how I feel about what happened.

The truth is, I'm spinning out a little. Darren was the only one I was completely honest with when I felt this way because he didn't worry about me. He said he never had to because there was nothing he and I couldn't get through together. Seeing him calm made me feel calm. It was a placebo effect. I believed it, so it was real.

If he were here, I'd tell him how I feel like I'm losing touch with myself. I'm sitting in a large, empty theater watching my life play out on a stage. If I'm being honest, I'm afraid meeting Brie right now, at this point in my life, hasn't been good for me. I feel guilty for only thinking about myself.

I'd tell him time stretches out like taffy now. Everything feels endless and undefined. I can't keep the days straight. When I close my eyes like this, I wonder what I'll see when I open them. If this is something I can wake from.

"Please don't sleep in the park."

At the sound of Hayden's voice, the curtain goes up and it's showtime again. I smile at him. He moves my legs out of the way so he can sit by me on the blanket. "I wasn't sleeping," I say. "It's too sunny." He's holding a small take-out box, which he sets in front of me. "What's that?"

"I can tell when you're in a bad mood."

I open the box. There are half a dozen assorted macarons inside. I don't know how he could interpret my mood from a text that said *at the park* and my location, but I don't question it. I choose a green one, pistachio I think, and eat it in one bite.

"My psychiatrist is an asshole."

He raises his eyebrows, and we both start laughing. I sit up, coughing from the piece of macaron I just inhaled. He pats my back until I stop. "Is your psychiatrist an asshole, or do you not want to hear what they have to say?"

I purse my lips. "Whose side are you on?"

"Are there sides?"

"Yes."

"Then yours."

He runs a finger over my ankle, tracing the flickering shapes of sunlight on my skin. It reminds me of sunbathing on the beach in the Hamptons. All the tentative little touches we exchanged, nervous about being so conspicuous when up until then, we'd kept to the shadows. Trying to learn who each other was in blinding light.

"You know what I thought about the other day?" I ask.

"Hmm?"

"I never asked my questions."

He's confused at first but then he remembers. Maybe he had been thinking of the Hamptons too. "Make them good."

I squint at him. He squints back. I wait for an intimidating amount of time to pass, and then I ask, "What's your middle name?"

"That's your first question?"

"Yes."

"I don't have one."

"You don't have a middle name?"

"No."

I nod, doing my best Richards impression. "And how does that make you feel?"

"Is that your second question?"

"It's a clarifying question."

He smirks.

I probably should have thought about what to ask, things I really want to know about him, but this is more fun. "If you could live forever, would you?"

"No."

"Are all of your answers going to be no?"

"You're asking very basic questions."

"Well, can you at least elaborate?"

"Why would I want to live after everyone I know is dead?"

"You'd meet more people."

"The world is getting progressively worse."

"True." The wind blows, whipping hair around. I search my bag for a hair clip. "Speaking of Earth, do you think Pluto deserves to be a planet?"

"Does Pluto want to be a planet?" He follows the motion of my hand, twisting my hair into a bun and securing it with the clip.

"I'm asking the questions."

"I bet no one's ever asked Pluto what it wants."

I fire off the next one. "When was the last time you cried and why?"

This time he thinks before he answers. His face scrunches as he tries to recall the last time he cried. What a privilege. "We lost a big game last season by three points."

I roll my eyes. "Boys only show emotion for sports. Your amygdala is so underdeveloped." I grab another macaron and lie on the blanket, taking small bites while I try to think of what I want to ask next. "Okay, final question."

"You're going to choke."

"Don't resuscitate. Donate my organs."

He sighs. "Your question?"

"Hard or soft cheese? You can only pick one and you can't have the other for the rest of your life."

"Seriously?"

"Choose. Quickly."

"Damn, okay." Of all my questions, this is the one Mr. Master Chef takes the most seriously. I think the answer is obvious because feta exists and who would choose to live without feta? But he says, "Hard cheese is more versatile, so I'd go with that."

"That's controversial."

"I stand by it."

"I know you so well now." I close my eyes, reaching blindly

for another macaron. "Did you secretly make these? Please don't tell me you bake too."

"Don't sleep in parks." His voice is closer than it was a moment ago. He pulls me up. I try to make my body heavy so he'll leave me where I am, but I don't think he even notices. "Especially alone." He lifts me easily, holding me against him so we're sitting with my back to his chest.

But I'm not alone because he's here. He found me here. I hadn't dropped a pin, just told him what area of the park I was in, and he found me. It didn't even take him long.

I yawn, turning my face away from the sun.

10

BECAUSE ART

There's an oil painting by John White Alexander hanging in The Met. I first saw it months ago, a few days after I moved to the city. A woman lounging on a chair in a billowing white dress. Chin resting on her arm, her hand in her hair. She's wearing an expression that I've read is meant to be sensual. I don't see it that way. She looks like she's hiding knives in the folds of her skirt.

An arm brushes mine. I lean in to examine the painting closer. "Does she look pissed off to you?"

"She looks like she read her husband's texts while he was in the shower."

"She just asked him where he's been all night."

"She's about to cook him dinner and splash hot oil in his face."

I raise my eyebrows at Trey. "What goes on in your house? Should I call CPS?"

He smirks. "My mom could never be that interesting."

"Hmm."

The next piece is a portrait of another white person, like every painting before and all the ones to come. Trey trails behind me. "What are we doing here?"

We're here because Trey texted me yesterday hounding me with questions about Brie. He knows I've seen Hayden several times since our run-in at the restaurant and I still haven't said anything to him. He wants to know how long he has to keep my secret and why he's keeping it in the first place.

We're physically here at The Met because I went for a walk and this is where I ended up. We were supposed to meet at my place but Sue and Dave weren't home and I couldn't stand the quiet apartment any longer.

"It's a museum," I say, my voice flat. "We're wandering aimlessly."

"Why?"

"Because art."

We round a corner and find a large, bronze sculpture of Thetis and Achilles. Trey studies it passively. I've been here for the past hour or so, reading every placard next to every painting between where I'm standing now and the door. It's mind-numbing but that is, after all, the point.

"How's your sister?" he asks in a tone that makes me grimace.

"Ew. Why'd you say it like that?"

"How did I say it?"

"Like, 'How's your sister?'"

"Oh, in my normal speaking voice."

"Exactly."

Brie's upstate visiting family with her parents. We're texting more frequently now, although we still haven't made plans to meet up again. Part of me wonders if it's because she's struggling with all of this as much as I am. Small talk is easier through the phone.

"Does anyone else know?"

"Not yet. It's . . . I'm feeling it out."

"Feeling what out?"

I tell him about how Brie and I only recently reconnected. I don't tell him I have no recollection of ever knowing her prior to this summer.

When I finish, he blows out a huff of air.

"Damn. Twelve years. That's—"

I cut him off. "Do you have siblings?"

He side-eyes me for that very obvious change of subject but goes along with it. "Yeah, a little brother."

"How old?"

"Five."

"Do you think you're a good brother?"

"I don't know." He moves past me, examining a small clay bowl in a glass case. I try to get into it, but it's a bowl. "The other day he told me, 'Sometimes you're sad, and then you just get a Popsicle.'"

"Is that all it takes? Popsicles?"

"Apparently."

Trey leans against a blank wall, giving me a look that says he's done with the bantering. It's a new look for him because all he and I do is banter. "What's going on, Melie?" I walk over and stand next to him so I don't have to look him in the face. "You don't have to talk to me, but you should talk to Hayden. He knows when something's off with you. It messes with him."

I know what he means. I've been in his shoes before and it sucks. I crane my head to steal a quick glance at Trey. He's staring straight ahead, watching people float from one exhibit to another. As I said, there really isn't anything to do here but wander.

"Why does he like me?"

He doesn't answer, just gives a slight shake of his head like it's not a question worth answering.

When I think about Hayden, all I know is, I want him here. I want to find a way to keep him with me for as long as possible, but I'm not dreaming of forever. Of weddings and children and one-story houses where we don't have to climb any stairs. I'm not imagining growing old with him, but I still can't fathom the end. I don't want to think about the fact that a day could come when I wouldn't have him anymore.

"I don't think it'll work between us."

Trey looks over at me now, his eyes pinning me to the wall. "Then you should tell him that."

I can't because it's not true. I think it would work. I do. We'd be good and maybe I'd be really happy. Happy enough to tie my every mood to his. To orbit around him like a fucking planet, dependent on him for light and warmth. So it's not about what we would be together. It's about who I would become and what that would do to him.

"I don't want to screw him up."

I don't know why I'm telling Trey this, but he listens. His face is more serious than I've ever seen it before. "You're not the only one with problems. He's got his own family shit going on. He doesn't talk about it much. He tries to play it like he has everything under control, but I bet he'd talk to you."

Trey and I have become unlikely friends. To be real, the bar is low. Like in hell. When we met, I expected him to be insufferable, and he's completely tolerable. Tolerable seems to be all that I require of the men in my life.

"I'm out." He gives me a one-armed hug. "You staying here?"

I nod, hugging him back. "You're weird, man."

I fold my arms over my chest as he strides across the long room, disappearing through the doors and out of sight.

What's the worst that could happen if I tell my friends about Brie? Rena and Cal already know and now Trey does too. I could call Hayden right now, send a text to my group chat with Shaine, Liv, and Justine, and it would be done. Everyone close to me would know about her. There'd be no going back from that.

Rena and Cal would always pick me over everyone but each other. In every scenario, even when I've fucked up. I know that from experience. But my friends and Hayden . . . those relationships are still too new. When I'm around them, I focus all my energy on pretending to be the better version of myself I created when I moved here. Someone confident and sure of herself, with cool clothes, an aloof attitude, and a heart that isn't bruised beyond recognition. I've gotten away with it so far. I'm afraid that, standing side by side with Brie, they'll see me as the imposter I am.

Maybe I'm being insecure, but besides Darren, Rena and Cal are the only people who have ever stuck around when faced with the reality of me. How can I risk everything I have now? I don't want to lose anyone else.

I take a seat on a nearby bench. I press my hand to my heart. I breathe deeply, in and out, trying to calm the panic building out of nothing.

Nothing is wrong.

Everything is okay.

I think of the worst panic attack I've ever had. The day I woke with my throat clogged with screams. I dreamed my heart had exploded. Blown up like a balloon until it filled the spaces between my ribs and popped.

I was fifteen, and I'd already lost control of my life. I didn't know control was something I needed until I was sure I didn't have it. I couldn't see how fast I was speeding until I wrapped myself around a pole. But I had Darren. For the moment, at least. And I warred with the part of myself that believed it was worth all that had come before.

My heart popped, and my lungs shriveled like dried petals. My fingers clawed at my neck, looking for an airway. Waiting for my chest to cave in. Everything was dark. I thought I was dying.

But I felt the heat beside me, so I reached for it with blue hands.

I'm dying. I'm dying. I'm dying. I'm dying.

I dragged myself over to him. I think it was the shaking that finally woke him. The violent shutters that tore through my body. I wasn't very concerned with those. I wanted him to feel past them to what was missing. The stillness where the dull thumping of my heart should be.

I'm dying.

The lights flickered on.

"Sit up." Darren lifted me by my arms. "Breathe."

That was the whole issue. I couldn't. My lungs didn't work because my heart was missing. The edges of my vision started to dissolve like ink in water.

He pulled me to him and I rested my head in the crook of his neck. I raised my shoulders up and down to convince my body that this was normal. Breathing was meant to be a reflex.

"Here." He put my hand against his chest so I could feel how easily it rose and fell. "In and out. You're okay."

I gasped, choking on the air. I coughed and wheezed and clung to him like life support.

With each drag of oxygen through my lips, I felt it return. Soft at first, but then a rhythmic boom deep from my center. I focused on counting the beats until the sun washed the dark away.

I'm free-falling again.

I search for my text thread with Justine.

Me: do you have rowen's number?

I kind of hope she says no or withholds it until I tell her why I need it. I want her to say something that will stop me from doing what I'm pretty sure I'm going to do. Crossing one of the few boundaries I've set for myself, for the second time in a matter of weeks. I know it's a bad idea. I'm hoping for an excuse to change my mind.

She doesn't provide one. She sends Rowen's contact, no questions asked.

It's why I asked her and not Olivia or Shaine. I knew she would.

Me: hey it's Mel from school

Me: you around?

I wait for Rowen's response and exhale when she texts back **no sorry.**

But my phone buzzes again.

Rowen: party friday

She sends an address for a place in LES.

Rowen: meet me there

11

MY HANDS ARE GLITTER

I'm only stopping by the party. Thirty minutes, tops.

It's a different crowd than I'm used to from my nights out with Shaine. All the light bulbs in the grungy warehouse glow red. It smells like fireworks and cigarettes. It's a little past 11:30, but everyone is one-a.m. wasted. The bodies on the dance floor move as one giant, tangled mass. I don't recognize anyone.

It doesn't take long to find Rowen leaning against a crumbling column, wearing an iridescent blue bra top and matching pants. Her brown hair is in two braids studded with tiny silver hoops. Her cheekbones are streaked with glitter.

She's in the middle of a deal, sliding the money into the inside pocket of her bag, when she sees me. She smirks, crossing the room until we're standing only a few feet apart. "I didn't think you'd come."

"Why?"

She shrugs, pulling a joint out of thin air and tucking it between her lips. She searches her bag for something and rolls her eyes. "Do you have a lighter?"

I shake my head. Rowen looks around, catching the glow of a match a few feet away. She leans over and holds the end of her joint to the flame until it catches.

"Come on, Ro," the owner of the match complains when the flame goes out. "That was my last one." Rowen waves her off, lighting the girl's blunt with her own.

I watch the smoke plume out of her nose and wonder if I'm actually going to do this. I have a complicated history with drugs, but a lot of that was exacerbated by Darren and his addictions. While Richards would be more than happy to put me back on my antidepressants, he would never prescribe me benzos. I'm not going to make a habit out of this, but if I can feel a little less overwhelmed while I adjust to everything that's going on, maybe it'll stick.

Rowen senses, as any good drug dealer can, that I'm having a moral dilemma. She grins. "What do you need?"

I hope it'll stick.

"Ativan," I tell her. A drug dealer is kind of like a priest. You expect them to take your problems to the grave.

"I have Valium and Xanax." She digs in the pocket of her backpack and takes out a bag with a bunch of smaller ones stuffed inside. Drops a baggie of blue pills marked with the letter *V* in my hand and another that contains nothing but a yellow gummy bear.

"What is this?"

She closes my fingers around them, the plastic crinkling in my palm. "Free."

"Don't flirt with me."

"Why? It's fun." I try to pay her, but she pushes the money away. What kind of drug dealer doesn't want to be paid? "Come find me later," she says, dancing into the crowd.

I stare at the gummy bear in my hand. I'm not stupid. I know I shouldn't take anything if I don't know what it is. It's just that when you're disappearing, the allure of tangibility is so strong. It's terrifying to feel so removed from yourself and not know what you're trying to connect to or how to do it.

I shake the gummy bear out of the bag and drop it on my tongue. Whatever it is, I hope it doesn't kill me.

I'm only two drinks in when it hits. The room explodes into colors. Bright purples and neon pinks. I've never seen anything more beautiful. Everyone is made of music. Their skin ripples. They dance on walls and drip from the ceiling like a thick paste. My hands are glitter. I drag them along the bar, leaving a shimmering trail in their wake. I inhale and the room shrinks. I exhale and it expands. Electric sparks shoot through the air.

I melt into the crowd, moving to a beat that I can taste on the back of my tongue. I find people and lose them. Everyone smiles. I dance until my legs disappear. I sit on the floor until they grow back.

I hear my name shoot by like a bullet.

"Melie?"

Blue eyes bore into mine. Not deep blue. Clear like the water you see in ads for cruise ships. Like frosted glass.

Darren?

"What are you doing here?" I slur. He isn't happy to see me. He's confused. I must be dead. He picks me up off the floor.

"Come on."

Where are we going?

Darren dissolves around me and I'm suspended in midair, floating in a deep and pulsating purple. I close my eyes and sink into it like sand. Maybe this is death, but at least he's here.

New York blurs past like oil paint smeared on canvas. I stare out the window with my head on Darren's shoulder. He's on the phone but I can't focus on what he's saying. I can't focus on anything but the lights burning through the black sky. The drops of water in the air. The taste of salt on my tongue.

The car jerks to a stop. The door opens.

"What is she on?"

"I don't know. She keeps talking about colors. Probably acid."

Darren passes me off to Hayden and it feels like some sort of ceremony. It feels like it means something. But when I open my eyes, it isn't Darren. It's Trey. He holds the door of the apartment building open for us.

"You got her?"

"Yeah."

We ride the elevator up forever with Hayden cradling me to his chest and my face against his neck. His body is rigid. He doesn't talk to me.

"She was alone?"

"She was with Rowen. They were dancing, but I didn't

realize it was her at the time. I didn't know until I saw her sitting on the floor."

Trey's voice is too loud in my ears. Like, why is he screaming? They both stare at me with giant eyes. The elevator opens directly into Hayden's apartment.

"We have to be quiet. My mom's asleep. Can you get her some water?"

Hayden carries me to his room and sets me on the bed, but I don't want to sleep. I'd get up but my legs haven't grown back yet. They hold cups of water under my mouth. Feed me bread that ends up on the side of the toilet and all over the bathroom floor.

Trey steps out of the room while Hayden helps me change into one of his shirts. I try to talk but my tongue is too big in my mouth. Whatever I say to him, he doesn't respond.

I close my eyes for a second. When I open them, my soiled clothes are gone. Down the hall, the washer is running. Trey's sitting on the edge of the bed. He sighs. "God, Melie."

He doesn't understand. I feel better. This is better.

12
THE FOUR SEASONS

I feel like shit.

I don't have to open my eyes to know I'm not home. These sheets are softer than mine. The bed is bigger, maybe even longer. Everything smells like Hayden. Last night comes back to me in muddled flashes.

There's a giant glass of water and a bottle of Tylenol on the nightstand. The room is eerily quiet and the lights are off. The heavy curtains are open just enough so that it isn't completely pitch-black, and even that's too bright for me. I burrow back under the covers, reaching an arm out and patting blindly until my fingers lock on the Tylenol bottle. I take two, not bothering with the water, and feel around again for my phone. It's dead. Of course.

What time is it?

I stay hidden away for a few minutes and then, with a groan, I arise like an ungrateful Lazarus. If death had me last night, it should've kept me. Or maybe this is hell. I think I'd recognize it if it were.

There's a charging pad on the other nightstand. Army crawling over with my useless phone, I set it down and wait for it to come back to life. Four missed texts.

Brie: I get back early next week. want to come over?

I heart Brie's message before I can think too long about what I'm agreeing to. That's next week's anxiety attack.

Rena: what a riveting morning podcast I've woken up to

Above that text, there are no less than ten voice memos from me to her. Two of which she saved, according to the notifications I received.

Rena: bet $50 your phone is dead. call me when you charge it

Rena: Nurse Calvin says drink water

My stomach turns, acid clawing up my throat. Nurse Calvin is the spirit that possesses Cal whenever Rena or I are sick, hungover, or PMSing. Without him giving us meds and forcing liquids and food down our throats, she and I would be content to wither back into the dust from which we came. I drink the stupid water.

After several futile attempts to turn on the lamp, my wobbly Bambi limbs carry me over to the window and open the curtains. The sun is like a slap in the face.

My clothes are folded neatly on the foot of the bed, along with a fluffy white towel, a washcloth, and a new toothbrush. It's at this moment I realize I'm not wearing my clothes and I must have changed into something of Hayden's. I don't want to think about why that would've been necessary but my suspicions are confirmed when I sniff my shirt and find that it's been washed. It smells like lavender breeze and humiliation.

I open doors until I get to the bathroom. Much like Hayden's room, his bathroom is huge. I knew he was rich, but my god, he is so rich. I can't process this right now. I have to pee and then I need scalding hot water running down my back for no less than fifteen minutes if I am to complete my ascension into the physical realm.

The Tylenol kicks in while I'm washing my hair with shampoo so luxurious I feel like I should only use a dime-sized amount. I don't. I found glitter in my hair, so I lather until I'm sure that even the essence of my bad choices has been rinsed down the drain. I emerge feeling like a new person who has never met the me from yesterday in her life.

I wipe the condensation from the mirror with the hand towel hanging on the wall and study my reflection. My hair is tangled because as nice as the conditioner is, I need more product than Hayden has to offer to force my curls to chill out. My skin is a little congested from sleeping in my makeup, but otherwise no different than usual. I grip the towel tighter around my chest and dig through the cabinets and drawers until I find lotion and toothpaste. They're stocked like a drugstore. Who lives like this?

The bedroom door opens as I'm brushing my teeth. I have a momentary panic attack at the thought of one of his parents catching me in a towel in their apartment like a slutty Goldilocks. I listen closely, wondering if I should hide somewhere, but decide to stand my ground. After all, the best defense is a good offense. Whatever that means.

To my immense relief, Hayden walks into the bathroom. That relief is short-lived though because he's pissed. I've never seen him angry like this. He doesn't look at me. He doesn't speak to me. I spit out the toothpaste, watching him quietly through the mirror. He must have just come from working out because he's sweaty and his skin is flushed. Without a word, he turns on the shower and walks back into the bedroom. I rinse the toothbrush off and then, unsure of where to put it, I throw it in the trash.

When I leave the bathroom, one of the closet doors is open. Why are there so many doors? I wait for Hayden to come out because this has surpassed the level of awkwardness I can tolerate, but when he does, he breezes past me like I'm not there and shuts the bathroom door in my face.

I laugh humorlessly and quickly get dressed. He may be mad, but what I'm not going to do is sit here and be ignored. I've just made my mind up to leave when my phone starts ringing with a FaceTime from Rena. I take a deep breath to quell my irritation and answer.

Based on the umbrella above her head, Rena's in her backyard sitting by the pool. She takes a big, crunchy bite of avocado toast and squints at the screen. "Where are you?"

"Hayden's."

Her voice drops to a conspiratorial whisper. "Est-ce qu'il est là?"

Teaching Rena French has been incredibly useful to us over

the years. She studied it in school all her life but never took it seriously until we met and realized it was a way for us to have private conversations in front of other people. That's not to say we don't occasionally encounter someone who understands us, but none of our friends do and that's what matters.

"He's in the shower."

She waves her hands frantically. "Flip the camera. Let me see his room."

"Why?"

"I need to be able to visualize while you tell me what the hell you're doing there. Are you having sleepovers at his place now?"

"Not intentionally."

I switch to the back camera so she can see, and she gasps. "Are you at Hayden's or the Four Seasons?"

For Rena, by far the bougiest person I've ever met, to say this is what I meant by Hayden being rich. His room is twice the size of mine, with a giant bed, a TV area, and two walk-in closets. Designer sweatpants and rare, collectible sneakers as far as the eye can see, all lined up neatly on custom shelves. The eerie silence I experienced earlier is due to the fact that this apartment is so far from the ground I'm sure even the oxygen up here is expensive. His neighbors are birds and God.

Rena throws her head back and cackles. "M."

"I know."

"The boy is loaded."

"I *know*."

There is now a breakfast sandwich sitting next to the refilled glass of water. Based on his attitude, he may have poisoned it, but my stomach is growling. If that's how this ends, so be it.

"Okay, I need a full recap of yesterday," Rena says. "The long version. Every detail."

The shower turns off. I was going to leave before he came out but I've changed my mind. You cannot feed me and treat me like I don't exist. I won't allow it.

"I don't . . ." The bathroom door swings open and Hayden comes out with a towel around his waist and water dripping from his short, curly hair. He walks straight into his closet without a glance in my direction. "J'me souviens pas."

Rena doesn't miss a beat, slipping back into her adorable, but extremely exaggerated French accent. "Rien?"

It's not that I don't remember anything, but what I do remember isn't very clear. "Non, j'me souviens . . ." I start to explain the fragments I've been able to string together, but maybe this is a conversation for another time. "On s'en parle plus tard."

Rena frowns at the suggestion that we discuss this later but she concedes. "D'accord. Je t'aime."

"Love you too."

Part of me believes that when I get off the phone, we will have the fight we are clearly building up to, but that doesn't happen. Instead, Hayden emerges dressed in gray shorts and a white T-shirt, plops down into one of the two armchairs by the TV, and loads a video game. Am I a phantom? I contemplate this while I scarf down the egg-and-cheese bagel to a soundtrack of gunfire and zombie screams.

My bag is on the floor by the bed. How I managed to make it out of the party with it is another question entirely. My keys and credit card are still inside, but the little baggie from Rowen is gone. Those pills were my entire reason for going to the party. How the hell did I lose them? I scan the floor around me, wondering if I dropped them somewhere, but I suspect that isn't what happened.

If he found them, that would explain his attitude, but who does he think he is going through my stuff?

"I'm leaving," I say, my voice clipped.

When he doesn't respond, I take that as my cue to exit. I make it all the way to the door before he speaks.

"Mel."

"What?"

He pauses the game, looking at me for the first time. I can't read his eyes at all. I have no idea what's going on in his head. He comes toward me, and I think he's going to yell, but he doesn't say anything.

Okay then. "Bye."

I open the door. He slams it shut. We glare at each other.

I lose it. "What is your problem?"

He doesn't back down, his temper flaring to match my own. "Since when are you friends with Rowen?"

"*You're* friends with Rowen."

Everyone's friends with Rowen.

"I'm cool with Rowen."

Semantics.

"What's the difference?"

"The difference is I don't do her drugs. I don't pass out on the fucking floor—"

First of all, "I didn't pass out."

"—and get dropped off at your apartment in the middle of the night."

"I didn't ask Trey to do that."

"Where was he supposed to take you?"

Anywhere else. "He could've taken me home."

He scoffs. "Really?"

Fine. Maybe not home.

"Or to Shaine's. He shouldn't have brought me here. I'm not your problem."

He looks at me like that's the most ridiculous thing he's ever heard. "Yes you are. What is wrong with you?"

What's wrong with *me*?

I open the door again. He slams it shut. Again.

"Move." My voice is quiet, but I'm so angry that I'm shaking. I want to be anywhere but here right now. His hand is still on the door, and if he doesn't move it in the next ten seconds, he'll be missing a limb.

"I don't want to do this anymore," he says.

At first I think he means argue with me. Unfortunately for him, it's too late for that. But when he looks at me, eyes smoldering, I realize that isn't what he means at all.

"Do what?"

"You were right." He lets go of the door, retreating a few steps. "I should've ended it."

He waits for his words to hit their target. To see how deep

they penetrate. Whether or not I care that he would say something like that to me. I smooth my face into an emotionless mask. I won't give him anything. No indication either way. I refuse to let him see that his aim was true. That he hit a spot I didn't know I'd left exposed.

I can't believe he'd threaten to leave me. I can't believe how much I don't want him to.

"You projected a relationship onto me that I didn't ask for."

He rolls his eyes. "Grow the fuck up, Mel."

"Do *not* curse at me."

My words ring between us like a struck bell. I won't let someone else talk to me like that. I won't let another boy make me feel like a child. My eyes burn with hot, unshed tears. I wrap my arms around myself, nails pressing into the skin of my forearms. Clawing toward something solid, like muscle or bone. His gaze lingers on my hands, flickers up to my face, softens.

"If this isn't a relationship, then what is it? Because you keep talking about how this started, but we are so far beyond that now. So what's going on?"

"I don't know! Okay?" The tears spill over and I let them. I don't wipe them away. This is what he wants, right? Emotion and theatrics? To pick the same fight with me over and over? To force my will to yield to his. Even if some part of me wants what he wants, I don't want to be strong-armed into it. I won't be. "If you're done, then be done. Don't threaten me."

"It wasn't a threat."

"It was. You know it was."

"This is exhausting." He slumps onto the bed, his head in his hands. "Are you not tired?"

"I'm not forcing you to do anything you don't want to do, Hayden. Don't put all of this on me."

"I'm not." He lifts his head, looking at me like a puzzle he keeps trying and failing to solve. "I care about you, even if you don't want me to. So no, you're not forcing me to do anything, but you could end it too and you won't. Why?"

Because I don't want to. I don't, but I can't tell him that. I won't let him use that against me.

He knows though. I know he does.

"What happened last night, you can't do shit like that again. All I kept thinking was what if Trey hadn't been there. Just . . . please. Don't do that again."

He definitely took the pills. My entire reason for going to the party. Without them, all of this was for nothing. I want to scream.

But I can't because when I look at him, I see me. At fourteen. Fifteen. Sixteen.

And now things are reversed. How many times did I look at Darren this way? How many times did I feel what Hayden's feeling? Wishing Darren would just talk to me. Tell me what was going on.

I don't know what I'm doing.

What am I doing?

"Fine," I say. "I'm sorry." And I mean it.

Still, we're at an impasse with neither of us willing to give an inch. I pick up my bag from where I dropped it. He tilts my chin up, examining my puffy, gross face like I'm something hanging in the Louvre. It's like the veil has been lowered. For the first time, I'm hit with the full force of his affection.

How did we get here?

It's too much. I hug him, burying my face in his shirt just to break eye contact and calm my racing heart.

We make it past Hayden's mom's office with no problem. The door is shut and from the sound of it, she's on a conference call. Neither of us expects to find his dad in the living room standing between us and the elevator.

I stumble to a stop. His dad barely looks up from the stack of mail he's holding, but when he sees me, we suddenly have his full attention. I've never been more thankful for clean clothes and a shower in my life.

Hayden clears his throat. "Dad, this is Amélie."

Hayden's dad turns to me as if to say, *Is that true? Are you Amélie?* Like, yes. Can confirm.

"Nice to meet you, Mr. Thompson."

"Likewise," he says, and I think that's it. I think he's going to let us go. I'm honestly shocked by this turn of events, but we only make it a few steps before he says, "Did you enjoy the Hamptons?"

Am I supposed to answer that? It's very clear I'm stepping into the middle of an argument that doesn't have anything to do with me. Can I pretend that it was some other girl Hayden fled to their beach house with to avoid his family obligation?

Eh, probably not.

"Yes," I say. "It was nice."

Mr. Thompson rips open an envelope, dropping the rest of the stack on the coffee table. The collar of his shirt is unbuttoned and his sleeves are rolled up. It looks like he's just getting in rather than heading out for the day. "Why don't you join us for dinner?"

Hayden glances at me like he must protect me at all costs. I really appreciate that. "We have plans."

"I didn't say tonight." His dad gives us what would, under different circumstances, be a very charming smile. "I'm sure your mother would love to meet the girl you've been spending so much time with. You won't even have to sneak her in."

At that, all words disappear from my vocabulary. I rack my brain for what to say because this man is firing shots, and I've been hit. All I can manage is, "Um, okay."

The second we're on the elevator, I squeeze Hayden's arm. "I don't want to have dinner with your parents."

His hands are clenched into fists. Without either of us touching a single button, the elevator whisks us down to the ground floor.

13

LIKE THAT SHOW FROM THE NINETIES

Hayden insists on accompanying me all the way back and yes, very sweet, but I suspect it's mostly because he didn't feel like dealing with his dad. He's quiet the entire way.

He invites me to meet up with him and a group of friends from school at Soho House. I know an olive branch when I see one, so I accept. I leave him in the lobby talking to his best friend, Fred, and head upstairs alone.

Good thing too because Sue's home. She looks me up and down and tsks. "Ah, the walk of shame."

"That would imply shame."

Her face falls. "I was kidding." She appraises me more carefully, noticing I am indeed wearing the same outfit from yesterday—a pair of cutoff jean shorts and a tank top. I have spare clothes at Shaine's place for impromptu sleepovers, so she quickly puts two and two together. "Wait, were you with a boy? I thought you were with Shaine." I could lie but I don't feel like it. I just stare at her. "Are you . . . uh . . ."

"You can make a walk-of-shame joke, but you can't say the

words 'having sex'?" She pales. Oh my god. "I was not out hooking up with anyone, no."

"But you were with a boy."

I drop my keys and bag on the kitchen counter. "Did you wanna have the sex talk, Sue?"

"I don't really—"

"Because we can have the sex talk."

She hesitates. "Are you being safe?"

"Do you have to use a condom every time?" My sarcasm is met with a look of sheer horror. "I'm not an idiot."

"No, I know . . ." She's relieved though, so maybe she doesn't know. "It might be a good idea if you go on the pill."

"I have an IUD."

Her eyebrows shoot up. "Really? I didn't know they do that for kids."

"I was never good about remembering the pill." And LCS doesn't take chances.

Although two forms of birth control have been confirmed and the general understanding that I am not stupid has been established, she frowns. "You can't sleep at your boyfriend's house."

"Would it help if I told you he's not my boyfriend?"

"I'm serious. And you have to tell us where you are. Even if you think we won't like it. We have to know where you are."

My phone vibrates in my pocket. I texted Shaine about Soho House during my ride up the elevator. She says she, Justine, and Olivia will meet me there.

I think I'm going to tell Hayden about Brie. The longer I wait, the more it becomes a thing I'm intentionally keeping from him. As long as Brie's around, there will eventually come a time when I can't avoid it anymore, and I'd rather do it on my own terms. Besides, after this morning I just want to have everything out in the open. I figure I might as well tell everyone at the same time.

"Mel," Sue says, voice stern. "Is that understood?"

Not Susan going parental on me.

"Yes," I say. "I'm still getting used to being under the guardianship of responsible adults. I will communicate better."

Her features soften. "Your other foster parents didn't check up on you?"

"Yeah, I mean if I was gone for days they'd probably text me." Except there were times when I lived with Cal's family when I was gone for days. At Rena's or with Darren. It was Cal who checked on me. "But then again, I was a kid. It wasn't like I was going anywhere."

"You're still a kid."

It's funny how you're a kid until the second you're not. To adults, there's nothing gradual about growing up. If I were eighteen, we wouldn't be having this discussion. I could turn eighteen tomorrow and the rules would change overnight. I'd go from being told I can't be responsible for myself to having my entire life packed up and dumped at my feet. How do they expect me to take any of this seriously?

"So," Sue says, a slight grin on her lips. "When are we meeting the boy?"

"At my funeral, standing over my dead body."

Shaine, Olivia, and Justine are waiting outside the Soho House entrance when I get there. I give them the quick, less mortifying version of last night's events so they're up-to-date. Now Shaine's scowling at me.

"No, because if you were raging with Rowen, where was my invite?"

"You guys are friends?" Olivia asks in a tone no one could mistake for casual.

Justine sucks her teeth. "Liv, no one wants Rowen."

"That's not what I'm saying! I just didn't know they hung out."

"We don't," I say.

"Which is why it's weird."

"I ran into her there."

That isn't technically a lie.

"And how did you find out about this party?" Shaine asks. "I didn't even know about it."

"Who cares," Justine says. "Shaine, give the woman your membership card so we can eat, please. I need ravioli. Stat."

Hayden, Trey, and a few of their friends are up by the pool, lounging around a spread of half-eaten food. We grab chairs from nearby tables and the boys shift to make space for us.

Hayden and Trey automatically scoot over so I can sit next to them.

"Melie," Trey says. "Lovely to see you alive and well. It was touch and go for a while there."

"Shut up."

Hayden pushes a plate covered with a napkin toward me. "I ordered you fries."

Shaine leans over from where she's sitting across from us and grabs a handful. "He loves you."

"If he loved her, he would've ordered the truffle fries," Justine says, dunking a few of Shaine's stolen fries in ketchup.

I'm not really hungry, but I pull one of the menus from under a stack of dishes. It's almost four p.m. and all I've had to eat is that breakfast sandwich. I tell myself that's why my hands are shaking. I just need to eat something. Then I will tell them about Brie and everything will be fine.

"You okay?" Hayden asks.

But I had good reasons for not telling them, didn't I? I still don't really know Brie. We've only hung out once. Who knows what we'll be to each other yet. And maybe it's better in the long run if I don't give them someone to compare me to. Someone more like them. More whole than I could ever pretend to be.

"Hey." Hayden dips his head close to mine, his voice a whisper. "What's going on?"

I have to say it or I won't. I have to do it now.

"I need to tell you something."

Trey snorts. "Are we talking about your sister?"

Shaine's eyes dart to me. I glare at Trey but part of me is relieved to not have had to be the one to say it. Besides, I'm kind of surprised he lasted this long.

He takes an unbothered sip of his drink. "You already told him."

"No, I didn't."

"Yes, you did," Hayden says. "Last night. I was going to let you bring it up again when you were . . . you know."

When I was sober. When I wasn't high out of my fucking mind.

"You have a sister?" Justine asks. "Since when?"

"Birth. Her name's Brie."

"They're twins," Trey adds.

Hayden doesn't look at all surprised, which means Trey must have told him about bumping into us at the restaurant. The rest of our table, on the other hand, is in an uproar.

"Twins?" Olivia screeches. "Like identical?"

Shaine points an accusatory finger at Trey. "Why does he know before me?"

Trey winks at her.

"He ran into us at a restaurant." Now that I think about it, why is Trey always randomly showing up where I am? I turn to him. "What, do you just follow me around the city?"

"In this heat? Be serious."

"She lives here?" Justine asks.

"She's in Brooklyn."

"Why haven't we met her?" Shaine demands.

"I just . . . reconnected with her the week after school ended." I try to phrase it in a way that will incite the least amount of questions. If I tell them I don't remember my childhood with Brie, it would open Pandora's psychoanalytical box, and I refuse. "We haven't seen each other or spoken since we were kids."

I steal a glance at Hayden as the pieces click into place for him. The night I asked him to stay over after seeing Brie in person for the first time. The shift in my mood over the past few weeks. The shit show that was last night. I don't have to tell him how hard all this has been for me. He's seen it—he just wasn't sure what he was looking at until now.

"I need visuals," Shaine says, whipping out her phone. "What's her handle?"

I recite it for her while she types it into the search bar. Olivia and Justine lean in and the three of them go through the pictures on Brie's profile carefully, like detectives solving a crime.

"Holy shit," Justine mutters.

"It's like that show from the nineties with those two twins," Olivia says.

"*Parent Trap*?" Shaine asks.

Olivia scrunches up her nose. "What?"

"*Parent Trap* is a movie," Justine tells Shaine.

"Then what are you talking about?"

"The show with the two sisters," Olivia says impatiently. "I don't know the name. That was like fifty years ago."

"The redheaded ones, right?"

"That's *Parent Trap*," Justine, the local authority on *Parent Trap*, reiterates.

I hate to interrupt this segment of Guess That Millennial Show, but, "Please don't compare my cataclysmic life to *Sister, Sister.*"

For the love of God.

"That's it!" Olivia slaps Shaine's arm. "*Parent Trap* is the other one."

They drill me with questions, and I tell them what's happened with Brie up until now. Shaine is aggrieved to have not been in on the stakeout. I promise her next time I stalk a sibling, she's the first one I'm calling.

And then the conversation shifts to something else. Summer vacays and senior-year plans. Hayden rests a hand on my leg, laughing at something Trey said. Olivia leans across the table to show me a video on her phone. I take them each in one by one. These people I hadn't even known six months ago who let me into their lives like I'd been there all along. How would I have made it through the spring without them?

Up until a few weeks ago, I had been figuring out my place in New York. Building something that might not stand forever but that I could find beauty in, if only momentarily. I had been proud of how far I'd come and that I was capable of more than tearing things down.

Learning about Brie was like a damn bursting. A great wave of anxiety and confusion. Streets flooded. Towns under water. All the things I was building, submerged. I was scared. I didn't know what to expect, telling them about her. Keeping it to myself felt like minimizing the casualties.

Hayden lets go of my leg, searching for my hand under the table. He's still talking to Trey, but when he finds it, he laces our fingers together. We don't hold hands, so I know this is his way of making sure I'm okay. He squeezes, and it's like a secret language between the two of us. My pulse is steady against his skin. My mind is clear. The waters are there but they aren't rising anymore. Whatever damage may lie beneath, that's something to be grateful for.

14

AN ACT OF MERCY

Brie lives in the type of house with family portraits lining the hallway and old holiday cards plastered all over the fridge. Fine china stacked next to homemade ceramic bowls brought home from camp. Dance trophies and middle school certificates displayed proudly in a glass cabinet by the TV. I didn't know people actually lived like this in real life.

After coming clean to Hayden and my friends about Brie, I felt less anxious about seeing her again. I'd told them and nothing changed. They gave me space to figure out how Brie could fit into my life and if that was something I really wanted. I texted Brie the next day to figure out the best time to stop by. That was four days ago.

I'm sitting on the couch of Brie's Brooklyn brownstone while she teeters on a chair to grab something off the bookcase. "Okay." She pulls a heavy silver photo album off the top shelf. "This is six through eight."

The book is luxurious, with The Mitchell Family carved on the cover. It looks like something people put on their Tiffany registry. When she opens it, the very first picture is her seated on her mom's lap, with her other mom's arm stretched out in front of them holding the camera. Her hair is in pigtails and her knees are scraped. She's smiling at her parents with more love than I can fathom. What must it have been like to believe someone hung the stars in the sky just for you?

She points to a picture on the other page of her eating pancakes at the kitchen table. "I cut my own bangs and it shows."

I never thought about how important it is to have these types of memories. Not for yourself, but for the people who want to know you. LCS must have pictures of me, but the only pictures I have are the ones I was old enough to take myself.

"That was the first day of second grade. The start of my social anxiety." She's standing in front of a brick building with a rolling backpack, eyes squeezed shut. "Look how I'm clinging to my mom. Ma had to convince her not to enroll in school with me."

There's a picture of her wearing a blue vest covered in pins. "You were a Girl Scout?"

"Mostly for the cookies," she says, flipping the page. "This is when I lost every single one of my teeth at the same time. Did that happen to you?"

"Nope." I lost most of my teeth at the Laurelle dorms. I dug them out with my fingernails and threw them in the trash. I'm sure her parents snuck into her room at night to trade her tooth for a few neatly folded dollars, which she probably saved in a piggy bank instead of blowing it on candy the way I would have.

"That's so weird when you think about it. Bones just fall out of kids' mouths."

"It's bizarre."

The security alarm chimes as the front door opens. Brie's dog, Rajah, comes running from her parents' room barking at the top of his little lungs.

We weren't planning on her parents coming home early. I don't want to ambush them. "Will they mind that I'm here?"

"Of course not," she says. "They've been wanting to meet you."

The woman who was holding Brie on her lap in the first picture starts crying as soon as she sees us.

"Oh my god, Mom. Really?"

"What's going o—" Her other mom stumbles to a halt, arms full of Target bags. Her eyes convey a thousand emotions at once, but the one that stands out the most is worry. In an instant, it's gone. Replaced by that parent smile. The close-lipped one that no one but their child can read. She sets the bags down on the floor and extends her hand to me.

"Amélie. It's so nice to meet you. I'm Erin. This is my wife, Rebecca."

Rebecca dabs her eyes with a tissue. "I'm sorry. I'm being ridiculous."

"So ridiculous," Brie mutters.

"It's nice to meet you both." They don't seem upset that I'm here, but they probably would've appreciated a heads-up. I'm sure they must have been in contact with LCS and Sue and

Dave by now, but I'm not sure how those conversations went, if they happened at all. "Brie, can I use your bathroom?"

"Yeah, sure. It's the last door on the left."

I hurry away, digging my phone out of my pocket.

Me: just met Brie's parents

Rena: !!!

Rena: you met Erin and Rebecca?

Why does she remember their names?

Rena: was it awkward?

Me: so awkward

Me: I'm hiding in the bathroom

Me: it sounds like they're arguing

Rena: about you?

I press my ear to the door. They are definitely arguing, but it doesn't sound like it's about me. They're talking about ballet.

Me: I don't think so

I can't hear exactly what they're saying, but Brie sounds defensive. Her parents sound like whatever they're discussing is not a topic up for debate. Something about her training schedule and Brie not holding up her end of a deal.

I stay in the bathroom until their voices die down, run the water for a second, and join them in the entryway.

"Ready?" Brie asks, her face impassive. She invited me to hang with her at the studio for a while until I meet up with Hayden.

She grabs her ballet bag and walks out without another word to her parents. I mumble goodbyes and thank-yous and sorrys, even though I don't know what I'm being so thankful or sorry about.

Outside, I want to ask Brie if everything's okay, but before I get a chance, she hits me with her own question.

"This guy you're meeting later. Is he your boyfriend?"

"I don't know." At this point, Hayden and I exist in a nebulous space where we're not dating but we're not *not* dating. She arches an eyebrow at me. "It's what he wants, but—"

"What do you want?"

I want him but I want it to be easier to want him. I don't want to feel like I'm standing in the middle of a bridge that's falling apart beneath me. I could move toward a relationship with him, or I could go back the way I came. But either way, I don't trust my footing. I don't know what part of the bridge will give out on me, and I'm having a hard time breathing up here.

"I think it's what I want too."

It's one of those rare New York summer days when it's still insufferably hot but not particularly humid. Everyone's outside. Joggers, street vendors, moms with strollers. It's only a few blocks to her dance school—I know this from when I stalked her—and as we're crossing the very street where I lost my shit on that fateful June day, she breaks the silence.

"I broke up with my first boyfriend because I liked him too much." I laugh but also I get it. "I was nine and he was perfect. We were a Taylor Swift song. I couldn't handle it."

"What happened?"

"The next day he was holding hands with Piper McKenna at recess. Apparently what we had meant nothing to him."

"You really were a Taylor Swift song."

"I cut all the erasers off of his pencils."

She says this calmly, like it isn't the academic equivalent of ripping off Barbie heads. I pause, stuck between terror and absolute admiration. "Why?"

"Because," she smirks, opening the door to the studio. "Some mistakes you can't fix."

An hour later, I'm lying on the floor of Brie's dance studio while she twirls en pointe to the beautifully sad melody of a Lana Del Rey song. Watching her interpretation of it makes me feel like she wrote it herself. It amazes me how her body can become music. You'd never guess how hard she works to move this way. It's what makes her feel the most foreign to me. It's like she's music now and had been before and will be in whatever comes next.

"Shit."

She wobbles over to me. I pause the song.

"You okay?"

She sits, rubbing her ankle. "Yeah my shoe is dead and I didn't have time to prep another pair. Can you hand me my bag?"

I slide it over to her. Brie's shoe-prep process is damn near surgical. She explains it to me as she goes, showing me how she cuts the ribbon into quarters and how she organizes everything—her stitch kit, toe spacers, and extra elastic all stored away in their specific places. I love hearing her speak about ballet. It isn't that I particularly care about a fouetté or jeté, because I definitely do not, but I've never heard someone speak so passionately about anything in my life. I've never seen someone work with that much focus.

"It's strange," I say, turning one of the shoes over in my hands. "Watching you dance."

She cuts the arch of the one she's holding with a box cutter, bending the sole until it cracks. "It helped me a lot when I was younger. I put a lot of pressure on myself to be great at something. I guess part of me felt like I had to be worth the investment, you know?"

"Yeah. I get that." LCS will do that to you.

"When I started dancing, it felt like what I was supposed to do. I became pretty obsessive as a kid. I just wanted to be perfect, but it freaked my parents out."

"Why?" She looks at me, and I can tell she's gauging how much she wants to say. "I've already claimed the role of the dark twin. There's nothing you can say that will knock me from my throne."

She smiles a little, placing her supplies carefully back in her bag. "I wasn't really taking care of myself. The only way they let me do it now is if I stick to our rules. I have to keep my weight up and manage my stress better. I have to at least attempt to have a social life with people outside the studio. My GPA can't drop below a 3.6, even though I don't plan on going to college."

"Is that what you were arguing about earlier?"

"You heard that?"

"I thought it might have been about me."

"No, they're happy to meet you. Really. They just . . ." She sighs. "It wasn't about you. It was about me. They're so protective. They worry themselves to death about everything, but they don't get it. I'm auditioning for SAB in September. Almost all the NYCB dancers are SAB alum. It's all I want." She folds her legs into a perfectly flat butterfly stretch. "What about you? What's your thing?"

"I don't have a thing."

"There's nothing you love to do?"

"No." I'd never really thought about it before. Most people have hobbies. Maybe my hobby is nurturing complicated relationships.

Right on cue, my phone vibrates noisily on the hardwood floor.

Hayden: here

"Hayden's outside." I knew when I told him to meet me here that I would introduce them. Now that the time has come, it's stressing me out.

Brie continues stretching while I trash the empty donut box from the bakery next door and gather my things. I know she wants to meet him, but I doubt she'd ask.

"Walk me out?"

"Really?" she says. I try to smile reassuringly. This is good. It's good. "Okay."

He's sitting on the steps texting when we come out. I get a sudden rush of insecurity, wondering if he will like her more than me. We have the same face, but she's in better shape. They're from the same city and probably have more in common than we do. She's kinder. More open. I see so much of what I like about him in her.

But when he turns our way, he only sees me. It's the same look he wore the other morning in his room. I can't believe I didn't see it before.

"Hey," he says.

"Hi." I hug him because hugging is a thing we do now. Brie hangs back, waiting for us to pull apart. When we do, they both stare at me expectantly. "Oh, you're waiting for an introduction. Okay. Sister, boy. Boy, sister."

Spare me. Please.

They grin at each other, at my expense, it would appear. But they decide to put me out of my misery. An act of mercy, really.

"Hayden," she says.

"Brie."

They hug lightly and exchange pleasantries while I astral project, floating somewhere above our heads. I can't listen to what they're saying because it's suddenly very important to me that they get along. Brie represents my past and Hayden represents the type of future I could have. Watching the two of them together is getting to know myself, right now in the present. How the different parts of my life may converge to form a whole.

It isn't until Hayden and I leave the school that I return to my body like a rubber band rebounding onto itself. I vaguely remember saying bye to Brie. Telling her I'd call her later. The way she'd stood at the top of the steps, watching us go.

We round the corner and Hayden immediately pulls me to a stop. He places his hands on either side of my neck and tilts my head up, reading my face like a book. He doesn't ask if I'm okay or why I was pretty much catatonic back there. He just gives me that Hayden smile that makes my heart flutter like a damn hummingbird in my chest and says, "Thanks for letting me meet her."

15

CLAIR DE LUNE

Hayden doesn't come over as often anymore. Not at night, anyway. Over the past few weeks, late mornings have bled into afternoons spent wandering the city. Hushed convos in the back of movie theaters. Picnics in the park. I come home, and he's on my clothes, in my hair like smoke. When I'm with him I worry less about the future and all the things I can't change. How futile it is to try. When we're apart, it all comes back again.

I can't sleep.

"Hey."

The phone in my hand glows brightly in an otherwise dark room. I didn't know if he'd answer. We don't FaceTime much.

"Hi."

"Is that Claudia from last night?" Hayden ignores Trey, whose laugh bellows over the sound of *NBA Live*. "Hey, Melie."

Hayden jerks back, his fingers stabbing at the buttons on the controller. The phone wobbles precariously on his lap. "Man, get that shit out of here."

"My guy thought he was making that from half court?"

"Delusion."

"Nah, he put his heart in it though. I felt that."

"What's up?" Hayden asks me. "You good?"

"Mm-hmm."

I'm supposed to have dinner with his parents tomorrow. I know it wasn't his idea and we would both rather it not happen, but the reality is, it is happening and it feels like a forced step forward in our relationship that I'm not sure I'm ready for. For the most part, Hayden and I have been living in a bubble of our own making, but bubbles are delicate things. I'm constantly anticipating a puncture.

"Hold on." He leans out of frame and comes back with one of his earbuds in. "Can you hear me?"

"Yeah."

"Can you hear Trey less?"

"My voice is melodic," Trey retorts.

"He speaks at a frequency too high for my ears to detect," I say.

"Put your phone on the side of the bed that you, for some reason, refuse to acknowledge exists."

I prop the phone up on the pillow he usually balls up under his chin. "No one with a mattress larger than a twin sleeps in the dead center of their bed."

"Now close your eyes," he says. I stare at his face, jaw clenched in concentration while he plays. His gaze never leaves the TV. "Your eyes aren't closed."

"Yeah, because I'm bored."

"You're also tired."

"I'm always tired."

"So close your eyes. I'll stay on the phone."

"While I sleep?"

"While you lie there and overthink."

I kick one leg from under the covers. This is stupid. "You won't hang up?"

"Nope."

He puts himself on mute so I don't have to hear him and Trey yelling at the game. At some point, sleep descends suddenly and without warning. When I wake in the middle of the night, he's asleep too. His breathing plays in my mind like a score. I dream of a saltwater pool. Of bicycles tangled in bushes. The last few seconds of sunset over the ocean.

And in the morning I roll over to reach for him, but there's nothing there but a dead phone.

Richards gave me my first journal when I was seven. He said the least I could do if I wouldn't talk to him was talk to myself. It did help, but it made me anxious to expel my thoughts onto a page that anyone could stumble upon. I'd fill notebooks only to bury them in the bottom of trash cans, pages ripped from their binding. Eventually, I stopped writing altogether.

I'm up on the roof with the journal I bought after Darren died. I can't bring myself to write in it. I always thought I'd use it once I was ready to talk to him again. I want to tell him what's been happening. How surprisingly well things are going with Sue and Dave. All about life in New York. He would've been the first one I told about Brie. I'd have run all my conspiracy theories about LCS past him, and he'd listen with that grin on his face. The one that, even when I was worked up, could always get me out of my head. He could make me smile when I couldn't find a single thing to be happy about.

But I can't talk to him. Not until I can apologize and live with the fact that I'll never get one in return.

My phone buzzes with a text from Hayden. I expect it to be him telling me he's downstairs, but unfortunately, he is incapable of following the simplest instruction.

He sent me a selfie, starring none other than Sue and Dave. All lounging in the living room, grinning at the camera like this isn't the very first time they're meeting. Like they've known each other for years. And you know what? Sure. Fine. If today's going to be that type of day, let's just lean into the madness.

I walk into the apartment cautiously, a rabbit being lured into a trap. "I hate everything about this." There's an empty plate of pasta in front of Hayden. Dave's mom would be so proud of Susan. "How long have you been here?"

"I don't know, twenty minutes?"

He looks to Sue, who shrugs, beaming.

Nope.

"We're leaving."

Sue sips from her mug of tea. "Hayden was telling us you're having dinner with his parents."

"Against both of our wills." I hold out my hand to pull him off the couch. He takes it but makes no move to stand. "Can we go?"

"Are you in a hurry to sit across the table from my dad?"

I'm not. He tugs my arm, and I slump next to him. Sue and Dave ask Hayden a thousand questions and Hayden has a thousand perfect answers. It's the stuff of late-night television. Like, sir. What are you here to promote?

"Can I use your bathroom?" he asks me.

"Sure."

He heads down the hall to my room. Sue raises her eyebrows. *Shit.*

She has the grace to wait until she hears the door close before she chews me out. "You can't have boys over without telling us."

Dave turns, confused. "What?"

"He came over, like, once."

"You're a horrible liar."

"I'm a great liar."

Admittedly, this is not my best work.

"He can visit when we're here. Door open."

"He's never coming back."

"You used to sneak me in," Dave says.

This is no time for nostalgia. Sue's face turns bright red.

"You're proving my point."

"Oh." As whatever memories he's recalling crystallize, his face becomes more and more horrified. "*Oh.* Yeah, no. Absolutely not."

"Ew." The second Hayden comes back, I'm out of my seat. "Let's go."

The boy is oblivious and incapable of reading a room. It takes a full three minutes before I get him out of the damn apartment.

"You couldn't have just asked where the bathroom was?"

He jogs down the hallway to catch up to me. "What?"

Not a thought between those ears, I swear.

I hadn't paid much attention to Hayden's apartment before. It's warmer than I remember. I see his mom's influence in the design—the soft colors, the choice of artwork on the walls, the way the layout seems to encourage conversation rather than entertainment—but it also feels like I shouldn't sit on anything. Now that I think about it, I get why we don't hang out here.

When we first walked into the lobby, which is an art museum in its own right, I asked Hayden what the hell his dad does for a living. It's not polite, but I'm over pretending to be polite. He told me his dad is in real estate and helped develop Hudson Yards into what it has become. Which is clearly unobtainable to mortals. He said it offhand, claiming they got in early.

"Who plays?" I ask, pointing to the white grand piano in the living room. It's tucked into the curve of a wall of glass that offers the most stunning view of the river.

"My mom mostly, but I can play a little."

"What's a little?" He shrugs. "You have to play now, you know that, right?"

I push him over to the piano and he reluctantly joins me on the bench. I watch his face while he squints at the sheet of music in front of him and starts to play. I recognize it as soon as I hear it.

"'Clair de lune.'"

He stumbles over a few notes but recovers well enough. "It's my mom's favorite. I only know the very beginning."

"Debussy's no joke."

He stops after the first few lines of music. I haven't played this song in years, but I think my fingers still remember the notes. I learned a slightly modified version because I was eleven and what can you really expect from a child? I place my hands an octave higher and start where he left off.

When I was a kid, I hated the piano. I hated the weight of the keys under my little fingers. I hated how it split my mind in two. The dissonance between my hands, one playing the treble clef while the other was playing the bass. I hated that I wasn't good enough to lose myself to the music yet. Every note took so much concentration. I hated that I couldn't hide what I was feeling when I played. The frustration of messing up. The longing to be good at something. The stupid pride I felt when I finally, after weeks, got something right.

I fell in love with it the way I fall in love with most things. Like flicking the light on while I sleep. Waking up in a bright room and having no recollection of when things changed. I love the weight of the keys. How sturdy they feel under my hands. I love that, no matter what piano I play, my fingers always find the notes. I love how my mind goes quiet. How music can express the way I'm feeling better than I ever could.

"I haven't played in a while," I say, self-conscious about the way Hayden's looking at me. He smiles and looks up at the same time that I notice something move out of the corner of my eye. My hands fall back to my lap when I see his mom standing in the entryway.

"That was beautiful," she says, coming toward us. "I was hoping I could sneak in without interrupting."

Hayden stands and hugs her. "Hey, Mom."

"Hi, Mrs. Thompson."

"It's nice to finally meet you, Amélie." I go to shake her hand, but she pulls me into a hug. Her skin is so soft. She smells like cinnamon and vanilla. Her hugs must be medicinal because I feel a little dazed when she lets me go. Like mother, like son, I guess. "Have you been playing long?"

How do I say, *Yes, whenever I'm returned to LCS by a family who's had enough of me, I take up piano as my mandatory music extracurricular?*

"Since I was five."

"I always wanted Hayden to stick with it." She brushes his cheek fondly. "He abandons every hobby I try to get him into."

"She wanted me to do watercolor paintings or row crew."

"I wanted him to try new things."

"Renaissance hobbies. She thought I was going to learn chess."

"You're not going to play basketball forever."

"Right, so let me take up needlepoint."

"You stuck with cooking," I say.

Witnessing the two of them together, how close they seem to be, I know he must have learned to cook from her. I can see little Hayden following his mom around the kitchen until she gave him something to do. Chopping veggies with his tiny kid knife and standing on a chair next to the stove watching intently while she worked. The thought alone is so cute I could cry.

The proud look on her face confirms my suspicion.

Hayden, on the other hand, rolls his eyes. "Because people have to eat."

I eat all the time and I never cook.

Mrs. Thompson checks the delicate gold watch on her wrist. "I'm going to check in with Henry. He may be running late."

Once she's gone, I take a careful seat on the shockingly plush cream couch. Hayden collapses on it, kicking his feet up on the armrest and laying his head on my lap.

He laces his fingers through mine and I imagine living in a home of my own with someone who looks at me like this. I don't need this kind of wealth. I just want a place that's mine, filled with my pictures on the mantel and my laundry in the hamper and my take-out boxes piled in the fridge. Still, if people knew homes like this existed, would they dream of them? If I knew boys like him existed, would I have dreamed of him?

"I'm glad you came," he whispers.

His mom reappears, crossing over to the china cabinet by the dining room, her lovely white sundress swooshing with each step. He watches her take out place settings, stacking them carefully on top of each other. His face is as peaceful and clear as a cloudless sky. But then I only count three settings, and I think he does too because a storm starts to gather over his eyes. There's thunder in the set of his jaw.

She looks at him and something passes between them. "It's just going to be us tonight." She turns away, and the china cabinet closes behind her with a rattle.

"What do you mean?" he asks, but I've only met his dad once and even I know what she means.

"He got stuck at work."

Hayden's entire body tenses. "This was his idea."

"Hayden." Her tone is exasperated and exhausted. They've been here before. Too many times. Her smile is thin, plastered there for my sake, but she's begging him not to react. To push whatever he's feeling down—the disappointment, the anger. "Let it go. Please."

This is where he gets it from. Why nothing ever seems to affect him. For the first time, when I look at him, I see through his calm facade. In his stillness and silence, there is rage.

His mom works hard to carry the conversation over dinner. Hayden's here physically, but mentally he's somewhere else. I try to keep up, but the energy is off. It's so obvious she's upset too. Her fork trembles in her hand. Her eyes drift occasionally to the door, like at any moment he may surprise them and show up after all. She fills her wineglass for the fourth time. Not a customary pour, but all the way to the top.

"I like your mom," I say once Hayden and I are alone in his room. I feel for her. I've obviously never been married, but

I know how it feels to be taken for granted. I know what it's like to wait for someone who isn't coming and wonder how you found yourself in that position again. His mom is strong, dignified, and kind. It's hard to be those things on a good day. Even harder when your world is falling apart.

"She likes you too." He can't know that. I don't think he heard a word she said to me, but it's nice of him to say it anyway. "I can't believe he didn't show up."

Again, I find this fully believable, but I've had a lot of practice with obnoxious, career-obsessed parents.

"It's probably better this way. Your dad's . . ." An asshole. "Intense."

"I hate him," he says, almost ruefully. An apology. He doesn't have anything to be sorry for. He isn't the first person to hate his dad. He won't be the last. "My parents are getting a divorce."

"Oh." It's all I can say.

"They don't know that I know. It should've happened years ago."

"My brother went through the same thing."

"You have a brother too?" he deadpans.

"Foster brother. Kind of. Calvin."

"Rena's boyfriend?"

"Yeah. I lived with them for a while when I was thirteen. They were going to adopt me."

Hayden and I don't talk about LCS. I've never told him about life at Laurelle or what it's like to bounce around from one family to the next. With Rena, Cal, and Darren it was easier because they saw it firsthand. I traded my room at Cal's for a room at Rena's. They spent days with me on campus and helped me sneak out of my dorm at night. Those memories are ours, and as painful as some of them are, they mean everything to me. They are memories I don't want to taint, not with anyone else's judgment or pity.

Hayden stares at me with eyes so dark brown, they're almost black. "What happened?"

I don't know what happened. Not the details, anyway. I just know from the moment I stepped into that house, I felt like the wrong solution to a complicated problem. Children know when they're supposed to be the tape holding something broken together. It's a horrible position to be in.

"Kids don't fix bad marriages. Even incredible ones like me."

Hayden smiles. I hate that he has to go through this. I know parents do their best, but for so many kids, they're the first source of trauma. They're the first people to teach you who you are and what you're worth. For so long, you're only someone's child. It's all you know how to be, and it's supposed to be easy because life gets harder later. Parents are supposed to make it easy.

"I love you," Hayden says. It isn't a declaration. It's just a statement. I've heard him mention things like the weather and how he did on a math test with the same inflection. It isn't the emotion in his voice that stuns me, it's the lack of emotion. How easy it is for him to say it. How many times he must have thought it.

"I do," he says, unfazed by my wide eyes and hammering heart. "Sorry."

It's not the first time someone has loved me. I've had the words wrapped around me like a blanket. I've had them thrown at me like a brick through a window. I've said it when I didn't mean it. I've said it when it was the only thing I knew to be true. I've said it when it didn't make a difference either way.

But I can't say it now, so I don't say anything. I don't want to be afraid of him, but I am because everything that has ever made me happy has broken my heart.

16

MIDTOWN

Hayden's dad didn't come home last night.

He asked me to stay and I did. Gave me a shirt and shorts to change into. A new toothbrush and a towel. I washed the makeup off my face. We brushed our teeth side by side. I put the toothbrush in the cup next to his because I'd need it in the morning.

His *I love you* shared the room with us. Took up space between us in bed. When he kissed me, it was softer than usual. Everything moved slower than usual. I felt more naked than usual. For the first time, I was scared.

I spent the night counting to a hundred and back down to one over and over again. I made mental lists of all the differences, big and small, between Hayden and Darren until I was reassured that this was not the same. This thing between Hayden and me is something new, and I don't have to be afraid of it. He is not Darren, and I am not the girl who Darren loved so recklessly. I don't have to be afraid. It's Hayden. I can do this with him. Can't I?

God, I don't know.

Hayden's dad wasn't there when we woke up. His mom didn't seem to care that I slept over. If she did, she didn't say anything. She made a large stack of pancakes, went into her study, and shut the door. I wanted to tell her goodbye before I left, but she never came out.

I grabbed a coffee at a café a block away. I texted Rowen and deleted the text thread so that by the time she got back to me, I could pretend I hadn't been the one to ask her to meet.

I'm at Shaine's apartment, giving her the details of last night while I change into a pair of clean clothes. I texted Sue yesterday to tell her I was staying at Shaine's, and even though I don't think she bought it, I want to sell it by not wearing the same clothes home.

"So, wait. Sorry. That boy looked you in the face and told you he loves you? Vocally? Out of his mouth?"

"That's all you heard, isn't it? Out of everything I said."

Shaine waves her hands impatiently. "Did you say it back?"

"Of course she didn't," Rena says over the phone. I called her so I wouldn't have to tell the story twice. "Not him apologizing afterward."

"I can't believe you didn't say it back. You're so in love with him it's stupid."

"I'm not obligated to say it back."

Shaine scrunches her nose. "You kind of are."

"*I love you. Sorry.*" Rena is in hysterics. "I'm dying. I can't believe you stayed. I would've expected you to repel out of his window like one of Charlie's Angels."

Shaine raises her eyebrows.

"I am not heartless," I say, collapsing on the bed. "Besides, his windows are very high up."

I was the first one to say "I love you" with Darren. Rena knows that because I told her right after it happened. It just came out, and I wanted to swallow the words whole. I wasn't ready for how they would change things, and they did. They changed everything. They became the binding between us. The thing that made me feel inseparable from him and special. They were the filter through which all the bad parts of us passed. Made us new each time we said it. Erased all the horrible things we'd screamed at each other.

But we said it too often until, over time, it became another horrible thing. Another weapon in our arsenals.

Shaine sits cross-legged next to me. "I know you like to pretend this isn't a relationship, but at this point, Mel, the wedding invitations are at the printers."

"I'd never have a wedding," I say. "I would hard launch a husband out of nowhere."

"I wouldn't have a wedding either. But I'd definitely throw a party for the divorce. I'd wear a black gown with a matching veil."

"Why be his peace when you could be his nightmare," Rena says.

Shaine grins. "Exactly."

I pick up food from my favorite Mexican restaurant on the way home. Brie and I were supposed to see a movie, but I'm tired.

I asked her to stop by instead. It's the first time she's coming over, and events such as these require empanadas and tacos with the extra spicy salsa. I thought we'd have the apartment to ourselves, but Sue's sitting at the kitchen island sorting through a stack of papers.

"I didn't know you'd be home."

She misinterprets my tone, eyeing the bags in my hands and my disheveled—but much better than it was two hours ago—appearance. "Hayden coming over?"

"No, Brie." I set the bags on the counter. I wasn't intending for them to meet today, but I guess it has to happen eventually. "Please don't make a big deal about it. I want to skip to the part where everyone knows everyone. If I have to formally introduce her to another person—"

"I get it," she says. "I'll be chill."

I take a seat next to her. "Want an empanada? I ordered for four people because I don't know how to order an appropriate amount of food." She smiles. I give her two because you can't just have one. "What's all this?" I ask, gesturing at the papers.

"A floor plan and vendor details for the garden party."

"You do this every summer?"

"It's a charity event that benefits a different sustainability organization each year. The first one went so well that we kept it going." She turns to me. "Why don't you invite some people?"

"Who?"

"Whoever. Friends."

"You want a bunch of teenagers crashing your party?"

"I want you to come. And yeah, I want to meet your friends. I want you to meet ours."

I can think of about twelve things off the top of my head that I'd rather do than attend a party full of rich thirty-somethings, but sure.

"How was dinner last night?" she asks.

"Hayden's dad didn't show, but I like his mom. She's nice." I'm not sure whether it's worth it to admit the next part to her, but I need to talk about Hayden to someone who can offer some perspective. "Don't be pissed, but I stayed the night over there."

She takes an ungraceful bite of her empanada, holding her hand in front of her mouth as she speaks. "I figured. I appreciate you telling me. We have to work on the whole telling-me-before part though."

"Sorry," I say. She looks more amused than mad. "Do you like him?"

"Hayden?"

"Yeah."

"I don't know him, but he seems like a good kid."

"He . . ." I can't bring myself to say the word love. "Likes me a lot."

"Is that a bad thing?"

"I don't know yet. It shouldn't be though. Right?"

Sue studies me for so long that I have to look away. "Mel," she says. "You have been through some impossibly difficult things. It's smart to be cautious. It's understandable for you to be confused about how you feel. But that boy caring about you isn't a bad thing, even if you don't feel the same way he does. Of course he cares about you. I've seen it in how he looks at you. You deserve that, whenever you're ready for it. Whether or not it's him."

I nod, eyes burning from the salsa or her words. "That was a great parent speech, Susan."

She smiles. "I thought so too."

By the time Brie knocks, we've eaten five empanadas and we're halfway through the chips and guac. I answer the door with a mouthful of rice and almost choke.

Brie's standing in the hallway soaking wet. Absolutely drenched from head to toe. The AC from inside hits her and she shivers.

"Did you swim here?" I ask.

"I walked. It's raining."

When did it start raining?

Wait. "You walked? From your house?"

"No. I was in Midtown."

"Why?"

She starts crying, which makes sense because you only go to Midtown if you're on the verge. I wave her in and shut the door. Sue takes one look at Brie and jumps out of her seat. "This is Sue."

Brie cries harder. "Hi. I'm sorry."

"No, it's okay," Sue says, running out of the room. "Let me get a towel."

"It's nice to meet you," Brie sobs.

Whew.

"My room's at the end of the hall. Borrow whatever you want. You can hang your clothes in the bathroom."

She leaves a trail of water in her wake.

I'm not usually anyone's first choice when they're approaching their dark place unless they'd like to stay there for a bit. The friends who know me well know I'm more of a cry-with-you friend than a cheer-you-up friend. There's always space on my bathroom floor.

But, no. I can be the cheer-you-up person. Or at least the emotionally composed person. I have tacos. I can do this.

"Is she okay?" Sue asks, handing me a stack of towels.

"Apparently not. She was in Midtown. Who the fuck goes to Midtown?" I grab the food and two bottles of water. "Sorry. For cursing."

Brie's sitting on the bed, her hair dripping onto one of my old sweaters. I toss a towel and expect her to catch it, but it smacks her in the face. This is going terribly. I don't know what to say to her. I open containers of food and place them in front of her like an offering.

She hesitates and then starts stuffing tacos in her mouth, barely chewing. "They're not letting me audition."

"For the dance school?"

"We got into it yesterday but I thought once they calmed down . . . I didn't think . . ." She dunks a taco in the spicy salsa and my eyes widen. "They're the ones who got me into ballet. They bought my first tutu and came to all of my recitals, but the second I start taking it seriously, it's a problem. They know how hard I've worked. They know what I've sacrificed to be as good as I am. I'm really good. I work out a lot, I know. But I eat! I'm eating."

Brie takes a big bite and immediately starts coughing because the spicy salsa is nothing to play with. She snatches one of the bottles of water and drinks half of it.

"Can you audition next year? You'll be eighteen. Will you need their permission?"

"That can't be my only shot. I've wanted this my whole life. More than I've ever wanted anything. What do I do if I don't get in?"

Wow. Is this how people feel when I freak out?

"My parents . . . I love them. I do. But sometimes it feels like there's a disconnect. I'm not always sure they see me, you know? When I was younger, all I wanted was for them to be proud of me. I worked my ass off. I was really hard on myself. I finished a recital once with two broken toes. En pointe. I know they're proud, but it stopped being about them. I need this. I really need it, and I don't think they see that."

There's still so much Brie and I don't know about each other. If we were closer, maybe I'd have the perfect words for her. Some way to help her put things into perspective. I should be able to do that. She's my sister. I should know what to say to her, but I don't.

I do understand though. We may have had vastly different experiences over the last twelve years, but we came from the same place. We have so many of the same wounds. Maybe that's why she's telling me all this. I may not be able to relate to what she's going through, but I can relate to the profound sense of anxiety she's feeling.

"I know what it's like to lose the thing keeping you here. Even if your relationship to it isn't as healthy as it should be."

She wipes her eyes with the back of her hand. "What did you lose?"

"It wasn't a what. It was a who. But you're not losing anything. You can still dance. Maybe it will be with that school, maybe it won't. Things don't always happen the way you think they will, but good can still come from it. If I hadn't . . ." If I hadn't lived through the last year. If I hadn't found a way to breathe through the pain. "Well, I wouldn't be here. We may never have met."

I don't know if it helps. I hope it helps because the truth is, if I had to do it all over again, it wouldn't have been worth the trade-off. But maybe I'll feel differently one day.

When Rowen texts me twenty minutes later, I make up an excuse about needing to help Sue with something and slip out of the apartment. Brie's too distracted, too lost in her head, to leave the room and notice I'm gone. I meet Rowen in the lobby.

"Your donut, extra sprinkles," she says, handing me a paper bag from a bakery with an actual donut inside.

Brie's in the bathroom when I get back to my room. I set the donut on the bed for her, open my drawer, and refill the wooden box all the way to the top.

17

THE KIDS ARE HAVING FUN

I only invited Brie to Sue's party, and to be real, I regretted it the second I did. But then Sue told Mrs. Aoki, who told Shaine, who demanded to come. She told Justine and Olivia and before I knew it, Trey and Hayden were coming. Rena and Cal are here to provide life-sustaining treatment in case I have a panic attack, which I'm pretty sure I'm having right now.

I felt the panic start to build this morning at the thought of having everyone I care about in one place at the same time. I couldn't conceive of all the different versions of myself I'd have to be. The social optics of being Susan and Dave Romano's foster daughter. The pressure of hard launching Brie to my entire group of friends at once and hoping everyone gets along. Having Cal and Rena meet Hayden for the first time. Can you be emotionally overstimulated?

I'm standing off to the side, hidden among the hydrangeas or whatever. I don't know flowers. I pull the satin fabric of the pink dress Sue picked out for me away from my clammy stomach. It's late July and the weather is mild today, but my skin still prickles under the warmth of the afternoon sun. My hair is styled in loose waves like an old Hollywood starlet. Borrowed diamonds stud my ears and shimmer against my wrists. Around me, couples walk arm in arm through the narrow passageways, glasses of champagne in hand. They nod cheerfully. I paste a smile on my face.

I'm like the bride before she leaves the groom at the altar.

"Are we hiding?"

I spin around and Hayden is standing there in a suit. A suit. Linen with a white shirt, no tie. I'm dying right now, but Hayden in a suit is something to live for.

"A little bit."

He looks around. "We're doing a terrible job. Everyone can see us."

He holds out his hand and I take it. To anyone looking, we're just another couple, wine drunk and in love. And maybe that isn't far from the truth.

Because I do love him, even if I still haven't told him yet. And I do want this, even if I can't say it out loud. Not just him, all of it. The family and the friends and the boy. I want the life being offered to me, if only I'd consent to it. But how can I without the guarantee that it will be okay? I need to know it'll be okay.

"You didn't have to come to this." I don't know why I came to this. "All these people. It's bright. So many flowers."

He hugs me. A tight hug that compresses my nervous system and calms me down. I slump in his arms. "The kids are having fun."

"Really?"

On the far side of the garden, Rena and Justine have posted up near the kitchen entrance, waiting for servers to exit with fresh trays of food. Brie, Olivia, and Shaine are all huddled around a cocktail table giggling uncontrollably. Trey's flirting with the bartender, from the looks of it. The woman pours half a dozen cups of what is definitely not water, which Cal helps him carry over to the girls.

"Are they . . ."

"The kids are drunk," Hayden confirms. Of course. "It's all good. Why are you freaking out?"

I've never gotten what I wanted. I've gotten what I craved, the things I've gone after, but never what I wanted. Not in a way that lasts. I think I'll fail him before we even get started. And Sue and Dave will see with time that this isn't what they want. Their life is full already. I won't be able to bear the resentment.

I pull away. "I just need a minute." He frowns, eyes searching my face, but I can't look at him. "Go hang out. I'll be right there."

I don't get a minute. The second Hayden walks away, Rena finds me. "There you are. I was looking for you, but I got distracted by the truffle mac and cheese. What's going on?"

"We're leaving."

"What?" She hurries after me, swiping a glass of champagne from a passing server. "Slow down. Drink. What happened?" I down the whole glass. "You really want to leave?"

Yes. "No."

"What do you need? What can I do?"

"Nothing." I smooth my shaky hands over my dress. "Everything's perfect. Everyone's here in one room together talking and getting along and that's so great."

"But?"

"There's no but."

She takes my empty glass and trades it for a full one. This time, I sip slowly. "I don't understand. You're stressed out because everything is perfect?"

"Do I look stressed?"

"Bitch, yes. You're visibly vibrating."

I climb over another plant I can't identify because I'm not a damn botanist and sit on one of the benches scattered throughout the foliage. "What if I mess this up, Ri?"

"Mess what up? What are you talking about?"

"All of this. It was supposed to be temporary and I was fine with that—"

"Who says it has to be temporary?"

"Come on. You know how this goes."

"No I don't." She drops her clutch and kneels in front of me, cream dress splayed out in the dirt. "Do you think everyone's just humoring you? That this is all some big performance? Do you think people have time for that? No one has time to pretend to love you. If I can love you, they can too. Get over it."

She pries my nails away from my arm, wrapping my fingers around hers instead. She keeps them pressed there with her other hand. My chin quivers. She knows I could never hurt her. Not even a scratch.

"Ri."

"I know. It hit me the other day too. I can't believe it's almost been a year." She rests her chin on our clasped hands. "You're going to be okay. He would want you to be. You know that, right?" Tears streak down my face. I don't want to do this here. I don't want to think about him. "We can leave if you want to. I'm sure Sue would understand."

"No. I'm okay." I fix my makeup in the reflection of my phone. "Can you get me more champagne?"

She smooths my hair and stumbles to her feet. Hayden was right. The kids are drunk.

"It would be my absolute honor."

While she's gone, I fish a pill out of my bag and chase it with the rest of my drink, which is 100 percent what you should not do, but it may be the only thing that gets me through the rest of the afternoon.

Sometime between the savory and sweet foods, my mind slips away like a face in a crowd. The slow, steady trickle of sounds. The irresistible lure of sleep or something like it. Darkness, quiet, peace. I hear my name.

There's a cup of water in my hands.

"Drink," Dave says. I do. "Nothing but water for the rest of the night. Sober up."

I nod, finishing the water.

"These parties are important for Sue."

I nod again.

"There you are," Sue says, coming up behind us. Dave kisses her cheek. "Mel, I'd like you to meet some people."

She drags me into a conversation with the editor of some newspaper. A British photographer. A woman with lipstick the strangest shade of coral. I try to keep up, but I'm floating.

I close my eyes and when I open them, Hayden's hands are cupping my face. We're alone again, but something's not right.

"What did you take?" he asks.

Hmm.

"I had some champagne."

He drops his hands, his beautiful face screwed up in a grimace. "Let me see your bag."

"What?"

"Your bag, Mel."

I hand it to him. He dumps it out on a table. There's nothing in there but lip gloss, a tampon, and my phone. He runs his hands over his hair. "You told me you weren't going to do this again."

Do what?

Hayden?

I blink again and he's gone. Maybe he wasn't here to begin with. My dress feels too tight. I pull the fabric away from my skin but it clings on, wraps around me like a serpent, and I can't breathe. I can't breathe. I can't fucking think. The more I fight the panic, the more it floats to the top like oil. Congealing into a thick layer I can't pass through.

I close my eyes and when I open them, I'm on the floor of a handicap bathroom stall, dress zipped down to my waist. Rena's huddled next to me, rubbing my back.

"Come home," she whispers. "Just for the rest of the weekend."

Black heels pound against the bathroom tile. The handle to the stall shakes. "Mel?" Rena unlocks it. Brie's eyes are wide. She pushes her way in, closing the door behind her. "Are you sick?"

I look at Rena. A silent question. She nods.

"Brie," I say. "You want to come to Connecticut?"

18

I MAY BE OVERSELLING IT

Cal rolls up at eleven the next morning with Rena hanging out the window. Brie stayed with me last night. They got a hotel room a few blocks away. The second the car stops, Rena hops out and throws her arms around the two of us. Seeing them together like this, I almost burst into tears. It should've always been this way. I feel robbed. How would things have turned out if I'd had them both from the start?

On the drive to Connecticut, Rena's fingers brush against the Band-Aid on my arm covering crescent-moon-shaped marks. Silently she tells me we'll talk about it later. I'm so tired. My appetite is gone. It doesn't make any sense to me because things have never been better than they are now. I've never been more content, but I guess that's because I've never had more to lose.

My head knocks against the car window. Brie watches the city fall away. It hadn't dawned on me that this may be strange for her, returning to New Canaan after all this time. I tap her shoe with my foot. "You're okay with this, right?"

"Okay with what?"

"Going back."

Connecticut is home for me even though our town is an emotional war zone now. There are land mines buried under beaches and along specific strips of highway and in the corner booths of certain restaurants. It may not be her home anymore, but that doesn't make it safe for her either.

"When I was a kid, I wondered what life would've been like there," she says. "Not at Laurelle, but in one of those houses with a garden and a pool."

"Wait until you see Rena's house."

Rena shoves Cal. "Shut up."

"It is beautiful," I agree.

"What was it like to grow up there?"

"Boring." Rena slips her sunglasses on. "Had to break my mother's vintage vases just to feel something."

"You think she's joking," Cal says. "She was Wednesday Addams."

"I was not. I just wore a lot of black."

"How long have you guys known each other?" Brie asks.

"Since second grade. I hated him until fourth grade."

"You hated everyone."

"We were best friends in middle school. Still not sure how that happened."

"Well, she was in love with me and—"

"False."

"—she would follow me around all day."

181

"I friendzoned him for years."

I roll my eyes. "They are insufferable and it's only gotten worse with time."

When we get off the highway, we hit a drive-thru for milk-shakes and fries. Rena points out the historic landmarks of our friendship as we ride through her neighborhood—a fence we hopped that ripped my favorite T-shirt. The spot on the side of the road where her tire blew out and "almost cost us our lives."

"It didn't blow out," Cal says. "It had been slowly deflating for days. You just refused to let me change it."

Rena snorts. "You can change a tire? Since when?"

"The only thing Cal changes is the channel from whatever you're watching to football," I tell Brie.

"That's not true. He also changes his mind five minutes after you order food because he wants to 'try something new.'"

"I'm about to try a new girlfriend," Cal mumbles.

The car turns into the driveway of Rena's home, with the rose bushes I used to throw up in and the front porch where we would drink coffee, hungover from a night of partying. It's just as I remember, like no time has passed at all. Three car doors open at once. Rena knocks on my window. "You coming?"

Her house is a land mine too. The biggest one there is. I may have lived at Laurelle for most of my life, but I grew up here. After I moved out of Cal's place and back into the dorms, my life became so tumultuous that it was hard for Debra to find anyone interested in taking me in. Those who were quickly changed their minds upon meeting me. I was a disaster, and as much as Debra and I tried, it was hard for us to hide it. Rena's house was the only place I didn't have to pretend to be someone else.

It's the first time I've been here since I moved, and it's exactly how I remember. It even smells the same, like citrus from the candles her mom keeps around the house. We settle in the kitchen. Rena pulls a bunch of snacks out of the pantry. She slides me some of my favorites, the chewy Chips Ahoy, jalapeño potato chips, and Swedish Fish.

"Where are your parents?" I ask her.

"I don't know."

Rena's parents are never home. It's the reason we all hung out here so much. Her mom is a photojournalist and her dad made a lot of money in investments when he was younger, so they spend most of their time traveling the world. Before he graduated and moved to California, her older brother was usually left in charge—which isn't saying much because he practically lived at his girlfriend's house. It's all mildly neglectful, but Rena seems to prefer it this way.

"Morocco," Cal says.

Rena grins. "They're in Morocco."

"Thanks."

"Ils me manquent vraiment."

Yeah right. She's never missed her parents a day in her life. "I bet."

Brie stares between the two of us. "I didn't know you still spoke French."

"Yeah. You don't?" French is our first language. LCS was very insistent that I retain my bilingualism. I'd have thought they would've done the same for her, but maybe she lost more than her last name in the adoption.

She shrugs.

"Okay." Rena claps her hands. "Cal, make yourself useful."

He mutters something about "the disrespect" but helps her carry snacks out to the back patio.

"We're going to throw our stuff in the room," I call after them. "Meet you out there."

I lead the way to my old room. It's technically one of the guest rooms, but I don't know if anyone else uses it. All my things still fill the drawers and shelves. Clothes and books that I didn't like to keep in the dorms and didn't want to bring with me to New York. I don't like to travel with too much stuff because the more things you bring, the more things you have to take with you when you go.

I tell Brie about the parties Rena used to throw. Trips to the beach. Nights spent lying by her pool and spontaneous photo shoots in the middle of empty roads. I may be overselling it a little, but I never focus on the good like this. It makes it less painful to be here.

Brie picks up a few old film strips from the dresser. I forgot they were there.

"Who's this?"

I don't have to look to see what she sees. Bright blue eyes. Dark, messy hair. A small scar on his right cheek that he refused to tell me the origin of. Me on his lap with my arms around his neck, wearing a glittery dress, a Happy New Year headband,

and the biggest smile. I was a different person then. I haven't smiled like that since.

"That's Darren."

"He's cute."

I take the photo from her and study the face that has not faded one bit from my mind in the year since I last saw it. "We had the worst fight, like, fifteen minutes after this. We were both drunk. I don't know what we were fighting about, but it was the first time I told him I hated him. The next day, neither of us could remember why. We knew we were supposed to be mad at each other, but the new year had wiped the slate clean. We went and got breakfast burritos like nothing happened."

"Is this the person you were talking about before?" Brie asks. "The one you lost?"

I nod, shutting the picture away in the top drawer of the dresser.

Rena stops me on our way to the backyard. "Can I talk to you for a sec?"

"The backyard's this way?" Brie asks.

"Yeah, through the family room."

Rena waits until Brie's gone before she says, "How bad is it?"

"What?"

"You were high yesterday."

"I wasn't."

"You can't lie to me."

I can, I just don't. I usually don't.

She grabs my hand, pulling me back into my room. Shuts

the door. "You never talk to me about him. I try not to bring him up because I don't want to upset you, but we all lost him. It's not the same as you, I get that, but we all feel it. I know the anniversary—"

"Rena."

My voice is cold. I don't know where it comes from. I'm never cold with her. It must be this town. Or this room. My body. All tombs housing the memory of him.

"M," she whispers. "Don't scare me. Please."

"Don't *scare* you?"

"You know what I mean."

I cross my arms. "No, I don't. What do you mean?"

So much of what I've done over the past few months has been for her. I've made so many promises, most of them to her. How can she look at me and still see who I was last year? Am I not different now? Am I not better?

"He was my friend." Her voice breaks. Tears gather in the corners of her eyes. "I can't forgive myself for introducing you two."

I push past her out the door.

Brie's on the patio with Cal. Rena's a few feet behind me. Cal looks to her first. Then to me. A long, assessing stare.

I need to get out of this house for a while.

"Brie, you want to go for a drive?"

I park Cal's truck outside the Laurelle Academy gate. Even though it's late July, the campus is bustling. Some kids take summer courses. Some are back early for fall activities. Some opt out of returning home for break. Others have nowhere to return to. This is their home.

It's surreal to be back.

Brie walks up to the gate, her face inches from the metal. "It's bigger than I remember."

"They're forever renovating. They just built a greenhouse last year. I don't have to tell you what happens in the greenhouse."

She laughs. I can't imagine that we could've existed here at the same time. That's the hardest part of all this for me to wrap my brain around. I can't see her here. I can't picture a time when we used to run through these halls or do cartwheels on the lawn. She's so removed from this life and better for it. But then she points across the sea of green to a building on the edge of campus.

"Was that our building?"

"Yeah, that's grades K through five. The building next to it is the nursery. Grades six through eight are over there. Nine through twelve are around back."

"It's kind of incredible."

I try to see it through her eyes and if I'm being purely objective, it's beautiful. Grand stone buildings with perfectly trimmed hedges and cobblestone walkways. Everything about its appearance is a facade, meant to sell the promise of a certain future. One you'd be stupid not to want and may kill yourself to attain.

"Trust me. It's not what it seems."

"I know. I get it, I just mean . . . no parents sounds nice. The freedom. I wish I had that."

I'm sorry. What? "You wish you didn't have parents?"

"That's not what I mean—"

"Really? Because it's what you said."

"I meant living away from your parents."

I know what she meant, but it doesn't make it any less ridiculous. "I'm sure the kids gentrifying our school would agree, but for those of us who this school was built for, we're not living away from our parents."

She flinches as if I slapped her. "You're saying that like I didn't live here too."

"Exactly, so what are you even talking about?"

"Why are you snapping at me?"

"I'm not. I just don't know how you're sitting here being all woe is me because you didn't get the privilege of growing up in an orphanage."

She scoffs. "An orphanage?"

"This is by definition an orphanage."

"Yeah, well maybe it's better than living in a cage."

Oh, *girl.* I wasn't aware that having two loving parents, a house with your height carved into the doorframe, and literally everything your heart could desire was equivalent to imprisonment. All because they won't let her audition for her dream school for twelve whole months. "Are you joking?"

"I don't know what you've been through, but you don't know what it's been like for me either. How lonely it's been. You have a good life, Mel. Maybe it wasn't always that way, but I've seen you with Sue and Dave and with your friends. Being around you and Rena . . . to be honest, kind of sucks. You're lucky you're not the one who remembers how things used to be with us."

We were babies. What is there to remember?

"The fact that you're romanticizing my life is insane. My life is a fucking mess. Don't compare what we've been through because it's not the same. The reason Rena and I are so close is because she was here when everything went to hell."

"I would've been—"

"I know. But you weren't. She's like my sister."

"I *am* your sister!" Her fingers tangle into the gate until her knuckles turn white. "It's not my fault we grew up this way, so different from each other. None of this is my fault."

"I didn't say it was."

"You don't get to invalidate my experiences because you chose a harder path."

"Chose it?" Anger burns through me like wildfire. What exactly did I choose? Which part of any of this does she think I wanted?

I've made mistakes. Too many to count, but I've always owned them. I've never blamed anyone else for my actions. The things I had to do to keep myself alive. The ways I coped with a fate plucked out of the stars. I have regrets about what I've done to try to regain some sense of agency over my life.

But I haven't told her this. Any of it. So how can she judge me?

"We're not family," I tell her. "Not in the way that matters."

I know it's cruel. I mean it to be.

19

GOING THROUGH THE MOTIONS

Brie and I take the train back to the city the same day. Rena pulled me aside when we got back to her house to ask what happened, but I couldn't articulate the way Brie's words hurt me. I couldn't justify how I could say what I said to her. I couldn't make things feel normal between me and Rena again. I didn't want to talk.

When the train arrives at Penn Station, we go our separate ways.

In my bedroom, door locked, I clutch the wooden box filled with white pills with random letters and numbers embossed on them. I took too much at the party. I was too conspicuous. I have to be more careful.

Rowen said it's Ativan, like I asked for the first time. Two milligrams.

I break one in half.

Two at night. One during the day. Half if Sue and Dave are home.

I wander through stores. Museums. Along the High Line. I tell Sue and Dave I'm with friends. I'll be home late. I've already eaten dinner. I'm tired. I'm going to bed.

When they're at work, I sleep. I set an alarm to be gone by the time they get home; out living the way they want me to.

I lose three weeks.

Half a pill when I'm with Shaine.

We text mostly, but when I see her, I let her dominate the conversation. We plan her birthday. I don't think about what else falls on that day. We'll have the party the night before. She tells me about the new beauty campaign she booked. How she's already stressed about senior year. She can't believe it's only a month away.

I lie on her bed. I nod. Tell her *Same*.

Haven't seen Brie since Connecticut. Things with Rena are weird. Hayden's not speaking to me.

It's August. Debra's here.

No pills for the home visit. My mind's a swirling black storm.

I want this so badly. This life. When did that happen? How do I make it last?

And is it enough? If I get to keep it, will it be enough? I'm living it now and I'm drowning. I'm fucking it up. I'm trying so hard.

Debra's finished. She's just waiting to speak to me so she can ask all the usual questions she asks during our calls. Sue and

Dave step out so we can speak freely. Debra sits across from me, her hands folded on the kitchen table no one uses. "Are you happy here?"

I know Sue and Dave check all Debra's boxes. Not a red flag between them. "Does it matter?"

"If you're unhappy, yes, that matters."

"I'm not unhappy."

But that isn't the same as being happy.

Half a pill, hours ago. Dave's off today.

He leans against the doorframe of my room, arms crossed. "What are you reading?"

"*Beloved*."

I read this book for the first time when I was twelve. Since then, coming back to it feels like what I would imagine it is to come back to a childhood bedroom. Old posters on the walls and stuffed animals on the bed. A truer version of yourself before you knew any better. Back when you did more dreaming than being. This book was the first book to shape me. I've been lost in stories ever since.

Dave hums appreciatively. "Toni Morrison."

"Have you read it?"

"Yeah, in school." He gestures at my Kindle. "I don't know how you read like that. It's not the same as a physical book."

"It's easier. You know, with all the moving around. I can't bring boxes of books everywhere I go."

My Kindle was a gift from my first LCS case manager,

Amanda. She was sweet and gentle, like a kindergarten teacher. One of the few people I felt comfortable talking to. I was nine when she left the company. I cried for a week. She came to visit once with a paper bag stuffed with glittery gold tissue and her personal Kindle, with all her favorite books downloaded. It was the nicest thing anyone had ever done for me. She moved to London with her fiancé, and I never saw her again.

"Can I sit?" Dave asks. I shrug, so he does. "I haven't seen Brie around lately."

I set my book aside. "We got into it at Rena's." He raises his eyebrows but doesn't say anything. "She just . . . pisses me off. When she says certain things, I can feel myself overreacting, but I can't stop it."

"What types of things?"

"I don't know. We're so different. I wouldn't have wanted her to live my life. I'm glad she grew up the way she did, but sometimes it seems like she doesn't understand how good she has it. I'm not saying her life is perfect, but a lot of people I know would trade places with her in a second, and she doesn't seem to get that."

Dave leans forward, bracing his elbows on his knees. "When I first moved in with my parents, before they adopted me, there was another kid who had been living there for about a year. He had to be around twelve or thirteen. At that point I was almost fifteen, so I'd pretty much checked out of the process. I was going through the motions." He smiles like he knows how very much I can relate.

"This kid made it his mission in life to make everything between us a competition. I ignored it at first, but eventually it got to me and I went off. I said some really ruthless shit to him. I still feel bad because now I know he was just trying to hold on to that last bit of hope. He thought I was standing in the way of his chance at adoption. Maybe I was."

"What happened?"

"My parents had been fostering for twenty years, so they'd seen pretty much everything. They sat us down and told us we were allowed to be angry about what we'd been through, but we had to learn not to wield that anger like a weapon. It was the first time anyone had said something like that to me. Until I met them, I didn't believe good people existed. Took me a while to break out of that mindset."

I know good people exist. I've always known that, even when I didn't count myself among them. If I didn't believe people could be good, I don't think I would have made it this far.

"Were you angry?"

He holds my gaze. "Yeah, I was. I still am sometimes. Are you?"

"That's not the word I would use."

"What word would you use?"

It's not that I haven't felt anger. I've felt it so intensely I thought it'd consume me. But it's always short-lived. A fire with nothing to catch on to.

"I haven't figured that out."

I could've had a life like Brie's. I had every opportunity she had.

"Well," Dave says, reaching for my Kindle. He examines it before handing it back to me. There's no trace of the life he lived before. It's hard for me to imagine him as a teen in the system, but maybe this is what healing looks like. "When you figure it out, whatever it is, you're allowed to feel that too."

"Hi."

I stare at Hayden through my phone screen. No pills, just tired.

"Hi."

"I'm sorry," I say.

His beautiful face is stone. His eyes give nothing away but pure exhaustion and a hint of something else. Relief, I think. At least that's how I feel hearing his voice after so long. I've missed him.

He sinks into the row of pillows at the head of his bed. "We'll talk about it later."

I pull my comforter up to my chest. "You want to hang up?"

"No. I just . . ." There's yelling in the background. "Don't really want to talk right now."

A door slams. His eyes shutter.

"Okay."

I prop the phone up on the pillow he usually balls up under his chin.

We wait for morning to come.

20

EVERYONE BUT LUCAS

I ring Shaine's doorbell for the fourth time, adjusting the heavy garment bags in my hands as my backpack slips down my arm. I'm holding too much stuff, and she's taking forever. The second the door swings open, I drop everything in a pile at her feet.

"I'm sorry," she pants. "I was in the shower."

"I called you thirty minutes ago and you were in the shower."

"That's what I just said."

Whatever. I pick the garment bags off the floor and shake them out so the clothes aren't all bunched up inside. "This one"—I check the name written in Sharpie on the tag—"is yours."

She rips it out of my hands, almost taking my finger with it. "Susan!"

"I haven't seen them yet."

Shaine starts to unzip it. "Wait." She hands me her phone. I open the camera app. "Okay." I hit record as she slowly, and very dramatically, unzips the bag.

"Happy birthday!"

A slinky sequin dress. Rose gold and sheer enough for Sue to include preselected undergarments, with a cutout that runs diagonally from shoulder to waist and a thigh-high slit.

"Oh, she's telling me to go off tonight. Copy. That." Shaine holds the dress up to her body, and even though Sue never did a fitting, it'll fit like a glove.

I put her phone on the counter, wet a paper towel, and drape it over my face like a sheet mask. I know people complain about winter in the city, but summer is worse. It's humid and clammy every day. The air is almost too thick to breathe. I don't like it.

Shaine hops over the couch to grab a bottle of tequila from the liquor cabinet. "Okay, open yours."

Mine is more modest because I'm a seventeen-year-old child and Susan is my legal guardian. It's a shimmering white top with thin straps that leaves my entire back bare. Paired with a pink miniskirt. I don't say it enough to her, but Sue's a legend.

"Oh." I dig for the envelopes Sue shoved in my bag. "There are styling instructions. Obviously."

Shaine grabs two glasses and pours an unregulated amount of alcohol into each.

"Eighteen." I tip my glass to her.

"Thank god."

And so it begins.

Shaine's apartment is never messy, mostly because no one uses the common areas. Her room, on the other hand . . .

"I told you I was bringing your outfit."

"Yes." She steps over the piles of clothes, still on their hangers, scattered across the floor. "And I trust Susan with my life, but I had to have a few backup options just in case."

"In case of what?"

"I don't know. A spilled drink. The drunken desire for an outfit change. I can't predict what eighteen-year-old Shaine will need. I can only prepare for what she *may* need."

I help her get ready, following Sue's glam instructions to a T. Sue doesn't just style. She creates a moment. You have to respect the artistry.

My phone buzzes on the bathroom counter. "Hey, are you guys close?"

"Are you serious? We've been ringing this doorbell for an hour."

"Really?" Apparently, no one can hear the doorbell from Shaine's bathroom. "Sorry, I'm coming."

"Hayden?" Shaine asks me.

"And Trey."

I race over to the door and let them in. From the looks on their faces, they may as well have walked five miles in the snow to bring us these backup bottles of Jack Daniel's.

"Sorry," I say again.

Even though this party is the last thing on Hayden's mind, he still volunteered to run errands for us. Hayden loving me means Trey loves me too. However, Trey does not love me enough to lug these bags through the city. He did this for Shaine.

"You want this stuff in the fridge?" Hayden asks.

"You can put it on the counter. There's no ice yet."

They unload the bottles and mixers, and I have no idea who's supposed to consume all of this or where they could've possibly gotten it.

"It's not going to be enough," Trey says. "You know everyone's coming tonight."

"Who is everyone?"

Shaine told me twenty people may stop by over the course of the night. Thirty, max. That was the story she gave her mom. It's the only reason Mrs. Aoki agreed to make herself scarce.

"The entire school."

I knew this would be a Shaine party, but I assumed she'd scale it back since we're in her apartment and not a nightclub. Why would you want everyone in your apartment?

"We barely told anyone. It was supposed to be a small thing."

Trey side-eyes me. "Melie."

He's right. Shaine Aoki is turning eighteen at midnight and the whole world must bear witness. I take another sip of the drink I'd abandoned on the counter.

"We'll go get ice," Hayden says, and I smile at him gratefully. At least that's one less thing to handle today. Is this how maids of honor feel, because who would ever agree to that?

I duck back into Shaine's bathroom, clutching the glass of tequila against my chest. She's carefully filling in her lashes with individual extensions.

"Did you invite everyone you've ever met?"

"No." She uses a pair of tweezers to place one of the lashes, fanning her eye to dry the glue. "Not everyone."

Everyone *but Lucas* is crammed within the walls of Shaine's apartment.

I grab the couch to keep from falling as someone pushes past me, spilling half their drink on my foot. My head is throbbing from the shots and the heat but also maybe from the Molly a bunch of us did in Shaine's bathroom forty minutes ago.

I edge along the perimeter of the crowd to avoid getting sucked back onto the dance floor that I finally managed to extricate myself from. Being the Meredith Grey to Shaine's Cristina Yang has me just about ready to keel over. I reach the kitchen, fill a glass with water, and drink the entire thing.

Now that I'm standing still, the room is starting to spin. I close my eyes, but it only makes it worse. Everything is too loud. The music. The talking. Whoever's laughing like that. Even my thoughts seem like they're yelling at me.

I need to cool down.

I find an empty bathroom. I splash water on my face. I stare in the mirror.

Someone knocks, but I don't answer. They knock again. I dry my face and open it. It's just Hayden. He locks the door.

"Too many people," he says.

He's wasted. I think I might be too.

"Yeah."

I drank too much. My stomach hurts. I thought it would help to be drunk tonight because tomorrow—

Hayden's hands are in my hair. And my back's against the towel rack. And our limbs are everywhere. And I love him and I think I tell him and I think he says it back.

But I drank too much and I don't know.

In the kitchen, Justine, Shaine, and Olivia are dancing on the island. My hair is a mess. I adjust the straps on my shirt. Hayden takes a few steps and stumbles.

I don't hear the banging on the door. I don't think anyone does at first. Suddenly Trey's pulling Shaine down and everyone is scrambling. There's nowhere to go because four police officers are blocking the only exit. Someone shuts the music off. Olivia's chanting curse words like a prayer. Justine throws up in the sink.

21

BETTER THAN DROWNING

Mistakes were made by all. When I open my eyes to the aftermath of last night's events, it's both as bad as I thought it would be and way worse.

I'm on the floor of Shaine's guest room halfway between the bed and the bathroom. I'm sure there's a reason for this but I'd rather not unpack it right now. Hayden's lying next to me wearing his hoodie backward with the hood over his face. I pull the hood off to confirm that it is Hayden because you can never really be sure about these things. I'm relieved to find him sleeping peacefully.

The sheets have been dragged off the mattress. There's a plate of half-eaten sushi on the nightstand. Just one glance at it makes me want to throw up.

I hop up, run into the bathroom, and dry heave into the toilet. The hopping up makes my brain rattle around inside my skull and now I'm sure I'm concussed. Everything's too bright. I can hear my pulse and it's deafening, like standing too close to the speakers at a concert. I gag one more time but nothing comes up. I must have eaten something. I would've been an idiot not to eat, but my hair is pulled back in a ponytail with what looks like a twist tie, so maybe this further informs the whole lying by the bathroom door thing.

I detangle the twist tie from my curls and splash cold water on my face. I have an in-person appointment with Richards today. Initially this wasn't a problem because my appointment isn't until two p.m. I assumed I'd have the morning to recover, but it's eleven thirty, and there's simply no way in hell I'll be human in time.

Three missed calls from Rena and one from Cal.

Rena: call me when you get up

Rena: I love you

Cal: love you

I skim their texts and a few others from my friends back home. They're all the same.

I love you.

I love you.

I love you.

I love you.

Did I tell Hayden I love him last night?

My stomach turns again. I take deep breaths until it settles.

Apparently Drunk Mel composed a variety of texts to Brie. I can't even bring myself to read them for fear of dying from embarrassment, but the last message between us is her agreeing to meet later today.

I shuffle through the discarded plastic cups and various food wrappers in the kitchen to the coffee maker. It's already filled with water and ground beans because I do have foresight when it comes to the things that matter. I press the brew button and lean my face against the cold steel of the fridge.

Trey comes stumbling out of Shaine's room, tugging his T-shirt over his head. He doesn't see me at first because the fridge and I have merged into one seamless, inanimate thing. The coffee maker dings, and he jumps.

"Morning," I say.

Do my eyes deceive me or does Trey look flustered? Maybe he thought he'd slip out of Shaine's room without anyone noticing. It's all I can do not to break into a slow clap.

He crosses the room, grabbing a donut from the box we hid in the pantry. Again, foresight. "You look like shit."

"You should see your friend. I've never seen him drunk before."

"Me either," he says.

"Really?"

"Not like that."

He starts toward the guest room. "Wait." I pour two glasses of water and hand them to him. "There's Advil in my purse. It's . . ." I gesture vaguely. "Somewhere. He's probably going to need it."

Shaine is still under the covers when I climb into her bed. There are a few individual fake eyelashes stuck to the side of her face. I offer her coffee, tucking my feet under my butt.

She groans and sits up a little. "I don't want to talk about it."

Yes, she does, but I play along anyway. "Okay. We don't have to. But I have a question."

She eyes me suspiciously. "What?"

"Did the cops come yesterday or did I dream that?"

"Oh my god." She bursts out laughing. "First of all, I want to know which of my neighbors is a snitch."

"What happened?"

"Nothing. They came and threatened to arrest everyone. Trey spoke to them, probably threw his dad's name around. They told us to shut it down and left. It was kind of anticlimactic, honestly."

It's all so very, very blurry.

"What does Trey's dad do?"

She yawns. "Something financial and boring, but he knows everyone. His sons could probably get away with murder."

I can't get a read on the whole Trey situation. She says she doesn't want to talk about it, but I can't help but notice how her energy has shifted in regard to him. The apathy is gone, replaced not by affection, per se, but maybe ambivalence. Some type of conflicting emotion that she's carefully trying to hide.

I mean, the boy spent the night in her bed. Something's clearly happening.

"I don't want to talk about it," she says again before I can ask. "It was a one-time thing. It's Sue's fault. I was possessed by the outfit."

Mm-hmm.

"Mel." Hayden calls from the doorway. Shaine waves him in, but he stays where he is. "I have to go. You okay?"

"Yeah. You?"

"Yeah, just a headache." I doubt that. "I'll call you later. Good party, Shaine."

"The best party," she yells after him.

I wait for Trey to make an appearance, but when the front door closes, I realize that's not happening. "So he just doesn't say bye to you?"

"He said bye." She brings the cup to her lips to hide her smirk. She laughs when I push her, sloshing coffee all over the sheets.

I barely have time to shower before I get a call telling me my ride is downstairs. A black town car with a driver named Raul. He doesn't insist on small talk as we make the hour-long drive to Stamford. I appreciate it because my head is pounding. He asks quick questions that require one-word responses. Windows or AC? Music or silence? I choose AC and silence, stretch out across the back seat, and try my best not to vomit all over the shiny black leather.

When we arrive at Richards's building, the car deposits me by the elevators in the underground garage. Richards's office is on the sixth floor. His receptionist, Nadine, greets me with a hug like we're friends. Nadine is twenty-five, but I think she forgets we're not the same age and I don't know her like that. It's probably my fault because I've definitely humored her from time to time by letting her ramble about her boring boyfriend or giving my solicited opinion on which selfie she should post, but that's called being nice. You really can't be nice to everyone.

"How are you? How's the city? I haven't seen you in . . . what? Five months. Wow, that's crazy."

"So crazy," I mumble, even though it's not. "Is he ready for me?"

"Yep! You can go right in. We'll catch up after."

Richards is sitting behind a large desk, knee-deep in what I can only assume is my file. He's in his typical black slacks and white shirt, with a truly horrendous blue tie. Richards has a thing for ugly ties. They work in perfect concert with his thick glasses and perpetually greasy hair in the effort to turn an otherwise fairly hot older guy into the annoying man seated before me. C'est dommage.

"Amélie. So good to see you. How are you?"

"Well. You know," I say, glancing around the room. It's very . . . functional. It isn't reflective of his tastes or personality; it just serves whatever purpose an office should serve. There are so few ornamental details, the room could belong to anyone. Richards is very good about keeping his personal and professional lives separate. "It's different in here."

"Yes. We made some changes. Added a few new pieces of furniture. Please, have a seat."

I think that's his polite way of asking me to stop prodding through the things on his bookshelf. I sit on the couch and watch curiously as he makes his way over to the coffee maker. He sets a steaming mug in front of me.

"Tired?"

I accept the coffee because yes, I am tired. I know Richards has a lecture on his heart. He's a worst-case-scenario kind of guy, so my appearance right now must be alarming. The last time he saw me the morning after a party, I thought he was going to have me committed. I should have thought this through, but what was I going to do? Not celebrate my friend's birthday because my psychiatrist would see it as a cry for help? Please.

"Don't be passive-aggressive. I don't have the energy for our usual back-and-forth today, Richards."

"Are you high or are you hungover?"

"Shaine had a birthday party last night. Everyone was drinking. It's not a big deal."

"But you're not everyone, Amélie. You have a history of substance abuse. You cannot do what they do. It's more dangerous for you. Do you understand?"

He's overreacting but that is, after all, his favorite type of reacting.

"It was a few shots. I wasn't doing lines of coke off a toilet seat. Relax."

He speaks carefully, the way you do to someone standing on the edge of a building. "I know today is hard for you. That's why I wanted to do this session in person. We've done so much work to prepare for this, but there's the anticipation of the grief and then there's the grief itself." When I don't say anything, he opens his iPad, scrolling through notes from our last session. "There is so much at stake for you right now. Debra says things are going well with Sue and Dave. Your grades have improved considerably. You've come so far. If things are becoming difficult for you again, please tell me."

Last year I had a bit of an emotional breakdown, but let us recap the circumstances that led to it. I broke up with a boy who I loved more than I had ever loved anyone. That boy found another girl in less than three weeks. I thought I was going to die, but he did that first. Overdosed in his bedroom at four in the morning. It was a nightmare, and I was a terror. Inconsolable and vicious. I took it out on everyone, but no one got it worse than I did.

"Have you been feeling anxious?"

Trick question. I'm always anxious.

"No," I lie.

"Depressed?"

"I'm fine."

"I want to take your word for it, Amélie, but I don't think there's any way you can possibly be fine right now." That's the problem with Richards. He needs things to not be okay so that he can have something to fix. "What is today?"

"Sunday," I answer stubbornly. It's not the answer he's looking for.

"Can you say it?"

On this day last year it was raining. I remember because I had left the window open and my roommate, Gabby, slammed it shut. That's what woke me. The ringing started a minute later. I sent the call to voicemail. It was barely six a.m. It rang two more times and then there was screaming. Crying. I fell out of bed.

I dressed in whatever I'd left lying on the floor the night before. My Laurelle uniform, I think. I ran down the hall, down the steps, through the foyer, out the front door. I didn't have a car so I called a Lyft. Six minutes away. A fifteen-minute drive. I pulled up behind the ambulance, two police cars, a stretcher. I didn't try to go in. I thought if I saw him, they'd never be able to tear us apart. I planted my feet, and I waited. And then they brought him out. His mom clinging to the stretcher. Cayla kneeling on the porch.

"It's okay to feel it," Richards says. "I know the mechanisms you put in place to keep yourself from feeling pain. You never truly settled things with Darren. There was so much left unsaid between the two of you. Scars that will not heal unless you address them. You have built a new life for yourself in New York. You've made so many positive, healthy choices. This cannot be a point of regression for you."

"I'm not going to regress," I say.

He continues on as if he didn't hear me.

"You can't dismiss your feelings. These things hurt, and that's the way it should be because that's what it is to be human. You have to learn how to process pain."

I glare at him. How dare he speak to me like I'm some naive little girl who's never been through anything? How can he trivialize all that I have endured, as if living through the past thirteen years hasn't been enough to produce a layer of callus over my skin?

"Richards, I'm done. I don't want to talk about it. Can you respect that for once? Please?"

I've dreaded this day for a year. Shot prayers into the sky for Darren and for me. Prayed that when I woke up today, my legs wouldn't collapse under my weight. I prayed it wouldn't come without warning. I didn't know what to expect, but it feels like I'm standing on the shore with my toes dipped in the waters of grief. I can do it. I can be here like this. It's better than drowning. As long as my head stays above water, I am okay.

Richards gives me an empathetic look. He closes the iPad and lays it conclusively on the table between us. "I want to try the antidepressants again."

"What? Why?"

"I appreciate that you believe you don't need them, but I have to go by what I'm seeing. You don't always communicate effectively when you need help. I have to look at your behavior. Substance use, the scratches on your arm, the changes in your diet and your sleep patterns—these are all cause for concern."

I don't know what's worse. The nausea and fogginess brought on by the meds or the inevitable nosedive off the highest cliff that my mood will take once I've gotten fed up enough by the side effects to convince myself I'm better off without them.

I won't take them. He knows I won't, but he scribbles the prescription down anyway and slides the script across the table.

22

AND NOW, AT SEVENTEEN

When I was a kid, I wanted to fit in. I wanted that more than I wanted parents. I didn't want to be one of the kids with school-issued clothes and nowhere to go during Christmas break. I wanted grades as average as everyone else's and not better. I wanted a brain that cataloged the good times as well as the bad. I wanted to laugh knowingly at inside jokes and trust the words people said to me. I wanted to be unremarkable.

At thirteen, it wasn't enough to fit in anymore. I wanted acceptance. I wanted people to see the things that made me different and love them anyway. I didn't want to have to work so hard. I wanted family more than I wanted parents. People who really knew me and could help me get some sort of grasp on this life. When I found them, I didn't want to let them down.

By the time I was fifteen, I'd let them down more times than I could count. It wasn't enough to be accepted. I wanted to be understood. I wanted someone to see how hard I was trying and tell me it wasn't all me. That I was this way due to a series of factors and circumstances, not all of which were within my control. There was one person who understood me completely, but it came at a cost I couldn't afford to pay.

When I was sixteen, I wanted to disappear. I learned there's an art to it, and I became a master. It took everything they had to reach into the darkness and pull me out.

And now, at seventeen, I want peace.

On the edge of Brooklyn, there's a quiet neighborhood where tree-lined streets are named after fruit. Raul drops me off here, outside a grocery store where I buy a bag of cherries and a blueberry muffin wrapped in wax paper. The cherries are a deep red and very sweet. I sit on a bench on the promenade to wait for Brie and eat until my stomach hurts.

We're supposed to meet at five. I haven't thought about what I'm going to say to her. We lost so much time. So much was stolen from us. I know what it's like to look in the mirror and not know the person staring back. How unnatural and disorienting that is. That's what it's like to look at her. I don't want it to be that way.

A few minutes later, Rajah comes bounding down the promenade, fighting the constraints of his leash. Brie herds him over to the bench and sits next to me.

"It's so hard for me to relate to you," she says after a while. "When I try, I just end up saying the wrong shit. I'd look at the pictures you posted and spend so much time imagining we would meet and it'd be like nothing had changed. We would fit together the way we did before, but that hasn't happened and it's not cool for me to take it out on you. I want us to be good. Whatever that looks like."

There are things I should say to her too. Apologies we should exchange. But looking at her, I can't speak.

I don't know what does it. Maybe it's the ache in my stomach. Maybe it's the fact that she's here so he can't be. Brie and Darren don't exist in the same world. Having her with me right now is proof that I don't have him. Or maybe it's the view of my new home across the river. The way the sun gleams off the buildings.

Maybe it's the water coming up to my knees now. Past my thighs to my hips. My chest. My shoulders. Part of me knew, as Richards did, that I couldn't stay on the shore forever. Tides rise and grief is inescapable.

Brie's speaking again, her expression growing more alarmed, but I can't follow what she's saying. The world around her is out of focus. I can't feel my hands.

She takes out her phone and dials a number.

The first time I couldn't pull myself out of it, couldn't hide it from everyone—the first time they saw me for real, Darren asked me, "How does it happen for you?"

Rena had gone by now. Cal too. I was lying on my bathroom floor. I hadn't answered a text in days. Hadn't eaten. Hadn't been to class.

I'd tried so hard to be okay, but now everyone knew. They saw how bad it could be, and they began to worry. Shame fed on my body like a parasite. Made me weak.

"What does it feel like?"

I told him it's like a spray of arrows filling the sky. Blocking the sun. Pinning me to the ground again.

This is that, but so much worse.

Four days in my sister's bed.

A NINA SIMONE SONG

There was something about his smile. Not the one he put on to appease me. His real smile. The one that reached all the way up to his eyes until they crinkled at the corners.

I don't know how to live in a world where it doesn't exist.

"Are you coming?"

I stood in the doorway of Rena's house in my pajamas. It was too early to be going anywhere, but Darren held out his hand to me and I stared into crystal-blue eyes and yeah, I was going.

I pulled him through the door and he grinned.

There was no sneaking out of Rena's house. We came and went as we pleased. I didn't technically live there, so Rena never questioned my absence when she woke to find me gone. She assumed I was with Darren or back at the dorms.

I peeked out from inside the closet. "Wanna tell me what's going on?"

"No."

"No?" I walked over to where Darren was seated on the edge of my bed and tilted his chin up. I checked the whites of his eyes and brushed my fingers over the thin skin under his lashes. His eyebrows

rose, and I felt guilty for letting the suspicious thought cross my mind. I kept my voice light. "Are we robbing a bank?"

"Why?" He kissed my collarbone. "Would you rob a bank with me?"

"Depends on how good the plan is."

"We're just going for a drive."

"At four a.m.?"

"It's actually . . ." He checked his phone. "Four thirty-four now."

He started to stand, but I wrapped my arms around his neck. I didn't want him to move. Whatever was happening, whatever this was, I wanted to stay in it for as long as I could. He slouched, resigned, and gazed at me patiently while my eyes roamed over his face again. It was like he was fifty pounds lighter. I didn't understand it. I wanted to press flat against him like I could curl around his DNA. Like if he had this energy in excess, maybe I could absorb a little of it through his skin. I didn't even want to be an inch from him. He was so warm. I didn't know how long it would last.

"You're happy today." I was afraid that if I acknowledged it, I'd get a little less of this version of him. But the observation only caused his smile to widen. It was contagious. "What?"

"Baby?"

"Hmm?"

"Can you put some fucking clothes on? Please?"

"Sheesh." I playfully pushed him away, but he tightened his grip on my waist and brought his face close enough for the tip of his nose to brush mine. I covered my mouth with my hand.

"I said please."

"Oh, well, since you said please."

He pried my hand from my mouth and kissed me until I forgot what I was supposed to be doing.

"Clothes," he reminded me.

"Right."

Sitting in his car as we sped down the quiet highway through the sparse early morning traffic, I hadn't known what to expect. I had resigned myself to whatever was happening, but as we veered right off the road and along a small clearing in the trees, a knot formed in my stomach.

"Where are we going?"

He grabbed a black duffel bag from the back seat and headed for the mouth of what looked to be an abandoned and overgrown trail. I hesitated, but only for a second. I had followed him down far shadier paths.

We hiked through the damp foliage for what felt like forever. I was just about over it when I heard the siren's call of rushing water. A waterfall.

It was a secret place. It wasn't but it was. No one was there at that hour. There was no reason to be because we were there, and it must have been made for us. I called it Eden, and like its namesake, I knew it couldn't last. I knew there'd come a day when I could never go back. But for now, we'd found paradise. Through the mist, above a thick canopy of trees, the sun sat low in an apricot sky. I wondered if I'd woken up that morning at all.

We swam for hours in cool water and dried ourselves along the rocks. My shorts lay in a wet pile with our shoes and his T-shirt. I wrung my hair out and twisted it in a bun. We stretched out on the blanket next to empty bags of chips and sandwich wrappers from our lunch. His head on my chest, arm draped across my stomach. My hand in his hair.

"My mom and Cay found a therapist they want me to see," he said.

"You're going to therapy?" I didn't mean to sound so shocked. He was always supportive of my treatment, but I never thought he'd consider it for himself. I tried to reassure him. "I think it's good."

"Yeah?"

"There's nothing I want more than for you to be happy."

"You make me happy." I didn't think that was entirely true. My fingers twisted tiny braids into his hair that unraveled as he sat up slightly to see my face. "You don't believe me."

I wanted to so badly. There was no way I could know for sure because he had never said something like that to me before. But he had also never lied to me. Darren was a lot of things, but he wasn't a liar.

He made me happy. He also made me sad and anxious and inse-cure. He made me all those things, often at the same time. It could be true that when that happened, my happiness was too obscured for him to see clearly. If he wasn't looking for it, he may have missed it entirely. He may not have realized that, just by being there, he put my whole body at ease.

It could be that way for him too. I wanted to believe that. I had never looked very hard. I wasn't brave enough to enter the dark parts of his mind to see what could lie beneath the surface. It's possible I could've missed it, and maybe that changed everything.

I had the strangest feeling he'd read my mind. He seemed to be able to do that somehow, so there weren't many secrets between us. Only what he kept from me.

He crawled up until his face lay right by mine. Three kisses on my neck, my cheek, the corner of my mouth. Three words we'd said so much we didn't need to voice them anymore, the meaning cracked and loose like the spine of an old book. My heart was so full, it hurt.

I curled into him. The sun beat down hot on my back. I closed my eyes and melted.

"I'm sleepy."

"You wanna go?"

"No."

I fought with my eyelids. I had water and wildflowers and him. How could my mind prefer sleep over this?

I yawned. "Hey."

"Yeah?"

This is my favorite day. *That's what I wanted to tell him. That day felt like a Nina Simone song. Like "Wild Is the Wind" or maybe "What More Can I Say?" I don't know what I wouldn't have given to stay there with him. I couldn't think of a single thing better than that morning.*

He was my entire life. You can't tell someone that. It's too much. People aren't equipped to be everything for you. And I didn't know how to love someone. I'd never done it before. It's just that he was made of the same stuff as me. I didn't have a choice.

I felt like I had loved him before and that this was inevitable. In all the infinite variations of how my life could've played out, there's no way we wouldn't have ended up there together.

It was the happiest I'd ever been.

23

A BUNCH OF WORDS

On day five I have missed calls and texts from everyone. My mind is clearer today, but I don't have the energy to deal with them. Rajah sleeps curled up by my side while Brie reads the texts to me. I listen passively, pulling at a thread on the hem of my borrowed pajama pants. People wanting to know where I am. What I'm doing. Am I okay? Why aren't I answering? Hello?

I wish our phones still hung on walls. I wish people didn't feel like they deserve access to you at any time of the day. I wish we didn't carry the world and all its problems in our pockets.

"You have to eat something," Brie says, rolling off the bed. "Should I blend a bunch of crap into a smoothie again?"

I nod. Once she leaves the room, I pick up my phone from where she left it on the nightstand and call Sue.

"Brie?"

"It's me." My voice is raspy. I clear my throat. "I'm coming home today."

I don't remember much about my first night here, but I know

Brie pled her case about me staying with her. Even with things still unresolved between us, she wanted me close. She brought me to her house since it was easier than taking me home. Her parents called Sue, and they all agreed it would be better for me to be in my own space. I didn't care. It didn't matter to me either way, but Brie was feral at the suggestion of splitting us up. She told them she could do this, and they must have conceded because here I am.

"Do you want me to come get you?"

It's simple questions like these that have been my undoing. Brie asking if I want bubbles in my bath. Rebecca asking if my salad has enough dressing. Erin asking if the AC is down too low. It's so stupid. I press the palms of my hands against my eyes, trying to force the tears back in. "No, I'm good." She lets me cry until I can pull myself together again. Sometimes that's all you need. Not a bunch of words that don't mean anything.

"Text me when you're on your way home," she says.

"I will."

I hang up and click through the rest of the text messages to clear the notifications. There are three unread texts from Hayden, all from five days ago.

Hayden: are you home from therapy?

Hayden: call me back

Hayden: can I come over?

I haven't thought about Hayden at all since I've been here. I haven't thought about anything. My primary goal, lying in this bed, was to not think. My mind is filled with secret passageways and trapdoors, one innocent thought leading to the next worry, the next heartrending thing. I slept a lot. More than I have in months.

Depression isn't just isolating. It's erosive. It destroys beautiful things. Feeds off the worst parts of you. For me, it flips on like a switch and builds until I can't see anyone around me anymore. When it ends, I have to tend to all the things I've neglected. The people who feel abandoned by me and the responsibilities I've failed to prioritize. It's exhausting, and even if all I've done for days is rest, I still never have the energy for it.

Brie comes in, handing me a smoothie that serves the same function as an IV at this point. Just nutrition to keep me alive. I reach for it but pause when I notice the tears in her eyes.

"Amie," she whispers. Her voice breaks against that name. I've heard it before. She's called me that before. "You don't have to go. You can stay."

I take the smoothie from her and wipe away the tears that are now dripping from her chin. "Why are you crying?"

I can't see her cry. It's horrible. The more I touch her, the faster the tears fall.

She sniffs. "Right after we moved into the Laurelle dorms, I busted my lip running up the steps. I knocked a tooth out and bled all over my shirt. You came with me to the nurse's office and then to the emergency room where I got three stitches right here."

She points to a faint mark on her bottom lip.

"When the doctor was done, he gave me a Band-Aid and

you said, 'Where's mine?' He said you didn't need a Band-Aid because you weren't hurt. You said yes you were. I was hurt so you were hurt. You made such a big deal about it that he gave you one just to shut you up. You wore a Band-Aid on your lip until I got my stitches out." She takes a deep breath but it turns into another sob in her chest. "You're hurt so I'm hurt."

I don't know what to say. Brie's been a rock for me these past few days. Strong in all the ways I couldn't be. I haven't seen her falter in that. Not once. She's done such a good job holding me together, I hadn't realized the things that affect me also affect her. I hadn't even thought about it, but wouldn't it be the same if it were reversed? If I saw her in pain, how could I not feel it too? I don't want that for her. I don't want her to feel everything I'm feeling.

"You can talk about him whenever you want," she says. "I know you may not want to, but if it helps. Whatever helps, okay?"

"Nothing helps. I don't know what to do, Brie." Now it's my turn to cry again. I clutch the smoothie in my hands, focusing on the chill of the glass on my skin. My body feels like an origami doll. Paper thin, folded tight on itself. All sharp corners and complicated layers. "We weren't supposed to be together. I figured that out. I was trying to learn how to be okay with that. I didn't know anything else. I was trying to learn a new way to be, I guess. But I hadn't learned it yet. I hadn't . . ."

I wasn't prepared. Maybe you can't prepare for death, but I wasn't even prepared to be fully without him. To live in this world where he was living too, separate from me. That's what I was working on.

"I planned his funeral. His mom, she can't . . . Me and Cayla, his sister, we did everything. I kept his ashes in my dorm room because his mom couldn't bear to have them in the house. I wasn't even his girlfriend anymore, but I still stepped in and did what they couldn't. Someone had to do it."

It took a certain level of disassociation that I knew, even at the moment, wasn't healthy. To-do lists and emails. Flower arrangements and an obituary and a eulogy. His girlfriend cried the hardest. They'd been together less than two months. I comforted her too. I did what I could so I didn't have to face it myself.

And when there was nothing left to do, it came all at once.

"I can't connect to who I was before," I tell her. She dabs my eyes with the sleeve of her sweatshirt. "It's not that I want to go back, but it's hard to know you can't. There's just after. I know I won't be sad about this forever, not the way I am now, but I feel like I shouldn't know it gets this bad. I'm really afraid this isn't the bottom. What happens if I lose my husband later or something? Or a baby? What happens if I lose you?"

"I don't know," she says. "I think about that sometimes too. I have no idea."

That's only part of it, of course. There's also him. Who he was. My heart softens, thinking of all the things that used to irritate me so much that don't matter anymore. "Darren was an asshole."

"Was he?"

"Yeah. He was also my best friend. More than anything, it's the friendship I miss."

Her smile mirrors my own. Wistful. Heartbreaking. "What do you miss about it?"

"We told each other almost everything, and what I couldn't say, he just knew. I don't think anyone will ever understand me the way he did." As I say the words, I know they're true. There are layers to the grief I feel around that realization.

How did I manage to let him know me better than I knew myself? At what point did we stop relying on words? At least when there were words, when I had to talk something out with him, I benefited from that too. But there were things I didn't know how to talk about. I didn't have the vocabulary for how dark it got sometimes. I still don't.

He and I struggled with different things, but he knew what it was like to have your drain pulled, to empty out on the floor. So after he'd seen what my darkness looked like, he learned how to manage it. And after I saw how black things got for him, I tried my best to become light.

"That's really fucked up."

"Yeah, that's pretty fucked up," Brie agrees, and I laugh for the first time in I don't know how long. The sound brings a little of the light back into her eyes. "You think you know yourself better now?"

"I guess so."

"Then maybe that was the point."

I don't know to what extent the point of a life is to impact another. Is it narcissistic to believe Darren walked this earth to help me? But I guess part of the reason I'm here is to love him. Maybe that was just one of my purposes and there are others I haven't discovered yet.

I wipe my tear-streaked face and gather my tangled hair into a bun. "I'm going to go see the living boy now."

It's time I really talk to Hayden. I hadn't warned him about any of this. Looking back, there are so many things I should've done differently. I should've told him about what happened with Darren. I should've warned him about what this week meant to me and what to expect.

I change into a pair of Brie's jeans and a ratty old tee. She walks me to the door with Rajah trailing after us. In the daylight, I see how tired she is. The bags under her eyes. The slight bend in her usually perfect posture from carrying the weight of us both all by herself. I wrap my arms around her and she hugs me back tight. A promise that, for me, she'd do it again and again and again.

I hope she rests now too.

24

ONE OF THOSE THINGS

I take the subway to Manhattan and get off at 14th Street. I haven't been outside in days. I want to walk.

My skin is sticky with sweat by the time I make it to Hayden's building. The AC blasts me in the face when I walk into the lobby. The receptionist looks at me like I'm something someone dragged in from the street.

"Hi. I'm here to see Hayden Thompson."

"Your name?"

"Mel." She waits for me to elaborate. I don't. "He knows who I am."

She exchanges a glance with the security guard standing nearby before searching for Hayden's name in the computer. Fred never treated Hayden this way, even from day one. It's a reminder that Hayden and I operate in this world differently. We may both be Black kids existing in primarily white spaces, but Hayden was born into wealth many white people can't fathom. He wears his birthright like an amulet. Credentials around his neck, affording him access without question.

"Hello, sir. I have a 'Mel' here to see you." I roll my eyes. She listens intently and frowns. "Thank you."

Begrudgingly, she walks me to the row of elevators and taps a card against the screen. The elevator arrives and I get in. I go to press the button, but I'm quickly reminded that this is no ordinary elevator. It starts its ascent automatically.

The shiny black door that serves as the barrier between the car and Hayden's apartment is already open, but he's nowhere to be found. I step into the foyer and wait, listening for the sound of approaching footsteps. There's nothing but the muted thud of a cabinet shutting. I cross through into the open living space. Hayden's in the kitchen making a sandwich. His back's to me. I drag the stool away from the island and sit. Neither of us speaks.

I wish he would look at me. Give me some type of reassurance that it's okay I'm here. That he wants me here.

"Hayden," I say, because he clearly doesn't intend to speak first. It reminds me of the morning after the party with Rowen and that night at dinner with his mom. He's shutting down. "I want to tell you something. I should've told you before, but I didn't know how." Finally, he turns to face me. He's never looked at me with such indifference before. The words almost recoil inside me, but I force them out anyway. "Darren died. A year ago on Sunday. I didn't mean . . ." As he processes this, his face transforms back into the Hayden I know. Soft, warm features. "I wasn't trying to ghost you. It was just a lot."

"You said you guys broke up."

"We did. A couple of months before."

He resumes his work, lost in thought. I wait for the questions he must have, determined to answer them, whatever they are.

"So you dated him for years, you broke up, and then . . ." He does the math in his head. And then Darren died. And then I met him seven months later. The understanding in his eyes breaks my heart.

"It was complicated."

"Yeah."

I never intended for things to get so serious between us. This is what I didn't want. This is what I was trying to prevent, but I'm glad it happened. I'm so happy I know him. I just wish I would've met him first.

He cuts the sandwich in half, cleans the knife, and returns it to the magnetic strip hanging on the wall. Puts the ingredients back in the fridge. Wipes the cutting board. All of this without a word. Without another glance in my direction.

"You're mad."

"No."

"You are."

"I'm mad at myself." He says it like a confession. More to himself than to me. "You had so many opportunities to tell me, and I understand why you didn't. Or at least I understand why it would be hard for you to talk about it. But I had so many opportunities to break this off and I didn't. It's too much, Mel. Being with you is too much."

I stare at him.

There are certain things that cannot be taken back. Can't be recalled when you don't feel that way anymore. This is one of those things.

It takes everything I have not to retreat into myself. To pick his sentences apart and study the space between each letter. "I should have told you," I say as calmly as I can. "I get that. But none of this was about you."

"Right. It's you and him. He's dead, and it's still you and him."

I see it, the moment the words register in his head. How quickly his eyes find mine. The apology they hold.

I feel like he just detonated a bomb in my chest. The kitchen should have exploded from the force of it, but here I am, whole and on fire. "It was the worst thing that's ever happened to me." I round the counter to face him, my flames licking at his skin. "The worst thing. What's the worst thing that's happened to you? Please tell me. We're sharing, right? We're telling all of our fucking business."

"I'm sorry—"

"You don't get to be sorry." I barely recognize my own voice, soft and molten steel. "You don't get to talk to me like that and then tell me you're sorry. You have never gone through something like that." His jaw tightens. "Do you know what it does to you? Do you know what it takes sometimes just to get through the day?"

"Pills?" He raises his eyebrows when I don't respond. Daring me to deny it. I glare at him. He grabs the plate and walks past me out of the kitchen.

I dig my nails into my palms and follow him. "They were anxiety pills. I don't even take them anymore."

He whirls around. Slams the plate on the counter so hard, I'm surprised it doesn't crack. "I don't believe you, Mel." There's the anger. The quiet rage that I've never had directed toward me. I knew he was capable of it because only someone who knows what it's like to lose it can actively choose peace. "Do you ever tell me the truth?"

"Just because I don't tell you everything doesn't mean I'm lying."

"That's exactly what it means."

"Oh my god." I run a hand through my tangled hair. "I don't understand why you feel like you have the right to know everything going on in my head. You don't tell me everything either."

"You don't ask! You're so caught up in your own shit, you don't notice what's going on around you."

My stomach turns. I could literally throw up. I take a deep breath, hold it for a few seconds, and let it out slowly. "That's not fair."

"No. It's not." There's so much pain in his voice. I recognize it because I've felt it before. The pieces of yourself that you lose when you rip yourself away from someone. You try to do it quickly so it hurts less. You promise yourself it's for the best. It hurts, but it's for the best. It hurts, but it's for the best. It's for the best. "My dad moved out."

I take in the apartment with new eyes. The wedding pictures are missing from the mantel. There are boxes stacked on the far side of the living room. The furniture is rearranged, like his mom is trying to bring new energy into the space.

How could all this have happened so quickly?

"When?"

He looks at me like I just proved his point. Is that why he was trying to find me? I wasn't there. I didn't know.

"I can't do this." He brushes past me, hitting the button for the elevator.

He's kicking me out. I came here to fix things with us and he won't even try. My body goes cold and numb, from the tips of my toes inward, pulling up all the way to my rib cage. I shouldn't have done it. I should've ended it before it started. I can't take it. I can't lose them both.

"You're breaking up with me over a fight about . . . what? What are we even fighting about? That life is hard? That shit isn't perfect all the time?"

"How could I break up with you?" he says, and there's no hatred in his voice. No malice. He's perfectly calm, and somehow that's worse than if he were yelling. "We're not together."

He's right, of course. You can't lose something that you never had. And it shouldn't hurt if it was never what you wanted. When the elevator arrives, I step in, and the door slides shut between us.

It shouldn't hurt. It shouldn't feel like this.

Sue is on the couch when I walk in. Dave's beside her. He says something to me, but I can't hear him over the pounding in my ears. He looks over, expectantly, waiting for my reply. Then he sees.

I am undone. Torn at my center. I'm cold.

Sue rushes to me, hands flitting around like flies, trying to soothe. I lean into her. My eyes pour. My legs shake. I lost them both in a matter of days. And Darren, I'll lose him over and over. Once a year, like it's never happened before. It's beyond my capability. It's more than I can handle.

"I need help," I cry, because I know how this ends. I think of Brie, and it gives me the strength to beg, to plead with them to take this seriously.

They do.

PART
TWO

1

SUCH A RELIEF

At night I lie still as figures haloed in dim yellow light scurry past the tiny window in my door. Back and forth and back and forth. It makes me so tired to think of what they must be up to so late that I stop thinking altogether, and I can finally sleep.

Mornings are bright and loud and everybody wants something from me. I have nothing to offer but my body for their exams and my silence as a response to their questions. Footsteps grow louder and fade away. The door opens and closes. It opens again. The footsteps are there, and I hope the door will close, but it doesn't.

"Amélie." The voice is soft but insistent. I'm not asleep. I'm waiting for the door to close again. "We have to get up today, okay?"

I don't move, so now there are two hands wedged between my body and the mattress, pushing me forward. I make my body heavy and dense as stone.

"Can you try to sit up for me?"

The hands move to my arms and gently squeeze, but I am

made of silence and stillness. There is nothing else. I don't open my eyes when it's light like this. I haven't stood from this bed yet.

"All right. Well, we'll try again a little later."

The footsteps grow fainter with each second. Finally, the door closes.

"You're awake."

The familiar voice belongs to an older woman with big blue eyes like pools of warm water. She smiles, the rise of her cheeks carving lines in the skin around her eyes. "How are you feeling?"

"Thirsty."

"Here, let's sit up and have some water." She holds a cup to my lips. I take small sips from the straw until it's empty. "Would you like to shower?"

"Sure," I say, because I think that's what I'm supposed to say.

I ease off the bed, leaning against her side when my knees buckle. She strips off my white sweats and holds my arm for me as I step into the shower and slump against the wall. I don't want her here but it's taking all my energy to stand. I focus on the tile under my feet and let the woman with the kind eyes scrub away and wash me clean.

I was so afraid of disappearing again. I didn't want to lose myself the way I have so many times before. Now it's all I want. To dissolve into nothing. To blot out the stain I've left on people's lives. All the trouble I've caused. All the ways I'm not enough.

It feels like I was made for this. It's such a relief and so incredibly heartbreaking to find out I'd been right all along. I belong here, alone and medicated and surveilled. Maybe I arrived into this world broken and my pain isn't anyone's fault. Not the result of some great trauma. Just a by-product of my creation. What do I do with that but lie still and let the growing despair wrap around me like a cocoon?

I didn't realize I had been fighting until I stopped. How much I invested in hope until it was gone, leaving me bankrupt. Even in the midst of my grieving, I'd anticipated a reprieve. I thought if happiness was fleeting, unhappiness must abide by the same rules.

But if life can be this anarchic, I understand all too well the desire to sink. Or float. Or simply fade away.

2

THE BEGINNING

"Hi, Amélie. I'm Nora."

I remember Dr. Christensen from a few days ago, when I first arrived at Roseview—a treatment center that, as it turns out, does not offer a view of roses. Sue and I chose it because it's all the way in Rockaway Beach. Still accessible but remote. At the time there was too much going on, so I hadn't gotten a good look at Nora. She's younger than I expected, with bright eyes and thick, brown hair pulled into a tight bun. The cut of her white blouse and jade-green wide-legged pants say she may be a young Black woman but yes, she is in charge. I can't imagine the microaggressions she probably has to deal with. She's one of those women who are so pretty, it would be intimidating if she weren't so nice.

My grace period for hiding behind my eyelids and communicating exclusively through grunts has expired. I've refused to see Richards for no particular reason other than I don't want to. Although I protested, I was told this appointment isn't voluntary. It was never implicitly stated, but it was strongly suggested that I need to talk to Nora if I have any intention of ever leaving this place.

Now that I'm here, I just want to get it over with. I don't have any fight left in me. I'll tell her whatever she wants to know. Everyone keeps saying she's good at what she does. I hope that's true.

Nora flips through my Laurelle file, which has been printed, bound, and organized with an array of multicolored Post-it notes. She has clearly spent a lot of time with it. "I understand that you've been seeing a psychiatrist since you were very young, so I won't bore you with any type of preamble."

"I appreciate that."

She leans back in her armchair, crossing one leg over the other. "What brings you here?"

"I was told I had to come."

She smiles. "Not to this session, to Roseview."

"Oh. I was sad."

"Was this sadness abnormal for you?" I shrug. She continues. "You've been diagnosed with major depressive disorder, panic disorder, generalized anxiety disorder, and PTSD in the past, is that correct?"

"Is that what my file says?"

"It is."

"Then sure."

Nora reviews her notes, underlining something in bright red ink. "A nurse asked you a series of questions when you were admitted. Do you remember?"

I do, but vaguely. Questions about my depression. How long the episodes last. How frequent they are. How dark my thoughts get. My instinct was to shut down, but I was so exhausted, the answers trickled out of me with very little prodding from the nurse. I told her things I knew could give them cause to keep me here for months. She wrote my answers down without judgment.

The nurse asked me other things too. About the nature of my relationships. How I connect with people. What I thought of myself. Those were harder to answer. I can't remember what I told her, just that it felt like bloodletting. Like she'd drawn a knife along my skin with a silent promise that the release of these things would cure me. I don't believe her.

"I know it's not a pleasant experience," Nora says gently, as if she can see the marks left by that blade. "But your answers provide us with an important foundation with which to build a treatment plan."

"A treatment plan for what?"

"I'd like to explore the possibility of a borderline personality disorder diagnosis. Based on your history and symptomatology, I believe it fits. To put it simply, it would mean you've been experiencing a significant sense of instability in your moods, relationships, and self-identity. Our goal is to help you learn to properly identify your emotions and regulate them in a healthy way, without the use of drugs or other harmful coping mechanisms."

I stare blankly at her because I don't know what to do with

any of that. Richards seemed to think I might be bipolar, but he never officially diagnosed me. What the fuck is borderline personality disorder?

"I don't want to overwhelm you with too much information," she says. "I promise we will go over all of this in detail during the next few weeks. For now, I'd like to start from the beginning. As far back as you can remember." When I hesitate because I'm not sure what she means, she sets down her notepad and pen as if to say, *We're just talking.* "Your earliest memory, no matter how random."

Memories are slick, oily things. When I think I've gotten a good grip on one, it slips out of my hands. I reach for another and feel stupid the moment I say, "Ice cream. I remember an ice cream cone."

Nora tilts her head. "Okay. Tell me more."

"I don't know how old I was. I remember chocolate. It's weird. I hate chocolate ice cream."

"Do you remember anyone else in that memory?"

I try to expand the scope of the memory. Ice cream melting down my arm, staining my shirt. The glare of the sun bouncing off rippling blue water. I don't hear any voices. I can't feel anyone near me. "No, but I have a sister. She may have been there."

"Aubrie." I guess that would be in my file. "And you don't remember her at all?"

I take a deep breath, blowing the air out in a huff. "I honestly don't have the energy for that convo today."

"That's fine. We can talk about her when you're ready. So

you were placed into Laurelle Child Services' care when you were four. What do you remember from that time?"

"I don't know. Life at Laurelle was tedious."

"Tedious how?"

"They raise very high-achieving kids at that school. All of the typical classes, plus etiquette, speech, music, language, art."

"That sounds like a lot of pressure," Nora says.

"It is, especially for LCS kids. We don't have parents paying our tuition. They're investing in us."

"The school?"

"Yeah. We have to do well. Adoption to some high-profile family is the end goal. It's what we're taught to want more than anything. It's what's supposed to make us happy."

Her pen starts moving again. "And how did you feel about that?"

No one has ever asked me that before. It catches me off guard. "I felt lied to." She allows me a moment to piece together the ways LCS has let me down. "I had some good families. I had families I really liked, and I wasn't happy. So what was I supposed to do? What else was I supposed to want?"

"What did you want? Outside of what they expected of you. What did you actually want?"

"To belong somewhere. That was the main thing for a while." I never realized until now how little I'd allowed myself to want. Just the barest, most fundamental necessities. Where would I be if I had wanted more?

But there was a time when I did want more. More than I

thought I deserved. I'd gotten what I wanted, and for a while I was happy.

To want and then get and then lose. That is unbearable. Maybe it's better to want nothing at all.

"Then I wanted Darren." There is no change in her expression when I say his name. No question in her eyes, or any sense of recognition. "You've seen him in my file too, haven't you?"

"Yes." Duh. Darren is my file. "I'd like to talk more about Darren if you're comfortable with that." When I don't protest, she continues. "Your symptoms increased drastically during that period of your life. From what I understand, it was a pretty volatile relationship. Would you say that's true?"

"Yeah."

"Then that's where we'll begin."

I pull the scrunchie out of my hair. Dry, frizzy curls fall around my shoulders, obscuring part of my face. Nora watches this curiously. "I don't know what to tell you about him."

"Whatever comes to mind."

The first thing Darren knew about me was that I was a liar. He told me later how he watched me from across Rena's pool, talking to one of her friends. How well I mirrored the girl's movements, molding my lips into an easy smile. Matching the lilt of her voice. Laughing at all the right times. I'd always done this when I couldn't find a way to really be there with them. Those times when it became hard to exist outside my head. But I was in pain. He told me it was my eyes that gave me away.

"I met Darren when I was thirteen. He was a year older than

me, but it felt like more. We had mutual friends. I'd see him around at parties. He was too smart, too funny, too beautiful. I didn't want anything to do with him."

Nora's lips twitch into a small smile. "Why is that?"

"He was intimidating. He also seemed kind of arrogant."

"How did the relationship begin?"

"Sometimes I'd get really anxious at parties and sneak away. He must have noticed because one day he followed me and found me in the middle of a full panic attack. He stayed with me until it was over. Read me some book from his phone. I don't remember what it was, but it worked. He told me later that he got them too. The panic attacks. After that we looked out for each other."

"You were friends."

My heart seizes at the word. *Friends.* "We were never just friends."

I was a kid. I hadn't loved anyone yet, but I was trying my best to be someone worth loving. Someone people wanted to be around. Someone people wouldn't leave. I had been told I was too much, which was incredibly ironic to me. How could I be too much when I was always gorging myself on other people to feel full? I needed to find some type of balance, but what would I do about the aching void in my stomach? I didn't know who to be. I was everything for everybody and nothing at all.

Meeting him was coming home to a place I'd never been. A layer of dust and thick cobwebs. Doors hanging on rusted hinges. Sheets tossed over furniture. Chipped china in glass-fronted cabinets. I stopped in the doorway, wondering how it could be both familiar and foreign. Like returning to a past life. He threw the windows open, and in the light, I saw that we were the same. He had been searching for home too.

We saved each other, just to ruin it all in the end.

"I honestly can't tell you how we started dating," I say, trying and failing to create any sort of timeline of our relationship. I've never had to do this before. Everyone in my life who knows the details of my relationship with Darren were around for all of it. "Once we were together, things were perfect. They weren't, of course, but I thought they were. I felt heard with him. Even when I didn't know how to say what I wanted to say. It's like I made him in a lab. He was the antidote to all the things that caused me pain. He could make everything better just by being there. I didn't know how to breathe without him.

"But I still got so sad sometimes and I'd pull him into it and we'd both disappear. So he showed me what he did to numb things when he was overwhelmed. He was always over-whelmed. I was never the antidote for that."

There's sorrow in Nora's eyes now. I can't imagine what she sees in my face. I can't control it. I've totally lost myself to the memory of him. I told him so many times how I feared we wouldn't survive our relationship. How the drugs had become a daily practice and my depression had grown wide enough to contain us both. I told him we exist in extremes. Too much light and we burn out. Too much darkness and we disappear. I told him I didn't think love could sustain us for long.

"It got to the point where I never knew which version of him I'd get. He could be cruel, and I would get so angry. I'd never felt rage like that. Only with him. We said horrible things to each other. I thought he hated me. I thought I'd done something to make him hate me. Then I thought maybe that's how love is for some people. Because when he was kind . . ." I don't know how to express that when your eyes adjust to darkness, the dimmest light can be blinding. "He was good, he just . . ."

"Take a few deep breaths," Nora says.

I inhale deeply through my nose and exhale slowly.

"I broke up with him last year in May. I said I never wanted to see him again, but I didn't mean it. But it was like he didn't care. He started dating someone else three weeks later. Not a casual hookup, a whole relationship. I was hurt, but more than that, I was fucking furious." I ignore the voice in my mind reminding me only a year has passed. This isn't a distant memory. Nearly no time has elapsed at all.

It was the first time I'd chosen me over him. Every day after, every minute that went by without hearing the sound of his voice—every second that expanded between us, forcing him a little deeper into my memory—I chose me over and over again. I still don't know how I did it. How I managed to muster up that much resolve.

Now that he's gone, I can't help but think about what Darren meant to me. What he represented in the midst of my mess. The space he held for me.

Suddenly I feel the urge to plead with Nora. I want to make

her understand because I feel so guilty. Once the tears start, I can't stop them. "If I hadn't broken up with him . . . He was alone. We promised we'd never leave each other alone like that. I'd felt that, before him, and for people like us, it's too much. If he would've told me he was hurting too, I wouldn't have stayed mad at him. I couldn't have. I just wanted him to be okay."

"Was it a suicide?" she asks.

"I mean . . . no. It's just hard to want to come back to this. If you don't have a very good reason, it's almost not worth it."

I've never been able to explain to anyone what it's like to feel your limbs petrify. To feel completely trapped in your body and so removed from it at the same time. It's almost as if the line between life and death becomes indistinguishable. It's like living in the space between the two.

"We had a scare once. I was with him and it was . . ." Terrifying. Seeing him unconscious like that. It was my greatest fear. "His sister was home. She got him back. I was high too. I just sat there with his head in my lap. I didn't know what to do." I wipe my nose with the tissue Nora hands me. "I asked him about it afterward. If he'd gone anywhere. How it felt. Did it feel like floating away? That's how I imagine it.

"He said it was more like sinking. The feeling of sinking forever. He told me coming back from that, settling into yourself again, it's one of the hardest things you can do." I've never told anyone this. I can barely get the words out. "But then he said if he had to choose between that and me, he'd choose me every time. He'd come back to me every time. I believe him. I think

251

he would've at least tried, you know, but I wasn't there. I wasn't there for him to choose me."

Nora leans back in her seat, absorbing the weight of my words. "Can you think of a good reason in your own life? Something worth coming back for?"

I can think of a few. That's why I'm here.

When Sue and Dave dropped me off, I told them I would try my best. I imagined I'd come here and I'd talk and it would be like an exorcism. I thought I'd find some peace, but I'm caught in barbed wire. The more I try to free myself, the more I rip myself apart.

3

PERFORMANCE ART

And so my days go like this.

6:52 a.m.

Wake up too early, but not early enough to go back to sleep. It's warm underneath the thick blankets. All three are piled one on top of the other because the weight helps keep me calm. It muffles the sound of pens clicking at the nurse's station outside my door. There's not enough time to sleep but I try. It only makes it worse when the door swings open.

7:00 a.m.

"Morning, Amélie. There's coffee."

I'm the first stop in Paula's morning checks. She's like an alarm you can't snooze. Someone barging in to make sure you're still alive. Still where you should be.

There's an understanding that passes between us. We both have expectations of how this day will go. She expects that I'll try. I expect that I'll fail. But I've got sixteen hours to kill before it's quiet again and sixteen hours is an eternity. She smiles and she's gone.

7:10 a.m.
I'm tired of staring at the wall. I get up and I shower until I'm tired of that too. Braid my wet hair into a thick rope. Brush my teeth. Sit on the floor by the foot of my bed until I see a messy red bun float past the door. I follow it into the hall.

7:45 a.m.
The entire unit lines up to be escorted to breakfast. I squeeze through the small crowd gathered at the nurse's station. Maddison hands me a lukewarm cup of coffee, swiping her bangs out of her face. She's leaving tomorrow and it makes me anxious to think of how I'll survive this place without her.

We fall into step next to each other. We're not friends, exactly, but it's nice to have the company. Besides, Maddison has a theory the center runs on a points system. According to her, being social earns you points. Spending time out of your room earns you points. So does eating, small talk with the staff, and expressing your feelings. The more feelings the better, she says.

She earned all her points in two weeks; and for this, she considers herself a prodigy. I think she's a bit of a narcissist. Still, I'm always trying to figure out how many points I have to earn to leave this place.

8:00 a.m.

My untouched bowl of cereal grows swollen and soggy with milk. A tech shoots a stern look at our table. Maddison is anorexic so sitting with her means my meals are monitored by association. I'd eat, but I don't eat this early. I peel a banana, or whatever random piece of fruit I happen to grab, and take small bites until some disturbance pulls the tech's attention away.

9:00 a.m.

The line at the nurse's station for morning meds is like Disney. I get there early to avoid the crowd. I still end up somewhere in the middle.

I know it'll take months before we even get close to a combination and dosage that works, and even that won't be perfect. I feel like a guinea pig. I feel like they're guessing. It's like my mind is at war with my body. Appease one and the other revolts.

9:10 a.m.

Sleep is not an issue for me here. Thanks to my meds, I can sleep just about anywhere—in the common room, in the cafeteria, in the hall—but my bed is the only place no one tries to talk to me. Where I can pretend things are okay.

I ask Paula to wake me before group and crawl back into bed.

10:30 a.m.

Support group reminds me of rehab. I've never been to rehab, but I threw it in Darren's face often enough to consider what it would be like. Sitting in a circle discussing feelings and regrets and impulses and triggers.

I resign myself to silence each day, and then remembering that this is a game and there are points to be earned, I talk briefly about my childhood. You know, the one I don't remember. Because I don't remember it, it doesn't hurt.

But I bake a quiver into my voice anyway. I bow my head and fiddle with my hands. I talk about the ache of losing a mom whose face I can't recall. The plight of the lonely or whatever. I peek between lashes at the slow nods and the chorus of *mmm*s. This registers as manipulative, but whatever. It works.

12:00 p.m.

By lunchtime I eat, digging into a pile of pasta. The food here isn't that bad. I sit next to a tortured Maddison, who's pushing a scoop of steamed veggies around her plate. A tech kneels in front of her. Begs her to eat. Says she can't leave unless she's willing to follow her nutrition plan. She glares through teary eyes and takes a resentful bite.

I eat as if the contents of my stomach won't end up in the toilet within the hour.

1:00 p.m.

I hold my arm still while the nurse draws a vial of blood. I don't have afternoon meds, but I still have to have my vitals taken. She retracts the needle and presses a cotton ball to my arm. I bend my elbow and she tapes it down.

She asks how I'm feeling. Takes my blood pressure and my temperature. I tell her I'm nauseous. Same as always. She makes a note for Nora. Promises we'll adjust.

1:30 p.m.

My session with Nora is my favorite hour of the day, aside from all the hours when I'm unconscious. Her hair is down, long brown coils pinned back from her face. She sits with one foot tucked under her butt and a cup of tea in hand, smiling warmly at me.

I don't edit with Nora the way I did with Richards. I don't feel analyzed by her. I don't even realize I've said anything worth analyzing until her pen glides across her notepad. I try to backtrack through my thoughts. What did I say?

I don't know what she writes down. We don't talk about anything in particular, but every day I feel lighter after seeing her. So maybe it helps.

3:00 p.m.

Cognitive behavioral group therapy is the hardest session to bullshit. You can't really lie to depressed people about your experiences with depression. Sometimes it's difficult to separate the sadness of others from my own.

Maddison says therapy is performance art. You give them what they want, you earn your points. She sits across from me, rolling her eyes whenever someone has a breakthrough. The second she's up, she puts on a show worthy of the closing night of a Broadway play. It's not her first time in a place like this. She jokes that it won't be her last.

CBT isn't just for the depressed, even though we are absolutely the majority here. It's also for people with compulsions and addictions. All of us who never learned how to separate thought and action. Who are constantly warring with our minds.

I shift in my seat, watching the most disconcerting performance take place in front of me. Both performers are in tears. They hug and cry into each other's shoulders. We murmur encouraging words as they take their seats.

The boy next to me traces a thick scar on his arm. He catches me looking and pulls his sleeve over his wrist.

5:00 p.m.
I spend dinner in the bathroom dry heaving into the toilet.

6:00 p.m.
I'm not seeing anyone except Sue and Dave. They stop by every few days. On the days in between, I sit in the doorway of my room watching visitors come and go. Caroline asks me again if I want to call a friend. When I tell her no, she says maybe I'll change my mind tomorrow.

8:00 p.m.
Dialectical behavioral therapy is the hell I deserve. It's basically CBT; but hey, while we're at it, let's unpack all of the relationships in your life. Let's talk about your inability to cope with your emotions and communicate effectively. Your tendency to

hide from the things that hurt you. Or, even worse, to latch on to them like a nursing child.

I cry every session. It's kind of a pre-bedtime ritual. Oddly soothing in a way. It takes it right out of you.

Nora said, of all my sessions, this is the most important. It's the most pain I've ever felt. I learn how my brain works. Why it's hard for me to let people get close. Why things always seem to feel so futile.

It hurts, and they make me sit with the pain. They've found all my hiding places. They cut my nails down to keep me from clawing at my arms. They ask me complicated questions so I have to be mindful. I can't run away.

I learn all my warped paradigms and I'm left feeling like I know nothing. Like I'm unprepared to face the world. Starting all over from scratch.

Nora explained the importance of demolishing the old to build the new. She promised that the dust does settle eventually. It won't hurt this way forever.

I worry they're breaking me into too many pieces.

9:15 p.m.
I swallow the pills in the paper cup. I don't ask what they are. I just hope they manage to do whatever they're supposed to.

9:30 p.m.
There's a TV in my room. I don't watch it, but I like the noise. It drowns out all the thoughts racing through my head.

I'm scared none of this will work. I'm scared that, even if I get through this, none of what I learn here will stick. How do I do this without a team around me reminding me to take my meds? Checking on me each morning? Keeping the darkness away? The structure they enforce here is numbing. In stripping me of my autonomy, they've stripped me of any responsibility.

But there are people waiting for me. I picture their faces in my mind, and decide I'm doing this for them because doing it for me doesn't seem worth it at all.

11:00 p.m.
"Amélie, lights out."

4
ISN'T THAT ADULTHOOD?

When Maddison returned on day seventeen, the news spread through the center like a plague. She's been back for a day and I still haven't seen her. I heard about how she came in sunken into herself like a deflated balloon. How she hadn't eaten since I last sat across from her in the cafeteria. How she cried and pleaded and when her pleading got her nowhere, stopped talking completely.

I thought Maddison had found a way around the system. I knew she wasn't better when she left, but I'm pretty sure we're all faking it. Pretending everything's okay. Trying to get through each day without someone calling our bluff. Without having to acknowledge all the ways we're falling apart. Isn't that adulthood?

Each meal consumed, each pound gained, earned Maddison a few more points. I was happy for her. It gave me hope. Not in the system itself but in the fact that, one way or another, it would end. We'd get to the other side.

But what would earn me my points? And even if I earn

enough to leave, could I lose them just as quickly? I attend my sessions. I take my meds. I speak more openly about my feelings than I ever have before. I'm doing everything I know to do but it feels like there's something they're waiting for.

I implored Caroline to explain this to me. I told her about Maddison's points theory. She said that's the wrong way of looking at it. It's about the work. I told her I'm doing the work. How can I know if it's the right work if I don't understand the rubric with which I'm being graded? She said it isn't a test. I told her it feels very much like a test, so maybe if she slid me some notes I could study up and get the fuck out of here. She asked me if I want to leave. I haven't spoken to her since because I'm determined that my first words to her be an answer to her question, and I'm still not quite sure what that is.

I knock softly on Maddison's open door. She's lying on the floor with her legs propped up on the wall.

"Long time, no see," she says.

There's a bitter edge to her sarcasm now. A light has been switched off behind her eyes. Her personality, which used to warm any room like a bonfire, has chilled. We sit silently, listening to her fingers tap against the bed frame.

"I don't know what I'm supposed to do," she says after a while. "I've tried to get better. I really tried the first time. I did whatever they wanted because they told me this could kill me, and I didn't want to die. I went through treatment, and they let me go. I thought I was okay."

She turns her face away from me. Her hair is pulled up in a

ponytail. There are patches of skin from where it has begun to fall out.

"I think I'm going to do this forever. In and out of treatment for the rest of my life." She dries her eyes with the hem of her shirt. "How am I supposed to do this forever, Mel?"

"I don't know."

I've had the same thought since I got here. How am I supposed to live this way forever?

But then I started thinking about points. I haven't allowed myself to look any further into the future than the day I'm discharged. When I try to look beyond that, I can't form a clear picture in my head. I wonder whether the reason I haven't earned my points is because I'm not sure this is a test I want to pass.

I'm not sure I want to live through this. I'm not sure I can.

The edges of my vision begin to contort, like running a hand through a cloud of smoke. I have the strange sensation that I'm slowly falling sideways, but as far as I can tell, I haven't moved. My back is still against the wall. The cool linoleum floor beneath my palms. Everything is as it was, so if I'm falling, the whole world must have been knocked off its axis.

"Are you okay?" Maddison sits up, leaning on her elbows. "You look like you're gonna pass out."

My chest is tight. Pulling air into my lungs feels like drinking coffee through one of those tiny black straws.

"Seriously, are you okay?" Maddison's kneeling next to me now. "Should I call someone?"

"No." I use what little air I have left to stand. "I'm fine."

I don't understand what my body is doing and my ability to coherently assess this in real time is only adding to my distress. I feel like a chasm has formed between my brain and my body. I can see across the gap just fine, but I don't know how to cross it. I don't even know how the crack happened to begin with.

I had just been thinking about points. About how to earn them and whether I wanted them in the first place.

Caroline intercepts me on the way to my room. I thought I was walking at a normal, inconspicuous pace, but maybe I'd been running because I nearly plow her down. I retract from her grasp so she won't feel the way my hands have begun to shake.

She studies my face. "What's wrong?"

"No. I mean, nothing. I just . . ." I need to walk very fast in circles like I can physically catch up to my body. I need there to be a reason why my heart is pounding in my chest. I try to move past her into my room, but she blocks my path.

"Amélie, will you sit with me for a moment?" There's a nearly imperceptible change in her voice, but I catch it. It goes from conversational—the Caroline who sits on the edge of my bed in the afternoon and tells me about the dog she just adopted or her recent trip to Tulum—to placating. Slow, articulate words dipped in warm honey. I sense a perimeter forming.

"No, that's okay. I'm just going to . . . I think I just need to rest for a second. My throat's just a little . . . so I'm, uh . . ."

I was determined that my first words to Caroline be an answer to her question. As she stares at me with those glassy blue eyes, I realize I answered her.

No. I know I don't want to be here. But I think I hate the idea of leaving this place more than the idea of staying. I hate the idea of coming back most of all.

I don't really want to be anywhere, and now my lungs burn like they're repelling salt water. I'm caught in a wave, tumbling around the ocean's floor. My legs give out and I collapse. Caroline calls for nurses and techs who come with machines and wires and vials of liquid.

I push them away with weak, leaden arms. I don't want to sleep. I feel like I've jumped off the edge of something very tall and, instead of falling, I'm suspended in midair. Locked in this moment, looking up at everything I've lost, and down at everything I still have to lose.

I think about Darren. The only person I've ever known whose darkness has even come close to matching my own. How often I found him floating this way, wondering if that would be the time he finally crashed to the ground. I imagine he must be close by now, but that doesn't bring me the comfort I would've expected.

Instead, it's something like cracking my ribs apart. It's violent, like reaching in and ripping my heart from its arteries. I'm hoping to pass out from the pain. To dissociate like I did when I lost him, but this is like nothing I've ever felt before.

There's an oxygen mask strapped to my face. Caroline's lips are moving, but I can't separate her voice from the other sounds in the hall.

I'm stuck, dangling off that thing I've jumped from. Above

me, they're working hard to get to me. The small strands of the rope they've thrown down snap one by one. I can see the panic in their eyes.

There's too much weight. I've never felt it all at once like this. All the little compartments of my mind have opened simultaneously and dumped their contents on me. So much love woven through so much loss. I'm embarrassed by how much stuff I've allowed myself to accumulate. No wonder my shoulders ache. No wonder taking on even the smallest emotional load feels like too much. I've been abusing myself. I don't know how I'll ever atone for the harm I've caused.

I'm hoping to pass out from the pain, but I'm still conscious and alert. I try to fold in on myself like I've done so many times before, but this isn't something I can escape.

Countless hands pin my writhing body to the floor. Caroline's face hovers over mine like the North Star. The rope scrapes against rock and frays. Maybe it could support me if I let some things go. If I let him go. If I let them help me.

Had I been paying closer attention, I would've noticed sooner that it shouldn't feel like this. It isn't this way for other people. I used Darren like a hallucinogen. Something to distort the world around me and make the colors brighter. To make everything feel a little more tactile so I could cement myself more firmly in this world.

I've never believed I could be any way other than the way I am. I've never had the desire to, but I have to try. It isn't good enough to try for them, the people whose faces flash in my mind whenever I'm tempted to loosen my grip. I have to want it for myself. Because what if they go? People go. What if they do? Would I cease to exist?

A stiffening spreads throughout my limbs. Hands pick me up from the floor and lay me beneath the pile of covers. It feels like a burial. Something I don't know how to begin to grieve.

The problem is the things I need to let go of are all that I know of myself. I don't know who I am and I can't understand how I've lived seventeen years as a stranger in my own body.

I let myself sink through the bed. The nurses are gone now, but Caroline stays with me until Nora comes. I don't want Nora to see me this way. I feel like I let her down. All our work has been for nothing if I dissolve at the mere idea of what life will be like outside these walls. I've been wasting everyone's time.

I was expecting disappointment, but there's understanding in her gentle gaze.

"Caroline, can you give us a minute?"

I watch through blurry eyes as Nora takes Caroline's place on the edge of the bed. My breath comes in quick, desperate gasps. The pillow at the nape of my neck is soaked through with tears.

"Do you feel it now?" Nora asks. I can't answer her. If I open my mouth, I think I'll scream.

She grabs my hand. "You feel this?" Her grip is firm. I nod. "You're still here. That's the important part. You're alive, and it can't kill you. When you feel this way, remember this night. The night it didn't kill you and you lived."

5

MORE THAN I CAN SAY ABOUT MOST

When I wake up in the morning, the first thing I notice is the sink running in the bathroom. It's a little past ten. I've slept through breakfast and meds. There's a covered tray of food on a rolling table to the right of my bed. The faucet squeaks, and the water stops. I assume it must be Caroline, but when the door opens, it's Sue that walks out.

I start crying the second I see her. Someone must have called and told her what happened. She climbs into the small bed with me and feeds me spoonfuls of yogurt once I've calmed down enough to eat. She helps me shower and washes my hair, braiding it into two neat plaits. We spend the morning in the courtyard sitting on a bench with my feet in her lap, face tilted up toward the sun.

Sue adjusts one of my slippers before it can fall off. "You know, I was pregnant once," she says out of nowhere, smiling at my wide-eyed reaction. "I was only a few years older than you. It was before Dave and I got back together. I was on and off with my boyfriend at the time, and neither of us were ready to be parents. I also could not fathom bringing a kid who would have to inherit all of our problems into this world. It didn't seem right."

She takes a moment to find her words. "I never wanted to give birth to a baby and for a long time, I thought that meant I didn't want to be a parent. I was scared this world wouldn't be good enough for my kid. And it's not. It's not good enough for any of you, but I'm so glad that you're here. I'm so grateful."

I don't know what to say. I'm so emotionally exhausted my body is beyond the point of producing tears. I'm trying so hard to be grateful to be here. I grab her hand, and she brushes her thumb over my knuckles.

Before Sue leaves, I make a deal with her and Caroline that I'll allow one friend to visit if they literally never ask me about it again. Caroline gives me cell phone privileges long enough to solidify this deal, hovering close by so I don't check any of the forty-two texts in my inbox. I have no desire to. I'm not even interested in the reply to the text I'm sending. I type out a quick message and hand the phone back to her.

By the time visiting hours roll around, my anxiety is truly showing off. My meds help but barely. I know it's too late to call it off, and it isn't until I hear footsteps stop in my doorway that I begin to relax.

"You look like shit, Melie."

I roll my eyes, but I can't help the tiny quirk of my lips at his words. No one else would've dared say something that blunt at a time like this.

I don't know if I consider Trey a close friend, but he has always looked out for me. Always made sure I was safe. I know that was mostly out of consideration for Hayden but still. It's more than I can say about most people.

He strolls in and unzips his backpack to dramatically reveal a bag from a burger place by Shaine's apartment. "Contraband."

"That bag did not make it past the nurse's station without getting thoroughly checked."

"Lifted the pickles off the bun and everything." I wrap a blanket around me and sit next to him on the small couch. He hands me a burger. "How you feeling?"

"Did you get that orange sauce?"

He pushes the bag toward me, and I fish through the sauce packets at the bottom. I think it's ridiculous to ask someone in a mental facility how they're feeling. Like probably not great because I'm still here. But maybe it's more rude not to ask. Either way, I let the question dissipate, and he seems to get the hint.

"I'm not gonna lie." He takes a big bite of his burger, wiping sauce off his face with a napkin. "I was surprised when you texted. Shaine said she hasn't visited yet."

"Talk to Shaine a lot?"

"Nah, it's not even . . ." I tap the burger logo. He smirks. "I was in the area."

Right.

His expression is amused, but I know I've hit a soft spot bringing up Shaine.

"She still likes you. You don't have to do that thing where you pretend to be all aloof and detached because you're afraid of getting your feelings hurt."

"I know you're not talking. A couple of weeks in here and you're a therapist?"

"It's a very accelerated program."

He rubs a hand over his neck. I've never seen him look this vulnerable. "I messed up before. I'm just trying to do things right this time."

"I know."

Given the sentimental turn this conversation has taken, I'm not totally surprised by what he says next.

"He still loves you."

I'm too worn out by the saga that is my relationship with Hayden to be annoyed with Trey. "I didn't invite you here to talk about him."

"I know, but we've been friends forever, and I've never seen him like this."

"Someone down the hall got discharged yesterday if he's looking for a place to process his grief."

My words come out harsher than either of us expects. He chews silently, waiting to see if I'm going to go off on him, but I'm not. Of course Trey would go to bat for Hayden. I knew that even before I texted him. I also knew he wouldn't push it once I shut it down.

I rip the bag open and dump my fries out, smothering them in three packs of the orange sauce. "How's school?"

He takes another huge bite of his burger. "It's school."

I spent the first week of classes in bed while Sue and Dave made arrangements for me here at Roseview. The life I'd carefully curated for myself over the past six months fell away like leaves from a tree, revealing the hard, unforgiving bark of winter branches. The things that truly made up my life, all gnarled and twisted onto themselves. Everything continued while I lay frozen in my room.

I wonder what Trey sees on my face. His eyes are unreadable. I'm grateful for that. I smile but it isn't convincing. "How's Shaine?"

"She misses you."

"Yeah. I miss her too."

"Then you should see her. I'm honored you chose me as your one phone call, but it was the wrong choice."

One phone call. What does he think this is? "I'm not in jail."

"Then why are you punishing yourself? It's self-inflicted solitary confinement."

I shrug. "I'm not ready."

"Shaine spoke to Brie. She wanted to know what was going on. Rena didn't even know. I think Shaine was hurt you didn't tell her."

I give him a look that indicates he's dancing very close to the edge right now.

"I'm just saying, it's hard for them too. If being apart is hurting you guys, how can it be a good thing?" We're clearly not talking about Shaine anymore. "You're being too hard on yourself."

I can't help but laugh. "Do you remember the chaos?"

"Oh no, I remember. But you were in pain. People understand that."

I think people understand pain conceptually, but just because you understand why someone did what they did doesn't change the fact that they did it.

"It doesn't make any of it okay."

"I didn't say it does. I said it makes it understandable." He scoops up all our trash and throws it in the can by the door. "How long are you going to be here?"

"Until they get what they want."

"And what's that?"

"I have no fucking idea." The points system is as elusive as always. "I've seen people get discharged since I've been here but only after a month or so of treatment. I don't know how to expedite things. I'm trying though."

I hope he can see that. I don't know why it matters. It's just that Trey has never bullshitted me. We've always been real with each other. Brie and Shaine would come here wanting to see the best in me. They'd give me more credit than I deserve. Rena would see everything, even the parts I try to hide from her. I don't know which would be worse.

"I never thanked you."

He scoffs. "For what?"

"I don't know. Everything, I guess."

"Like?"

I purse my lips. "You're going to make me list out the reasons?"

"Isn't that part of your recovery?"

"I'm not in rehab, Trey. Technically. I'm saving that for my next spiral."

He lies back against the cushions, kicking his feet up on the table. "Cool. Thank me then."

I wrap the blanket tighter around myself. As bad as things were this summer, they could've been worse. I can't let myself think about that for too long. When I do, all the alternate endings of that chapter run on a loop in my mind, and I see that each one destroys something. A relationship. A future. A life. It's too much.

"Thank you," I say, because I have to. Not later, right now. Because I don't know what comes after this.

"Don't worry about it."

Later, after group, I find Caroline at the nurse's station and ask to use the computer to email Brie.

"I think that's a wonderful idea," she says, coming around the counter to walk me to the computer lab. "I'm sure she'll be very happy to hear from you."

I find an empty chair in the back corner of the room and log in with my credentials. While I wait for the computer to load, I pick at my thumb until the cuticle rips open. Caroline places her hand over mine.

"What do I say to her?" Brie should've been who I asked to come. I know that. It was easier to talk to Trey than to have to look into my own face and admit how badly I've failed. "I know

I'm not supposed to need anyone, but I do need her. What if she doesn't want to come?"

"All you can do is ask."

I stare at the blank email in despair. How do I do that? I run my fingers over the keys, trying to compose the words in my mind. It feels inadequate, but I write the one thing I know to be true. For whatever it's worth.

Brie,

I miss you.

6

I MAY FALL ASLEEP

Brie comes to visit a few days later. I wasn't sure if she'd accept the invitation to join my session with Nora, but she wrote me back almost immediately. She'd been waiting.

"Aubrie." Nora reaches out to shake her hand. "Thank you so much for coming."

"Of course."

Brie gives me a shy smile, but her eyes are scanning me like a computer. She hugs me, and it makes me feel stronger to be this close to her. Maybe I can do this after all.

"How are you?" Nora asks her once we're all settled, Brie and me on the couch and Nora in her usual chair across from us.

"Me? I'm fine."

Nora turns to a blank page in her notebook. "The reason we asked you here is we're hoping you can provide some context for Mel about your childhood together. Whatever you can remember would be very helpful."

"Okay."

"I want to start with your reconnection. How did it feel to see Mel again after all these years?"

Brie fidgets nervously with the strap of her purse. I guess this is as uncomfortable for her as it is for me, considering she's the one in the spotlight. "Well, I didn't think she wanted to see me, so I was surprised."

"Why did you think she didn't want to see you? Had you tried reaching out before?"

"No. I wanted to but I was scared. When I saw that she was in the city, it felt like the right time. I sent her a message, and she didn't respond. I didn't know she hadn't seen it or that she didn't remember me."

"How did it feel to realize that she didn't remember you?"

"It was confusing. We did everything together when we were kids. We were never apart. But . . ." Brie steals a glance at me. "I don't know. She's been through a lot. So." The pain in her voice is almost too much for me to bear, but as hard as it is for me to hear about it, it must have been that much harder for her to live it.

"Do you remember your birth mother?" Nora asks.

"Yeah," Brie says. "Not well, but well enough."

"What do you remember about her?"

"She was funny." Brie's talking to me now. Painting a picture of our mom since my memories seem to have fallen into the folds of my brain. "We laughed all the time. She used to play with us. Not the way adults do, but really get down on the floor with us and roll around. We ate a lot of chicken nuggets. Our apartment was tiny. She gave us the bedroom and slept on the couch. There were toys everywhere. Barely any furniture but a ton of toys."

"What do you remember about Mel?" Nora asks.

Brie clears her throat. When she speaks, her voice quivers. "We were really close. I was the more sensitive kid. She looked out for me."

"No," I interject. "I don't think that's true. I mean, I'm sure we looked out for each other, but I doubt you were the sensitive one."

If she was, I don't know how we reversed roles so completely over the years.

"I used to cry all the time," she says.

"Yeah, but I remember . . ." A memory of her little hand tugging on mine flashes in my mind. A tiny, determined voice pulling me out of my head. Frizzy curls flopping over big, round eyes. *S'okay, Amie.*

"What do you remember, Mel?" Nora asks.

"You called me Amie."

Brie grins. "Yeah I did. You called me Abie. We couldn't pronounce our names that well."

"I remember you telling me, 'It's okay.'"

"You would get sad sometimes, but you weren't emotional about it. Just quiet. You would kind of stop speaking."

Nora jots that down. "Really?"

"Yeah. I would make a fort in the hallway with covers. We'd lie in it, and I'd tell her stories. We usually fell asleep there and woke up in our bed."

It can't be normal to have such a clear recollection of life before five years old. "How do you remember all of this?"

"I thought about it a lot. When they split us up, I kept reliving everything in my head. Eventually, it was hard to forget."

"What do you remember about the time right before you were brought to Laurelle?" Nora asks her.

"Nothing. It was a normal day until an ambulance showed up at the house. Someone took us to Denny's. We got milkshakes. And then we never saw our mom again."

I think of the ice cream cone I remembered in my first session with Nora. "Did I get chocolate?"

Brie's face scrunches. "No, you hated chocolate. I got chocolate and you got strawberry."

Maybe it was Brie in that memory. Her arm holding that ice cream cone. If so, maybe the memories of us together aren't lost forever. If I work on it, I wonder if I can get them back.

"You said an ambulance came?" Nora scribbles more notes in red ink.

"Yeah, with sirens and everything. People rushed into the house, but I don't know what happened. We were playing with our dolls and then we were being carried to a car. It felt oddly normal."

That doesn't seem right. "It didn't feel normal."

"How did it feel for you?" Nora asks me. It's starting to come together in my head. The ambulance. Dinner at Denny's. But there's something missing. There's a big part of this Brie's leaving out. "Mel, what do you remember?"

Why would an ambulance have been there? Who called th—

My chest tightens, and it all pours over me like a waterboarding.

The fear that coursed through my little body. The woman's voice on the other line of the phone, asking me how old I was. If I was alone.

"I called them."

Brie's nose scrunches. "The ambulance? Why?"

"Um. I don't know."

Nora leans forward, putting her notebook and pen on the table next to her. "Close your eyes and try to put yourself back there. You're home with your sister and mother. What happens next?"

"I don't know." I never understood how I could forget everything, but now I get it. Now that I remember, I want to forget all over again. "I don't want to do this."

Brie scoots closer. When I look at her, I know I'm seeing my own expression mirrored back at me. "Maybe we should stop," she says.

"We can stop if you want, Mel."

I found her lying on the bathroom floor. She was sweating so much her hair was sticking to her face. I was frozen in the doorway. I couldn't move. I wanted to run to her, but I was terrified. Despite the pain she must have been in, she still smiled at me as best she could.

"Ça va, baby," she said, voice strained. "J'ai besoin que tu fasses quelque chose pour moi, d'accord?"

I couldn't take my eyes off the blood. There seemed to be so much of it, dripping down her leg. Staining her bright yellow skirt.

"I need you to get the phone, dial 911, and tell the person who answers our address. D'accord?" Her eyes closed, and it looked like it took all her strength to open them again. Her golden-brown skin was pale like a ghost. "I may fall asleep, but you just tell them our address and everything will be okay."

"She was bleeding. She told me to call 911. I took the phone into the bedroom. I didn't want to scare Brie."

Brie shakes her head, confused. "But we were together when they came to the apartment. You didn't say anything."

I should've gone back and checked on her, but I was afraid of what I would see. "She told me I just had to call and it would be okay."

Nora crosses the room, taking a folder off her desk. "Do you remember who came to tell you what happened to your mom?"

"No."

"I don't either," Brie says.

"I knew though," I say. Kids may not understand everything, but on some basic human level, I think they can sense when a life is ending. "I knew as soon as I saw her. I just wanted to believe her."

"That must have been very scary for you," Nora says.

It was scary, that fear and helplessness. I still can't see her face clearly when I think of her, but I do remember the way our mom made me feel. I was safe with her. No matter what happened, I knew everything would always turn out okay in the end. I felt that until she was gone, and then I never felt it again. From that moment on, the world was random and uncontrollable. It felt ruthless and then it proved itself to be so time and time again until I forgot what safety was.

"Aubrie, how are you feeling?"

I see Brie's younger self in the set of her face. Determined to get us through this. "It's just a lot, you know. Um, but . . ." She wipes my cheek with the palm of her hand. "We're okay."

She believes it so stubbornly, I start to believe it too.

"I have something I think you should see." Nora slides a manila folder over to me. "I managed to get a copy of this from LCS. It's about your birth mother, Audrey."

Audrey.

I stare from Nora to the folder and back again. I don't know if I want to see it. I have no idea what it is. If it's from LCS, why haven't I seen it before? I swallow the lump in my throat and pick up the folder, angling it so Brie can see too. There's a single xeroxed page in there. A copy of Audrey Cœur's death certificate. Why is she showing us this?

"Look at the cause of death," Nora says softly.

"It says she died of complications from an ectopic pregnancy." I skim the page, looking for more details. "What does that mean?"

"It means she was pregnant, but the baby was growing outside of her uterus. She might not have known until it was too late."

I think of the young woman lying in the middle of the bathroom floor. "That's what I remember? I saw her bleeding out? I should've—"

Nora cuts me off for the first time ever. "You took care of yourself and your sister. That's more than anyone could've reasonably expected of you at that age."

"But I didn't help her." Maybe if I'd gotten to the phone quicker. Or if I'd found her sooner. Maybe she called out for me. Maybe I didn't hear her. "Do you think she was afraid?"

"She was probably afraid, yes. But I think she was mostly worried about her girls. I'm sure she just wanted you both to be okay."

I knew our mother was dead, but part of me fantasized that she was somewhere living a happy and prosperous life without me. I wish it had been a choice she made because with time she could've chosen differently. It would've been more painful but at least that way she'd still be alive.

"I couldn't get any information about your birth father," Nora says. "But I did get this." She hands me a black-and-white photo, printed on computer paper. "Your mother moved to the States from Montreal, but she was born in Toulouse. When she died, there was no one to claim you. Ending up in LCS was a good thing, regardless of how you may feel or how justified those feelings may be."

I hear what she's saying but my brain is still playing catch up. Repeating the same facts over and over, trying to make them make sense. I trace my finger over the photograph of Audrey.

"I've never seen her picture before," Brie says, eyes rimmed with tears.

Nora leans over, and I hold it out for her to see. "You two look like her."

It's a shitty photo but I can see we have her eyes and her smile. Her hair is a little curlier than ours. Cut shorter than Brie's and pinned back behind her ears. I don't know where they got this picture, but she looked happy. She was so beautiful.

I didn't realize how much I needed to know about Audrey, to see her with my own eyes, until now. Maybe she wanted us. Maybe she was a great mom. Maybe we were happy.

They let me skip group to spend time with Brie. It's windy on the beach, the breeze kicking the sand up at our feet. The spray of the ocean on our faces. Soft tufts of grass under our legs. She rips a weed up by the root and rolls it between her fingers.

"I'm going back to therapy," she says. Her eyes look more like mine than hers. Darker, almost amber. "If the audition next year . . . If it doesn't go well, I need to be okay. I need to be okay either way."

There are times when I imagine myself in different scenarios. Living at different times in history or born into different families. Who would I be if I'd had two parents? If I'd loved different people? Was I always going to end up this way? Would she and I have found each other? We were together from the beginning. Could there be me without her?

"What do you think it would've been like if we got to grow up together?"

"I think about that a lot," she says. "I don't know."

"You think we'd be close?"

Her smile is wistful. "How could we not be?"

She builds a little mound of sand and crushes it with her foot. This story is mine, but it's hers too. Because she carries it differently does not mean it isn't heavy for her. She's had to live with it all this time.

"I think the reason I don't remember everything you remember is because I couldn't. Losing her and then losing you. I knew they were both my fault."

If I had been different, maybe I could've kept them. If I had made better choices, maybe I wouldn't have ended up so alone.

"There was nothing you could've done that would've made a difference, Mel. We were kids."

I know that, but I can't help how it feels. "I lose everyone."

We watch the push and pull of the waves. Cool water tumbling onto shore. "You should let Rena and Shaine come." She glances at me, waiting for a response. I wipe my tear-streaked face with sandy fingers. "If you push people away, you lose them for sure. Is that better than trusting that you can love them and they'll stay?"

I'm so tired. I feel like I've been sprinting for seventeen years. Tripping over every hurdle. Twisting ankles and scraping knees. "How am I supposed to do this? How is this my life now?"

Brie stands and dusts off her pants, reaching a hand out for me. "It's the same life."

7

TWO MINUTES APART

Brie and I were born two minutes apart, according to our birth certificates. We weren't born, so much as removed from Audrey in what I imagine to be some banal and unceremonious way. There is no father listed on the hospital documents. No one holding her hand or assuring her that everything was okay. That things were going according to a plan they'd made together. She was alone.

And so, as we came into the world, there was only the sound of two wailing things she'd created. Tiny and wrinkled and already needing so much from her. Two spotless lives that she, at age twenty-one, was fully responsible for. It hurts me to try to put myself in her shoes. To imagine how it must have felt for her. Maybe she cried too. And maybe that was the start of everything.

I requested my full file from Richards. I never realized that was a thing I could do, but it is, after all, mine. Mine in a way so few things are. He agreed, but only if I would allow him to visit. The file arrived in my inbox an hour ago with many of his personal notes redacted. My entire existence to date, summarized for quick consumption like a scientific abstract. Something for people to read and then decide, with total confidence, that they know what's best for me. To qualify them to make unilateral decisions on my behalf.

"It's a lot of information. Take your time," he says. "We can go over whatever you'd like when you're ready."

"Give me a second."

It's the first time I've spoken to Richards since checking myself into treatment nearly a month ago. I've refused to see him until now. Richards is hardly my favorite person in the world, but it still makes me uncomfortable to feel estranged from him. What has elapsed in the time since we last spoke has made me new. In that way, we're strangers.

"I know these past few weeks have been very challenging—"

"I'm trying to read."

My mind is determined to fictionalize the information in my file. I go over each line carefully, word by word. I hope, by doing so, it'll feel more like something that belongs to me. Something that truly happened in this exact way, that I can recall at will like a memory.

Nora said it may help to take a more objective approach. To resist my tendency to vilify myself and instead try to absorb the facts like a news report. These things happened and there is no use in projecting alternate endings onto a story that was written long ago. It simply provides context with which to move forward. Just look at the facts.

This is what I know to be true.

Brie and I were born two minutes apart. Audrey died at twenty-five, leaving behind two daughters with no family to claim them. The social worker took pity on us. She brought us to Laurelle Academy, and since we had no history of trauma or abuse, they took us in.

"There are a series of physical and psychological tests performed when LCS first acquires a child," Richards says. "The results of these tests, when measured against the qualities we've found to be most compatible with prospective parents, allow us to calculate the likelihood of adoption."

"We didn't do well on your tests? That's why you split us up?"

"One of you, despite identical upbringings, ranked significantly higher."

I don't understand. "Brie got a higher test score than me so you decided we couldn't be family anymore?"

He flinches. A fleeting reaction, but I catch it. "LCS is an effective system, and for a system to work, it must have its rules. The goal for every one of our kids is adoption. Everything we do is a calculated means to that end."

He says this in defense of LCS's methodology and the role he has played with little consideration for the impact his words may have on me. To know I had been the flawed one. A piece that had come loose and rattled noisily inside an otherwise functional machine.

"I remember the night my mom died. I was the one who called 911. Did you know that?"

"Yes."

Of course he did. My fingers tighten around the iPad. "Unbelievable."

"When you were brought to Laurelle, you wouldn't speak about what you saw. You passed the physical tests with ease, but something in your psychological evaluation concerned us. Statistically, the longer a kid is in the system, the lower their chances of adoption. We wanted both you and your sister to have the best chance at finding a home, so we separated you. Over time, you began to have trouble recalling much of your childhood. You didn't ask for Aubrie. We didn't think it would be helpful to tap into those repressed memories before you were ready." He sighs. "You were a very sad child, but we were hopeful."

I return my attention to the file briefly before clicking out of the document. "Well, I'm sorry I didn't live up to your expectations. I wouldn't have chosen you either. I wouldn't have chosen any of this."

"We truly do want what's best for you."

"You really believe that, don't you?"

"I do," he says simply. "Yes."

It's hard for me to see it that way. It's hard to see the merit in the practice of splitting two sisters up because one didn't meet some arbitrary criteria. I wonder how many other families have been fractured. How many people like me the system has produced. People who believe themselves to be broken because they were never taught that perfection is a false reality no one can truly belong to.

"Thank you for keeping me alive, Eric." My voice cracks. "But we're done. I'm done."

I can't look him in the eye. Can't face what's irreparably broken between us. The trust that now lies in shreds at our feet. He's the closest thing I've had to a father. I don't want to lose another person, but I can't heal with him. I can't heal like this.

I want to heal.

"Amélie—" he starts, his voice uncharacteristically thick with emotion, but I stand up and walk out.

Squeezing my shaking hands into fists, I practice the breathing exercise Nora taught me. I can't catch my breath. I can't console my heart, which is beating itself bloody against my ribs. I can't make it understand why it was halved and then expected to keep pumping. A thing split in two. It never had a chance.

Because by age six, one of us had been adopted. I could've gone my entire life never knowing something so constitutive, so integral to who we are as people. Something they never intended for me to know.

Brie and I came into this world together. Tiny and wrinkled and already needing so much from each other.

We were never meant to be alone.

8

GUILTY OR SAD OR WHATEVER

It's been important to me since leaving Roseview two weeks ago that I spend more time with Sue and Dave. I want to make an effort. Show them I appreciate how hard they've been trying with me and I don't take it for granted.

We've decided to spend Saturdays together doing "TV-family shit," as Dave calls it. My friends have an open invitation to join whenever they want. Today it's Rena and Shaine. Sue uses it as an opportunity to whip out all her fancy party dishes and cover the coffee table with an assortment of snacks and, as of this week, Halloween candy. It threw me off a little to realize it's now October. I thought September would never end.

There's also hot chocolate. Dave spikes his with whiskey, even though I told him whiskey is not part of the classic TV-family aesthetic. He said we're a streaming TV family, not a network TV family, so it's fine.

We're halfway through the first of tonight's movies when the doorbell rings. Dave glances over his shoulder as Sue opens the door. When his eyes meet mine, I know exactly who it is.

Steeling myself, I set my mug on the table, but Dave puts his hand protectively on my knee. Neither of them knows exactly what went down between me and Hayden, but his absence hasn't gone unnoticed.

"It's okay," I say.

Dave lets me go. Sue steps away so I can pass, but not before shooting Hayden a look I can only interpret as *Hurt her and you die.* I step into the hallway and close the door, keeping my hand on the doorknob in case I need an out.

The last time I saw him, my whole world fell apart. I replay all the things he said to me. All the times he didn't listen to me. Even now, standing here when I haven't answered a single text or picked up the phone when he called. Can he see what he's doing to me? Did he think about that? Does he care?

"I know I shouldn't have just shown up like this, and I get it if you don't want to talk to me right now. I understand. Really. Just . . . don't hate me. Please don't hate me."

I let go of the knob, take a few steps away from the door, and sit. He sits across from me, leaning back against the opposite wall. We're both silent while he picks at the fibers in the carpet.

"You look tired," I say. "Are you sleeping?"

He shrugs. "Sure." He isn't. I can tell. "You?"

"Yeah."

"That's good. I'm glad."

I would have thought he'd have more to say, considering he was so determined to come here, he didn't find it necessary to

make sure this was something I wanted. It seems like he's looking for absolution. I figure he's done enough for me during our
time together. I can give him that.

"I don't hate you, but you're right. I don't think you should
be here. I . . ." I want to find the right way to say this. "I'm not
ready for the conversation we need to have. I don't know when
I'll be ready, and in the meantime, I can't . . ." *I can't do this.* His
voice plays in my mind like an old, warped record. ". . . see you.
Not yet. You should go."

My heart twists at the despair he's trying so hard to conceal.
He looks like he wants to say more but he doesn't. He just nods
and gets up to leave.

"Hayden," I call after him, because I can't send him off this
way. "I'm okay. You don't have to feel guilty or sad or whatever.
You were right. We were never together. You don't have to feel
anything. It's okay."

They're his own words, but they cut through him like an
axe. Would this have been easier for us if I'd been the girlfriend
he had in his head? Would we still have ended up this way,
haunting each other like ghosts? Stuck between a past life and
whatever lies on the other side of this. I'm praying for heaven,
but is heaven with or without him? I don't know.

The TV clicks off when I walk back in. I head straight for
my room with Rena and Shaine close behind. I shut the bathroom door between us and lock it.

The second I'm alone, I fall apart. I squeeze my hand over
my mouth, digging my fingers into my cheeks to muffle the

sound. My whole body convulses from the effort of keeping the sobs inside.

"Mel?" Shaine calls from the other side of the door. I can't draw oxygen into my lungs. I gasp and it feels like I'm suffocating. "Are you okay?"

I wipe futilely at my tears but they won't stop.

"Can we come in?" Rena asks. "Please?"

I don't open the door. I can't move. I lay my cheek against the cold tiles, pull my knees into my chest, and wait for the storm to pass.

A few hours later, I'm lying in bed replaying Hayden's first voicemail, trying to feel something definitive for him and our situation. Rena's asleep next to me and Shaine's swaddled in a nest of blankets on the floor. They sat outside the bathroom until I cried myself into a stupor, refusing to leave even when I told them I'd be okay.

"Hey, Mel. I know I probably shouldn't be calling, but I just want to make sure you're okay. I'm so sorry about everything. I really want to see you. Call me back when you get this."

The rest of the messages are more of the same. I delete each one in turn.

I walk over to my window and crank the glass open, welcoming in a gush of wind. There's a bookshelf next to the window now. Dave had it built for me while I was away. It's huge, stretching from floor to ceiling. Empty except for my Kindle and the brand-new copy of *Beloved* I found sitting on the shelf when I got home. I haven't been able to bring myself to fill it with books.

Shaine rolls over, blinking into the pale moonlight. "Are you okay?" she asks.

I put my finger to my lips. We're careful not to wake Rena as we teeter through the dark room and out into the kitchen. I turn on a small light over the stove, bracing my elbows against the cool marble countertop, my face in my hands. She takes a seat at the island.

"Are you okay?" she asks again.

"I'm so tired." She waits for me to go on. I rub my eyes. "I've slept so much lately, and I'm still so tired."

"He shouldn't have come," she says.

"No."

"Are you upset he did?"

I don't know what I feel. I had no expectations for what he would do. I have no way of knowing what's going through his mind, and I don't have it in me to ask Trey. He's probably the only person Hayden would talk to about any of this. The two of them are similar in so many ways.

"Why did you forgive Trey?" I ask Shaine. She blinks at me. "I know it's not the same situation, but . . ." I hate how small my voice is. Just on the verge of breaking. "What made you trust that he wouldn't hurt you again?"

She exhales, slouching a little in her seat. "Cheating on me was a fucked-up thing to do, but we were young. We're still so young. I knew why he did it, even at the time. He cared about me, and it scared him. It doesn't excuse it, but I understood because I was scared too." Her face softens. "I'd never liked someone the way I liked him. When things ended, part of me was relieved that I wasn't the one who ruined it."

"Why did you think you'd ruin it?"

"Mel, I'm a textbook case of daddy issues. I'm pretty sure boys can sense it from a mile away. It's embarrassing."

"You never talk about him," I say, coming to sit beside her. "Your dad, I mean."

"He's not worth talking about." The thin smile on her face does nothing to disguise the shadows brewing in her eyes. "There's a lot you and I haven't talked about."

Hayden accused me of being selfish. He said I never notice what's going on with other people. All the ways my friends may be struggling. Besides Cal and Rena, I've never confided in them. I can see now how unfair that is because I want them to know they can confide in me too.

"Do you think I'm selfish?"

"Yeah," she says. "You are. I am too. I don't know, maybe it's a self-preservation thing."

Maybe it's what happens when you're left to raise yourself.

"I'm sorry I didn't let you visit." I should've let her come to Roseview. Her and Rena. "I'm sorry I didn't tell you what was going on. I'm sorry I made you worry." A tear slips down her cheek. She quickly wipes it away. "I don't know if I can talk about everything now but I will. One day soon. I promise."

She rests her head on my shoulder. "You know, with all my

boy drama, I've never had love the way you've had it. I know what it feels like to lose someone whose name you won't remember in five years. But what you went through . . ." Tears dampen my shirt. "I hate that you had to feel that. I can't imagine."

When we get back to the room, Shaine burrows into her makeshift bed. I can feel her eyes on me as I take my place by the window again, staring at the city until I hear her breathing even out into a soft snore.

Only once I'm alone do I take the journal I bought for Darren from my desk and finally begin to write.

9

SELF-AWARENESS IS EXHAUSTING

Nora's main office is much warmer than her office at the center. There are abstract paintings hanging in expensive frames, a diffuser spitting out jasmine-scented clouds, and windows that reach from floor to ceiling giving you a snow globe view of Manhattan.

As she goes over the latest updates to my treatment plan, I arrange the magazines on the coffee table alphabetically and then reorder them by size, color, and weight.

I was doing pretty well since leaving Roseview, but seeing Hayden kind of fucked me up. I haven't been able to sit still. I can't slow my thoughts down. My brain is splintering, and I can't keep track of all the pieces.

"What's wrong?" Nora finally asks.

Self-conscious, I put the magazines down and pick at the polish on my nails. "I'm thinking of taking a gap year." She raises her eyebrows. "Rena has decided she's going to be a travel influencer. I figured I'd go with her for a while."

"Is that what you want?"

"I don't know what I want. That's as good a reason not to go to college as it is to go."

Finishing the first semester of senior year online is putting a lot of things into perspective. It's giving me space to think about what I want, not what I'm told I should want or what I've convinced myself I need to be okay. I don't want to get accepted into an amazing school and show up as the same aimless person I am now. I'm not sure where that leaves me, but it can't be any worse than where I've been.

"If it will make you happy, I think it's a good plan." I try to read her face for any sign that she may not really approve, but her smile is as genuine as always. "Do you want to tell me what's bothering you now, or is there something else you'd like to discuss?"

I rack my brain for something else and come up empty. "Hayden stopped by yesterday."

Nora twirls her pen absently between her fingers. "What was it like to see him again?"

"Confusing. I thought I'd know what to say to him. I'd gone over it in my head a thousand times. I thought I'd be angrier. I expected that. I know none of my problems have anything to do with Hayden, but there were so many things left unsaid between me and Darren. I don't want to live with regret again. I wanted Hayden to know how I felt." I can still see that devastated look on his face. It rips me apart. "But he looked so sad. We were both so sad."

I'm sick of being so damn emotional all the time. I'm tired of my brain catastrophizing everything. Things end. People break up. Life goes on. Why can't I ever just move on?

"Can I tell you something?"

She nods. "Of course."

"Don't freak out, okay?"

"I won't."

"I never thought I'd make it to eighteen," I admit. "It never mattered to me much what happened after high school because I couldn't imagine I'd be around to see it. It's not like I want to . . . I never . . ." Only the smallest bud of a thought. Nothing has ever sprouted from it. "I just couldn't imagine it."

"Can you imagine it now?"

"No. Not really."

Recovery is hard. You feel unequipped to cope without the mechanisms you've become accustomed to because part of you remembers the comfort they provided. It's like being stripped of your superpower and kryptonite all at once and told to live a normal life.

Mostly it's hard because of all the possibilities. I'd been living with the expectation that my life would play out a certain way, and now everything has changed. Anything can happen.

Nora passes me a box of tissues. "It's different for us."

"What?"

"Life. The way we navigate it as women. As Black women. It's different. It takes incredible resilience and a strong sense of self. The things you've been through, they're part of your story, but they're not the sum of your identity. You have to plant your identity deep enough for it to take root because the world will try to define you. To tell you who you are and what you're worth. It isn't always easy to stay grounded in what you know to be true. You have to remind yourself constantly. No one knows you the way you do."

"That's the problem. I don't know anything."

"Think about the work you've done over the past month or so. Was it difficult?" I roll my eyes. There were several times when they had to physically pick me up off the floor. Difficult is an understatement. "Why do you think that was?"

"Because you guys are relentless," I mutter.

Her lips quirk. "You've learned so much. You have to debride a wound before it can heal, and that's often the most painful part. What you're doing isn't easy. Many people will never know themselves the way you do now. You're not perfect. You never will be because no one is, but you should give yourself credit for how far you've come."

I really like Nora. She helps me organize the compartments in my head, to decide on what can stay and what should go. We seal them with clear lids so I can see what each one holds. This self-awareness is exhausting, but it's my responsibility. It's the work that earned me my points.

I let the sharp edges of Darren go and packed away the parts that made me feel warm and alive. I'm learning to accept my diagnosis and remember it's something to be managed and not who I am as a person. To push all the qualities I love about myself to the front and throw out all the stories I've written about being inadequate and undeserving of good things. I've left the compartments they occupied empty to fill with new stories I've yet to write.

Not having a place for Hayden leaves things unfinished. I don't know where to put him or even how to begin to organize the elements of our relationship. Should I pack him away or let him go?

He said this wasn't what he wanted. I wasn't what he wanted. What's changed since then? I'm doing better now, but I'm still, at my core, the same person I've always been. He has proven that when things are hard, I can't rely on him. I can't guarantee a life without hardship.

"What do I do about Hayden?

"What do you want to do?"

I don't know how to be alone anymore. I don't want to be with someone because I'm afraid to be alone. But I do miss him. I don't want to lose him. "What's the point of any of this if we don't end up together?"

"It's not about a boy, Amélie. Darren or Hayden. It never has been." Her words go in one ear and right out the other. She changes tactics. "Loving someone doesn't mean you're supposed to end up together. But not ending up with the person you love doesn't mean the love you shared wasn't significant."

If it's significant, then the loss of it is also significant. All that wasted potential. "Would I be an idiot to take him back?"

"No."

That may not be the right thing to do, but on some level, it's what I want. Maybe Trey was right. Can this be what's best for me and Hayden if neither of us is happier apart?

"You're not going to tell me what to do, are you?" Nora shakes her head. I groan. Of course not. "Why?"

She trades her notebook for the cup of tea she's been drinking. "Because you don't need me to. It seems to me you're really looking for me to tell you it will be okay."

"Will it?"

"Yes." She smiles. "It will be."

I hope she's right.

10

HAPPY TEARS, LOTS OF HUGGING

I am writing an email. An email to this boy. I am writing this boy a fucking email.

Ugh.

I'm not going to send it, but I figure it may be a way for me to at least work through my feelings until I'm ready to see Hayden face-to-face. I plugged his email address in to really drive my anxiety to its breaking point. I'm using my thrashing heart as a metronome. It's soothing in a psychotic sort of way.

I've spent every morning since last week's session with Nora sitting here, trying to find nearly seven months' worth of words. This is further complicated by the fact that I'm not sure what Hayden wants. I know he wants to see me, but I don't know if it's to salvage things between us or end on better terms. Just because I feel stupid doesn't mean I want to look stupid. We've been through so much in such a short period of time. We haven't even known each other long enough to have wrecked each other the way we have.

Sitting at my desk, I scan the email I've spent the last hour tripping over. I don't think I'll ever get it right, as it's more of a feeling I have rather than a cohesive grouping of sentences in my brain. I hit delete, and have a moment of pure panic that I may have accidentally sent it. Just as I'm checking the trash folder, my phone vibrates loudly. It's absolutely the most dramatic thing that could've happened at this moment. I almost fall out of my seat.

Gabe: Court seven.

I send a quick text back, confirm that the email is indeed in my virtual trash can where it belongs, and grab my duffel bag from the closet.

Sue and Dave come out of their room just as I'm stepping into my sneakers by the door. There's something ominous about the way they're staring at me.

"Hey, do you have a minute?" Sue asks, in a tone much higher than her normal speaking voice.

"I'm meeting up with Gabe."

"Oh, that's right." She takes a hard left, pivoting away from whatever topic seems to be causing them physical discomfort. "How are the lessons going?"

Gabe and I have been training together twice a week at Dave's athletic club. Since I've been avoiding Hayden—and by extension most of my social circle—Sue and Nora conspired to get me out of the house by any means necessary. Tennis lessons were our compromise because hitting things with a racket appeals to me greatly.

"Fine. Good." I don't know what else to say. We settle into a charged silence. "Is everything okay?"

"Everything's great."

"Mm-hmm." I send Gabe a text letting him know I'll be running late and drop my bag on the floor. "What's up?"

Sue looks at Dave. He gestures toward the couch.

"Okay." She takes a deep breath once we're all seated with the two of them sitting across from me like an intervention. "We've been thinking a lot, you know, with everything that's been happening. You know how much we care about you—"

"It's okay." I cut her off. "I get it. We don't have to do this. Really, it's fine."

"Just hear us out," Dave says. I want to run.

I don't blame them. Not after everything I've put them through. Who would sign up for this knowing all that it entails? But I don't want to have this conversation. I don't want to hear them say it, or see all the things they'd never say out loud etched into their faces. I can't.

"Please," Sue says.

I've felt this before. That's what I remind myself, clasping my hands tightly in my lap. I've felt this before and I got through it. I always get through it.

"We know we haven't known you very long, but we've been through a lot as a family, even in this short time. The past few months . . ." Unable to articulate exactly what she wants to say, she looks to Dave like she's passing a baton.

"We didn't know where any of this would go," he says. "But we feel like you're our kid. We know we're not your parents and you're basically an adult, but we feel responsible for you. It's a responsibility that means a lot to us."

Sue nods fervently.

This isn't how I expected things to go.

"So we were wondering if you'd be interested in officially becoming part of our family."

I let his words hang in the air for a moment while I adjust my attitude. I had begun to shut down, and rebooting that quickly isn't an easy thing to do.

"Oh. Um. That's not . . . I mean, I appreciate it. Really. But you don't have to do that."

"We want to," Sue says in a small voice. I can tell this is not the reaction she was expecting either. Now all three of us are confused.

"I already consider you my family, but you're right. I'm almost eighteen. You don't have to legalize it. Paperwork won't change the way I feel about you."

"The paperwork matters, Mel," Dave says. I would expect nothing less from a lawyer.

"I mean, yeah. But—"

"If something happens to you . . ." Sue's voice cracks. Dave rubs her back soothingly. She closes her eyes, and when she opens them again, they're pleading. "I need people to know who I am to you. I need them to let me see you. We both need that. The paperwork is important."

I've imagined this moment a thousand times, without ever believing it would happen. It's something that used to play in my head like a scene in a movie. Predictable dialogue, happy tears, lots of hugging.

With each family I lived with, I'd plug them into this scene. Kind of the way girls imagine the proposals of the people they date. Some of those fantasies were so ridiculous, it was laughable. But others started to crystallize over time. When that happened, it always hurt that much more when things inevitably fell apart.

"You don't have to answer now," Dave adds quickly. "It's a big decision. We'd understand if this isn't something you want."

It isn't a question of whether I want them. I just never thought it would really happen.

"No, it's not that. It's just . . ." I struggle with the part of me that wants to talk them out of it. To tell them that it'd be too much. There's an easier way to live. But they want to be here. They want me. "Are you sure?"

"Yes." Dave smiles. "One hundred percent."

This is where the hugging would go if we weren't all participants in an unspoken competition where the only rule is to show as little emotion about this highly emotional event as possible. Sue loses.

Before I too can succumb to the tears welling up in my eyes, I check the time on my phone. "I gotta go. Gabe's been waiting."

"Right."

"Okay."

Then we all stand at once because there should be hugging, and we can't avoid it anymore.

11

YOU CARE SO MUCH

I called Brie after tennis yesterday to tell her about the adoption. I'm going to be Amélie Romano. That's so weird. I asked her what it was like when it happened for her. She was only six so it's obviously different, but I wanted to know if she had any reservations about changing her last name. It seems momentous and necessary, but I can't help but feel like I'm leaving an important part of myself behind. She said she never really thought about it. It's been so long since she was Aubrie Cœur.

I was joking when I suggested matching tattoos. I didn't think there was a chance in hell Brie would say yes. It was probably the fact that I didn't think she'd do it that made her want to do it.

She gaped at me when I produced not one, but two fake IDs from the state of Vermont. Both with the same birthday so I wouldn't get them mixed up. To be fair, I did tell her I was a recovering degenerate. A tattoo is probably the least illegal thing I've used these IDs for.

The second we walked through the door of the tattoo parlor, Brie's stubborn resolve dissipated like smoke. I had to laugh.

The tattoo artist, Nila, sketches our simple design and prepares her materials. She's supposed to be great at what she does, according to her social media and Trey's recommendation.

"I can't believe we're doing this." Brie grips my arm. "This is insane."

"It's tiny. Who's going to see?"

"I'm not good with needles."

"It'll be quick. I'll go first."

I start to climb up on the table, but she pulls me back. "Oh my god. No. I can't watch you go and then go."

I shrug and step aside. It doesn't make a difference to me. She lies down and rolls her shirt up, tucking it into the band of her bra. Nila cleans the area over her rib cage with alcohol and stamps it with the design.

"You ready?" she asks.

Brie eyes the collage of tattoos on Nila's arms. "On a scale of one to ten, how horrible is this about to be?"

"It's three letters," Nila says. "It won't be bad. I promise."

Brie groans and I giggle at her pinched face. The theatrics. "Just squeeze my hand."

Nila turns on the tattoo gun and Brie squirms. "Try to stay still," Nila says. Brie buries her face in the crook of her free arm and squeezes my fingers until they're numb.

"Didn't you tell me you broke two toes and still finished a recital en pointe?" I ask her.

"Those were just toes!"

"Okay."

Brie whines excessively, earning several exasperated glances from another client in the shop, but she gets through it.

"You're up," Nila tells me once Brie's bandaged and looking quite proud of herself.

"It honestly wasn't that bad," Brie says.

I roll my eyes. "Mm-hmm."

I take my place on the table and she extends her hand. I don't need moral support, but I take it anyway. The sensation of the needle is annoying, at most. She's so dramatic. It's over before I know it.

"Check it out," Nila says, waving toward the full-length mirror on the wall.

I turn to the side to examine her work. It's simple, dainty, and beautiful. Exactly what we had in mind. Brie stands behind me, arms around my shoulders, grinning at me through the mirror.

We got them in the same place. Three tiny little letters written across our ribs. A monument to the girls we once were. Who we are, still.

ABC. Amélie Belle Cœur. Aubrie Bette Cœur.

Brie and I had just made it back to her place when I received a barrage of texts from Shaine demanding I come over. It's to be expected. Shaine has been very understanding, all things considered, but Halloween is her favorite holiday, and I knew at a certain point I'd have to meet my festivity quota.

She answers the door in a flour-dusted apron. I stare at her.

"We're baking cookies," she says by way of an explanation.

"You don't bake. None of us in this apartment bake." I turn to Brie. "Do you bake?"

"No."

We step in and shed our jackets in the doorway.

"I found a recipe online," Shaine says. I've never seen her touch an appliance in her kitchen. Not even her coffee machine. But now she bakes. "It's, like, five ingredients. Between the six of us, I think we can figure it out."

Olivia's digging through plastic bins of fall decor in the living room. Justine is pulling ingredients from the fridge. And Trey is just . . . here.

"Okay, I need you two with me." Shaine grabs our arms and tows us to the kitchen. "Justine doesn't know the difference between baking powder and baking soda."

Justine arches an eyebrow. "What is the difference, Shaine?"

"One is needed for this recipe and the other is not."

Olivia comes over to grab scissors from the drawer next to the kitchen sink. "Mel, how's life on the outside?"

Shaine rolls her eyes. "She wasn't in prison."

"She kinda was," Trey says.

"Like Martha Stewart prison." Justine rips open a bag of sugar. "Didn't she have an en-suite?"

I smile. "And really soft sweat suits."

"No drawstrings, I'm sure."

Brie's eyes widen at Trey's joke, but inappropriate humor is the glue that bonds him and me. What good is four and a half weeks in an asylum if you can't joke about it after?

"I always thought I'd be the one in the group to be institutionalized first," Olivia says, carefully unwrapping the Bubble Wrap from a crystal pumpkin.

"I did too," Shaine agrees.

By some miracle, we get the cookies in the oven and they don't look terrible. You never think about how useful cookie cutters are until you use them.

Trey helps Shaine load the dishwasher while we lay out all the tubes of icing and jars of sprinkles that Shaine, for some reason, had stashed in her pantry. Again, the girl does not bake.

I didn't think I'd get to have a real Halloween this year. I expected bowls of candy at the nurse's station and witches' hats in group therapy. I thought of what it would be like to have turkey and stuffing in the cafeteria. To open Christmas presents on the small couch in my room under bright fluorescent lights. Back when my time in treatment seemed like it would stretch on forever, this is what I hoped for. But now, with all my friends around like this, it's painfully obvious who's missing. Even if no one has brought it up.

"It's weird that he's not here," I say to no one in particular.

Trey dries the bowl and clicks it back into the stand mixer. "Do you want him to be?"

"I feel like I got the kids in the divorce."

"Well, no," Shaine says. "We were kids from a previous marriage. You're just babysitting Trey."

"Is it over between you guys?" Olivia asks.

"Remember the part when he broke up with me and I had a mental breakdown?"

"Yeah, that was wild," Trey says. Shaine hits his arm. "What? It was."

"So . . . just, like, done?"

"I don't know, Liv. I guess."

"Eh." Trey bites his lips as if he has to physically keep himself from saying something he shouldn't.

"What?"

"It's not my business. I just think you both have some things you should say to each other."

"Like?"

He looks to Shaine for help. She shrugs. "I say fuck him."

"Wow," Trey mutters.

"What? She better say the same thing about you when we break up."

"*When* we break up?"

"Yeah, we're not gonna last. Besides, Hayden's your best friend but to me, he's the ex-situationship of my best friend. I'd like to make my allegiance clear."

"Stand down, Shaine," I say, although this is the energy I need right now. "We don't hate him."

"Is he coming to your Halloween party?" Olivia asks Shaine. Shaine turns to Trey. Trey turns to me.

"What?"

"He's not going to come if you don't want him to."

"I don't care if he comes."

"Don't you though?"

"I do not care."

"You care so much," Shaine says, untying her apron and tossing it on the counter. "It's fine. Listen, I'll make it easy. He's not invited. Done."

"Unless you want him to come," Justine says.

"Yeah, then he's totally invited."

I don't want to be the reason Hayden can't hang out with people he's known longer than I have. I also don't think I could be in the same room with him and pretend everything's normal. I hate this.

Trey comes over and hugs me. Not one of his side hugs, a full-on, rib-crushing one. "He'll follow your lead, Melie. Whatever you want. He just wants you to be happy."

I don't doubt what Trey is saying is true. He knows Hayden better than anyone. What scares me is that after all this time, after everything that's happened, I'm still not sure what it means to be happy.

12

NORMAL AGAIN

New York City during Halloween is mayhem. It's nothing like Connecticut, where kids go trick-or-treating, and then once they're all in bed, the rest of us abuse the holiday for what it is. An excuse to blame your behavior on the fact that, for just this one night, you're not yourself.

Brie's on her knees in the back seat of the car stabbing bobby pins into my hair. The driver swings a quick right. She loses her balance and one of the pins nearly punctures my scalp.

"Ow!"

"You have too much hair. This is why I cut mine." She uses her teeth to open another one, tucking a chunk of hair back into my tight ballet bun. "Okay, I think that's good."

Neither of us wanted to dress up this year, but when Shaine insisted costumes were mandatory for her party, we decided to cheat the system. I lent Brie one of my old Laurelle uniforms. She found extensions that match the color and texture of our hair and pinned her bangs back. I'm wearing her black leotard, a pair of purple tights, a charcoal-blue mesh top, and scuffed ballet slippers.

"Roll your skirt," I tell her, smudging her eyeliner a bit for the authentic sad-girl aesthetic. If it wasn't for her perfect posture, I might actually believe she's me.

"We should go as each other every year."

"This is my last year in a Halloween costume."

She smirks, putting her seat belt back on. "Tell that to Shaine."

I crack the window, careful not to roll it down too much and mess up all of Brie's work. I'm glad she came over to get ready with me. I know tonight is important to Shaine, but it was hard for me to muster the energy to come out. This isn't how this was supposed to be. It's the first time I'll be seeing a lot of my classmates since Shaine's birthday, and although I'm ready for things to be normal again, nothing about this is normal without him.

"Are you thinking about Hayden?"

My head jerks up. Brie's staring at me like a psychic in Union Square. "Ew, don't do that."

"Sorry. It's not a telepathy thing. I'm just looking at your face."

I start to rub my eyes, and then remembering the carefully applied smoky shadow, I smooth my hair instead. "I need to talk to him."

"Is he going to be there?"

"No. Trey said he's staying home."

Brie leans forward. "Hi." The driver turns the music down. "Can we add a stop to our ride?"

I grip her arm. "What are you doing?"

"You said you want to talk to him."

317

The driver stares at us through the rearview mirror, which is deeply concerning because he's still speeding.

"I didn't mean right now."

"If you do it now, you can use the party as an excuse to leave."

I slump back in my seat. I don't know how long I can avoid Hayden, but I was hoping I could do it forever. "I'm in a costume," I whine.

"Do you want me to go in your place?"

She could. He may not even notice. Ugh.

"Fine." I type Hayden's address into the app and a new route snakes out in blue on the screen. "If it goes badly, I'm not coming to the party. You can be the one to explain that to Shaine."

"I'm not afraid of Shaine."

When the car stops in front of Hayden's apartment, Brie glances up at the tower wearing the same exact stunned expression I wore the first time I came here. Sober, I mean.

"Do you want me to come with you?" she asks. "I can stay in the lobby."

"No. I'll text you when I leave."

"You sure?"

I'm not, but I tell her I am anyway. She squeezes my hand through the window. Once she's gone, I immediately FaceTime Rena, but it's Cal who answers.

He grins. "Hey, Brie."

"Shut up."

"I can't decide if that costume is lazy or genius."

"That's because it's both."

I wrap my free arm around myself, bracing against the cool autumn air. I don't have to do this. I can call another car and go to the party. I can talk to him another time.

"What's up?" Cal asks, worry creasing his brow. "Why does your face look like that?"

"What? Stunning, glowing, and well moisturized?" He isn't amused. I groan. "I'm outside of Hayden's place."

"Are you going in?"

"I don't know." My words come so fast, I can barely keep up with them. "I don't know what to say. I don't know how I feel about anything. I always make such shitty choices, Cal. What do I do? How do I talk to him? I'm—"

"Is that my phone?" Rena's voice rings through the speakers. "Who are you talking to?" Her head pops into view, but her smile drops the second she sees my face. "What's wrong?"

"She's at Hayden's," Cal says.

Cal passes her the phone, but she keeps them both in frame.

"I'm going to throw up," I mumble.

"Okay, well. Don't do that. You don't have to go in if you're not ready."

"I'm already here." I don't want to run or hide anymore, I just . . . "I need a minute and then I'll go in." I walk over to a nearby bench and sit with my head between my knees to settle my stomach.

I'm being ridiculous.

"M, look at me," Rena says, her voice stern. I lift my head slightly, peeking through my fingers at her. "If you need to leave, then leave. If you decide to stay, just go in and say how you feel. Whatever you're feeling, it's not wrong. You loved him, and all of this, the entire situation, is complicated and hard. It's okay for you to be confused. Just say how you feel, listen to him, and you'll know what to do."

I let out a shaky breath. "Okay."

"Call us if you need us," Cal says. "Love you."

"I love you guys too."

"I love you the most," Rena says, blowing me a kiss.

I smile at the two of them, my family, and hang up.

In the lobby, I'm greeted by the same receptionist as last time. She saw me leave in tears, so she's not as much of a bitch to me today. Only a boy who knows you intimately could invite you into his apartment and send you away sobbing in less than twenty minutes.

"I'm here to see Hayden Thompson."

"Your name?"

"Mel."

She calls up and then buzzes me into the elevator. I brace myself to see him, but when the elevator opens, it's Mrs. Thompson standing in the entryway. I stop short, blinking at her.

She smiles warmly at me. "Mel. It's good to see you."

I don't know why I'm surprised she's here. She lives here. I clear my throat. "Um, hi . . . is he . . ."

"He should be home any minute." She steps out of the way and gestures for me to come in. "You can wait for him if you want."

I take a few reluctant steps in and try to breathe through the pain of being here again after so long. She rubs my arm, and I see my loneliness mirrored in her eyes. It's almost enough to make me fall apart right here in the living room.

I wander down the hallway to Hayden's room. The door is cracked, and all the lights are still on. The scent of him knocks the air out of my chest. It's so clean in here. All his textbooks are lined up neatly on the desk. His bed has been made army-style with the sheets pulled tight and the edges tucked under. I've never seen Hayden's room messy, but there isn't a single thing out of place. It looks like no one has been here for months.

Something on his nightstand catches my eye. A Polaroid poking out of a small black notebook. It's one of me on the beach in the Hamptons. My fingers tremble as I ease it out from where it's wedged between the pages like a bookmark. The angle of the camera is low, but I'm staring up, beyond the lens, at him. He tried to sneak the picture but I caught him. Instead of a candid, he captured my taunting smirk before I snatched the camera from his hands, snapping picture after picture of him until there was only one photo left in the cartridge. Then I took one of us.

I feel him before I hear him. I can sense his uncertainty in the way he holds himself on one leg, unsure whether to step forward or backward. Like I'm not the one who invaded his space without so much as a warning. He makes a decision to move forward, as I knew he would, toward the conversation that could very well be the end of us. I haven't thought through how exactly to go about this. I keep my eyes on the photo as he takes a seat on the edge of the bed.

"I'm so sorry about everything," he says, blurting the words like they've been clogging his throat. Like he's been choking on them. "You didn't deserve that. I was stressed with everything going on with me and you, and then the shit with my parents. Things just felt out of control. I was angry. Mostly at myself, because I couldn't figure out how to fix any of it. But what I did, what I said to you, it wasn't right."

I allow myself to look at him now. Into those eyes that used to burn my heart into dust. I used to want him so badly, even before I could admit it to myself. I still do, if I'm honest, but so much has changed.

"I wanted to see you while you were . . . but I didn't think—"

"No," I say, too quickly. The thought of Hayden at Roseview makes me want to drive off a cliff. "I wouldn't have wanted that," I add, with slightly more composure.

He drops his gaze, nodding to himself. "Yeah. I figured."

"Not for the reasons you think though. I needed space. I needed to go through that alone so I could figure some things out."

"Did you figure them out?" he asks, his voice tentative.

There are tears stinging my eyes now. A lump growing in my throat. He asked me before if I ever told him the truth. I thought I had, but I didn't know it myself.

"Yeah. I, um . . ." He's patient while I try to organize my thoughts and quell the panic in my chest long enough to let him know me in a way so few people do. "I never really felt like I had . . . a place in the world, I guess. I was never really sure I wanted one. I've always known on some level that it shouldn't be that way. That something was wrong. That everyone doesn't walk around the earth wondering what horrible thing they did to have to be here."

I can't believe I'm saying any of this out loud. All those years I spent in therapy with Richards never really dealing with my shit. To be able to be honest this way for the first time in my life is a high I've never felt before. It's also excruciating.

Hayden's brown eyes are deep, dark pools, dragging me under like a riptide. They never leave my face. He barely blinks. Just listens.

"The thing about Darren was he was the first person to make life feel less like a consequence and more like an adventure. I needed the turbulence. I needed to feel like it was dangerous. Like I'd either be really alive or not alive at all. I didn't want anything in between. But what I didn't realize was the highs made the lows unbearable."

Reflexively he reaches out to touch me, but I flinch away and his hand falls back to his side. When we're this close, it's difficult to make our bodies understand that they don't belong to each other anymore. He shifts like he's not sure what he's supposed to do with his arms if he can't hug me. I squeeze my hands into fists, careful not to dig my nails into my palms. I'm not trying to hurt him. I'm trying to tell him how I feel.

"I loved Darren catastrophically. We loved each other like

we were crumbling and gluing each other together and crumbling. Confusing my pieces with his and wondering why there were so many holes. I don't ever want you to compare what I had with him to what I had with you. Loving you was different. I just hadn't figured out what to do about the crumbling."

He's quiet for a long time. An agonizing amount of time. Enough time for me to replay every word I said in my head on an unending loop until I wish I hadn't spoken at all. Then he says, "It's hard, Mel. It's not hard to be with you. I should have never said that. I didn't mean it. It's hard to hear you talk about yourself like this. To know that you feel this way and not know how to help. You don't understand how badly I wish I would've handled things differently."

I do because I wish the same thing.

I wish we could've figured it out. But I think it needed to happen this way. The breaking and the healing.

"I know you want to help me, but if I let you then I'll start to need your help and I can't live like that." I don't want to lose myself in other people anymore. I don't want to disappear because I haven't learned to live in my own body. "I have to find a way to help myself. I have to want to."

What I need now is to be alone. To learn how to be alone. I know that, but knowing it doesn't make it any easier for me to say these things to him.

"I hope you want to," he says.

"I do."

I stare at him and he stares back. Memorizing each other's

faces. Finding all the small changes that mark our time apart. Things that would be imperceptible if we hadn't spent so many hours studying, searching for things we didn't know to just ask for. If we hadn't, at one point, known the other's face so well.

It makes me dizzy. Breathless.

It breaks my heart.

When he pulls me in, I go willingly because that's where I want to be. I don't know if that's good or bad, if it'll make this all the more painful later, but right now it's what I want.

"I'm sorry I hurt you," he murmurs, and I cry.

We stay this way for a long time, with his arms around my shoulders and my head against his chest. I cry because I know where I need to put him. What space I can allow him to occupy in my life right now. The compartments of my brain shift in anticipation, like the shuffling of books in a library, and now there is nothing left unsorted.

We both know, so we can't let go.

"I'm sorry I hurt you too."

ACKNOWLEDGMENTS

It is impossible for me, a Cancer, to write coherent acknowledgments during the season of my birth. I told my editor as much. You can blame her if things go off the rails.

First of all, I can't thank anyone before I thank God and my parents. Daddy, you are my best friend in the entire world and the reason for my sense of humor. Mommy, I got my strength and perseverance (and bone structure) from you. I love you both so much it terrifies me.

I dedicated this book to a boy—a very ironic thing for me to do. To Alex Charles Bridge (See, I'm crying already. We're off to a great start.), all the good parts of Hayden and Darren and none of the bad. I'm sure you know, wherever you are, what losing you did to me. But I hope you also know I'm doing better now. Thank you for the best three years.

And now for my team. I only wanted one agent and it was Pete Knapp. Reader, if you only knew how his clients speak of him in our group chats. We are all so lucky and I have not quite gotten over the shock of having him as my agent. Thank you, Pete, the one and only Stuti Telidevara, and my incredible Park & Fine family for fighting so hard for me and trusting my instincts.

If anyone understands Amélie the way I do, it's my wonderful editor, Emilia Rhodes. Emilia, thank you for believing in this book and tolerating my very dramatic emails. You know I love to catastrophize. A huge thank you to the rest of my team at HarperTeen/HarperCollins: Briana Wood, Sarah Mondello, Erika West, Mary Magrisso, Julia Tyler, Alison Klapthor, Trish McGinley, and Taylan Salvati. Working with you has been a dream.

To Lisbeth Checo. I would say this cover left me speechless, but the reality is I will not shut up about it. Thank you for this masterpiece. I am so in awe of your talent.

To Sarah Marie Hawkins, my creative partner in crime. Thanks for all the work you've done for this book behind the scenes. And thanks for letting me storm into your room when I need to talk through writer's block and for crying whenever I read you literally anything I wrote.

This book would not exist without Lane Clarke. The very first person in the industry to bet on me. From Pitch Wars mentor to friend to agent sibling. I'll always look up to you.

To Isi Hendrix, Danielle Parker, Taj McCoy, and Kiana Nguyen. You talked me down from every publishing-related ledge, and your transparency gave me the courage to fight for what I want. Thank you for paving the way for me.

To my brother Johnny, the first of us. I miss you so much.

To the rest of the seven: my sister Egypt, brother Nike, and my cousins who are really my siblings, Hunter, Haven, and Honour. There will never be another group like us.

To my family: my grandmothers, Marlene and Joy; my stepmom, Arlene; my aunts, cousins, nieces, nephews, my sister-in-law, and my uncle Butch, who was my favorite. I love you all so much.

To my Renas: Morgan Daluz, Siena LeCorps, Natalie Allen, Serene Ball, and Saba Abbasi. You've been with me through the best and worst moments of my life. Thank you for showing me what friendship is.

To my Shaines: Sarah Hawkins, Yogi's Angels (Annie May Gay and Adrienne Rose White), God's Faves (Sarissa Thrower and Waverly Coleman), Erika Latimore, Alex Portée, Christina Ward, Michelle Li, Nila Frederiksen, Rachel Watson, and Roth Wagner. You made LA home. Thank you for everything.

To the rest of my friends: You are such an important part of my life. I wish I could list you all by name, but please know I would not be the person I am without you.

A few of my friends (and my mom) took the time to read what were absolutely chaotic (by my own personal standards) drafts of this novel throughout the years. Adrienne, Serene, Erika, Alex, Nila, Lane, Isi, Jen Carnelian, Alyssa Villaire, and Emily Charlotte: I appreciate you so much.

Thank you to Lane Clarke, Danielle Parker, Elise Bryant, and Jade Adia for taking the time to write such beautiful blurbs for the book. The texts and DMs you sent while reading are saved in a folder I open whenever I start to doubt myself and my work. It's an honor to see your names alongside mine on the cover.

I was discouraged from dedicating this book to Taylor Swift or Lana Del Rey, but just know I thought about it. I can't express what their music has meant to me and the way they've shaped my writing. Special thanks to all the other Sad Girl artists whose albums constantly rank on my Spotify Wrapped.

I am being absolutely serious when I say *Twilight* is the reason I'm an author. Thank you, Stephenie Meyer, for those blank pages in *New Moon*. They changed my brain chemistry.

My therapist deserves her own dedicated page for keeping me in one piece during the publishing process, but that page would be heavily redacted. Thank you, Tiffany.

To the Calacs and Anora Schaer, you were the best bosses I've ever had. You've supported me in so many ways throughout the years I spent writing this book. Thank you for always being so encouraging and understanding. Also, thanks for the money and snacks.

Thank you to Scott Gratson at Temple University for letting me "intern" for myself and write this book in NYC. (Brooklyn Heights, you will always have a special place in my heart.)

I took up French for Mel as a quarantine hobby, and I'm so glad I did. Special thanks to my very French teacher, Pearl Mboyo, for the private lessons, and to my very Canadian friend, Alexandra Raymond, for proofreading the few French scenes that made the cut.

In the early years of writing this book, I was convinced I was writing a character with bipolar disorder, but it never quite fit the way I needed it to. Turns out, that's because she has borderline personality disorder. Thank you to the countless mental health professionals I've learned from and the people living with BPD who have been so open about their experiences. Mel is in no way a perfect depiction of this complicated condition. Still, I hope I did right by you.

Finally, to the readers. I started writing this story when I was seventeen. I just turned thirty-two. By the time you're reading this, it's yours now. I've grown up with Amélie. We got each other through some very dark times. I am forever grateful to you for making space for her. If you can relate to the things I've written in these pages, I'm sorry, I see you, and I hope you're okay.